I HATE YOU, I LOVE YOU

PART 1

BAILEY B

Copyright © 2020 by Bailey B and Christina Beggs

ISBN: 978-1-959724-47-6

ASIN:B0834H3976

EbookISBN: 978-1-959724-17-9

Discrete Duet ISBN: 9781959724018

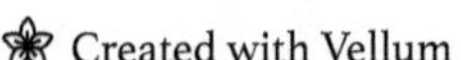 Created with Vellum

I rewrote this story a few different times trying to find the best way to paint the full picture of Danika and Logan's relationship. I ended up splitting the story into two parts because I felt It wasn't enough to see their past through flashbacks. You needed a full painted picture to understand the decisions they make later in life.

I warn you, IHYILY part one is set before we meet Piper and Rex in Beautifully Broken. This means we get a glimpse at one of Piper's darkest moments, but hers is not the worst we see. There are some potential triggers including but not limited to —bullying, suicide (not graphic), drinking, smoking, drug usage, foul language, sex, childhood trauma, near sexual assault (not graphic), blood, and molestation (not graphic)— but these key moments are handled with care.

Logan and Danika's relationship does not come without struggle because each have their own burdens to bear. Also (don't hate me) this book ends on a cliffhanger, but I promise that by the end of part two they will have their happily ever after and you'll understand when I say... she didn't do it.

I rake a shaking hand through my hair, dark strands slipping through my fingers like restless shadows. My new neighbor looked familiar, but I couldn't place why. At first, I brushed it off—maybe we'd hooked up, maybe it was nothing. But that round face, those long dark locks, they clung to the edges of my mind, refusing to let go.

Then, this morning, passing her on the way to first period, the scent of rosewater shampoo ignited something in me. A memory. A name.

Danika Winters. My middle school best friend. After more than three years, she's back.

But instead of relief, my skeletons are knocking.

A lump lodges in my throat, heavy as a cannonball. My pulse hammers. My vision blurs. And suddenly, I'm seven years old again, small and shaking in a therapist's office, his icy fingers curling over my shoulder.

I blink hard, forcing the ghosts back into their graves.

I can't let Danika tell anyone about that night. Can't let the past resurface. No one besides me, her father, and the two other men in that room know the truth.

And I intend to keep it that way.

I twist an unlit cigarette between my fingers, my gaze drifting to Danika as she steps into the cafeteria. She moves toward the food station with Sarah Archer, and I don't know how I missed it before. She looks exactly the same as she did in middle school—just older. Same olive skin. Same hazel eyes. Even that single dimple on her left cheek when she laughs is still there.

A sick sense of déjà vu washes over me as I watch her bypass lunch entirely, opting for just a Coke. Lunch was our thing back in middle school—sitting on the stage, splitting a peanut butter and banana sandwich, and then washing it down with a soda. I still remember the day she told me her mom was sick. She cried the entire lunch period, never once touching her half.

Being the nosy fuck that I am, I've already noticed there's only one car in the driveway next door. Now that I know Danika is my neighbor, it doesn't take a genius to put the pieces together. Her mom didn't make it. Whatever they were doing in California all these years didn't work. And I doubt it was cheap, which is probably why they bought the renovated two-bedroom mother-in-law suite next door.

Tad Parker drops onto the tabletop beside me, shaking me from my thoughts. "You look like you're out for blood. Who pissed you off this early in the year?"

I don't particularly like Tad, but playing football together all through high school has forced us into a strange sort of camaraderie. He thinks we're friends. I don't.

I slip the cigarette between my lips and light it up. "No one."

Lunch trays clatter onto the table behind me. I don't need to turn around to know who it is. Tad only associates with a specific breed of entitled pricks and no one dares to sit with him uninvited.

I scan the cafeteria again, searching for Danika's distinct shade of brown. It's rich and threaded with natural highlights. Too pure to come from a bottle—something I didn't appreciate at thirteen.

I take a slow drag from my cigarette, exhaling a stream of smoke toward the ceiling. I need to stop thinking about Danika like this. Like she's still the girl I shared my secrets with. The girl who was once my best friend.

I take another drag, letting the burn in my lungs anchor me. It makes tuning out the cafeteria noise easier—until I hear her name.

"You guys remember Danika, right?" Sarah sets her tray beside Tad and glances at my tablemates.

Danika is greeted with a collective murmur of uninterested hellos. Good. No one remembers her. She'll have to prove she belongs, and judging by the fact she still wears pink Converse low-tops, Melody is going to eat her alive.

Melody Fox, self-proclaimed queen of St. Anastasia's High, has earned every bit of her title because she's mean. I can't stand her, but for some reason, she's convinced we're a thing. Everyone knows I don't do relationships—especially not ones that come with the expectation of exclusivity. Just like she knows I fuck whoever I want, whenever I want. Yet she still clings to the idea that we're together. At this point, arguing with her takes more effort than it's worth, so I let her believe whatever she wants.

Melody's voice turns syrupy sweet when she says, "You're like, really pretty."

It's a trap. One Danika is sure to fall into. I almost feel bad, but Melody is making my job of running Danika out easier. Growing up, Danika was quiet and folded in on herself when met with confrontation. Our personalities back then were so similar. We were two halves of a whole.

Looking at how Danika's cheeks are flushing, I doubt she's changed. I give it a day, maybe two, before she finds another lunch table. Hell, maybe she'll find another school.

Melody tilts her head, her beady brown eyes rolling over Danika's features again. "Who does your hair?"

"Um." Danika runs unmanicured fingers through her long strands. She's nervous and every instinct in me screams to put an end to whatever Melody is doing, but I don't. I let Danika hang herself socially as she says, "I don't dye it."

Melody snickers. "So, that's natural?"

Rachel Moore, Melody's ever-loyal sidekick, cackles beside her. They exchange a glance—silent conversation passing between them. I've never understood how girls do that. If guys have something to say, we just say it, while girls can tear down reputations with a single lift of an eyebrow.

"She's probably too poor to dye it," I add on an exhale, the words heavy on my tongue, but I can't stop thinking about what Danika might remember. I need her on edge. Maybe even afraid of me. Maybe then I can keep her quiet. "Have you seen where she lives?"

"No!" Melody gasps. "Where?"

I take another drag and then let out another exhale to numb my mind as a shiver of guilt ripples through me. "The shack next to me."

Melody cackles and then gasps for air, her words coming out as a breathy squeak when she says, "You mean Mr. Andrew's old guest house?"

The weight of Danika's stare burns into me. I turn my head, meeting her gaze with a cold glare. She needs to understand I'm not the same scared little boy she left behind. I will burn the world down to keep her quiet. She may have been my friend when we were kids, but now she is my enemy.

"Whatever. Poor or not," Gunner Wells cuts off Melody's laughter, his gaze sliding over Danika's curves before settling on her face. His lips curl into a smirk. "You're fucking hot."

Danika isn't hot. She's beautiful. Always has been. Only now, she's grown into her body. She developed early. I know that's strange to say, but come on. I'm a guy. I notice these things. Especially on a pretty girl who leaves her table to sit with the weird, friendless kid who had a stutter in the sixth grade.

That kid was me.

Awkward as fuck, thick-rimmed glasses, and quieter than a church mouse because damn near everyone picked on me when I talked.

I was in therapy for years to correct my speech. Although, looking back, I'm not sure if those sessions helped my situation or made it worse.

Tad crushes his soda and tosses it at the trash can. It circles the rim and then falls onto the cafeteria floor. He grunts, probably remembering how shitty he was on the basketball team as a freshman. "Yeah, at least she's not like Piper."

"Don't fucking talk about Piper," I quip. Tad smirks, realizing he's gotten under my skin and I'm reminded once again why I can't stand him.

Piper Lovelace, my on-again-off-again foster sister, doesn't deserve to be treated the way she is. Part of her reputation is my fault. I started the rumor that she slept with, I don't even remember who, as a joke last year when I considered her to be nothing more than a nuisance. Before I knew what she was going through. Not that that's any excuse.

I never expected the rumor of her being easy to stick because most of the things people say about Piper are forgotten in a day or two. It didn't help that soon after she started hanging around with a bunch of different guys, adding fuel to the rumor fire. Even so, everything they say about her is wrong.

Piper is a good person. She's just been dealt a shitty hand in life.

"Let me guess, Piper's fucking both you and Cooper now that she's moved back home again?" Tad digs a joint out of his cigarette pack and lights it, not caring about the cafeteria monitors.

They won't do anything anyway, a perk of going to the most expensive school in the county. *Certain* kids could probably murder someone in cold blood on campus and damn near get away with it.

Tad sucks in a breath, holding the smoke in his lungs, then passes the rolled paper to Gunner and says, "Tell me, is that bitch as good in bed as the rumors say she is?"

I toss what's left of my cigarette to the floor and jump off the table, ready to kick Tad's ass, but Cooper—my twin brother—beats me to it. He comes up from the left, catching Tad in his blindside, and throws a jab at his face. Tad falls off the table and clutches his cheek like the little bitch that he is. Serves him right. Piper is family, and you don't fuck with family.

I sit on top of the table again and light another cigarette to calm my nerves. I'm anxious, full of unused adrenaline, and I need something to take my mind off stomping Tad's face into the pavement.

"Damn it, Cooper!" Tad yells, but anyone within earshot has gone back to talking with their table mates. Everyone on campus knows that if you mess with Piper, talk to Piper, hell even look at Piper the wrong way, you'll face the wrath of Cooper. He's more protective of her than a starved watchdog with a steak.

Our principal, Mr. White, grabs Cooper by the arm and escorts him to the office with Tad in tow. Mom will be pissed when he gets suspended for the rest of the day, but she'll understand. She always does. Cooper spends more time out of school than in and she barely bats an eye.

But when I get in trouble, all hell breaks loose.

Melody groans and rolls her eyes. "Always with the drama."

From my peripheral vision I see Gunner make himself comfortable next to Danika. I don't like the way he's looking at her or the way he whispers into her ear. I hate how she playfully shoves him and they both laugh.

I have no right to be pissed, but being around her sets me on edge.

Besides, I saw her first.

ompared to the toothpicks on campus, I'm not a tiny girl. At one hundred and fifty pounds my hips are thick, but I have the ass to go with them. My stomach has more fluff than most, but the double-Ds I've been blessed with make my waist and tummy look smaller than they are. I have my assets and I know how to work them.

That being said, I don't openly flaunt what I've got. I make it a point to cover up because guys, young and old, have gawked at me since I was eleven years old. Back then, my figure seemed to develop overnight, and I didn't know how to handle it.

Back then, Logan was the only one who never made a big deal about my body, even though I know he noticed.

In the cafeteria today, I knew who Logan was the second I laid eyes on him. My heart soared when I realized Sarah and I were about to sit at the same table. Even more so when I realized that he had friends.

In middle school, Logan was always a social loner. Any time Cooper was around, Logan was surrounded by people, but the moment Cooper was sick—or any where Logan wasn't—those friends disappeared. Everyone wanted to be around the smooth-talking football prodigy, not the quirky kid with a speech impediment.

All things considered, I'm not surprised Logan outgrew his awkward stage. It helps that he's absolutely gorgeous, but he's always been cute.

From what I can tell, both Harris boys have long, lean bodies, muscled in such it's obvious they still play some kind of sport. While Cooper's hair is the color of gold and buzzed short. Logan has locks, so dark they're almost black, that fall into his eyes. Sitting on top of the table at lunch, he looks like a living sculpture. Too beautiful to be real. Too flawless to be human. In California, I'd have argued that no one looks *that* good unless they've had work done, and yet Logan defies my logic.

I shake my head, still stunned that little Logan Harris turned into the kind of man my mother warned me about—dark and magnetic. Every fiber in my being is drawn to him with a pull I've never felt before. Mom said she'd only felt an attraction like this once and it wasn't to my dad—their love was pure.

Wherever this feeling stems from is dirty. I hate it. *I love it.*

Too bad Logan doesn't remember me. Or worse, if he does, that means he consciously chose to be a jerk. Although, I can't for the life of me figure out why. I'll have to ask him after school. Perks of being neighbors.

Coach Rae blows his whistle, signaling for us to get ready. I widen my stance and intertwine my fingers, prepared to hold my own once the first serve is sent over the net. Volleyball is a good sport for big-breasted chicks. There's minimal running, which is great because even with two sports bras on my boobs bounce and it hurts.

I'm in the first row, center, with Melody to my left and a redhead to my right. The ball goes flying over the net and behind me. We volley it back and forth a few times, until the other side scores. We go a few rounds, my team holding its own against our opponent until Melody sets up to serve.

She tosses the ball into the air and spikes it straight into the back of my head. "Sorry."

Bitch. I rub the sore spot with my palm and hold up my other hand to signal I'm alright so the game can continue. We are tied with roughly fifteen minutes left in the period and I hate to lose. I've been competitive for as long as I can remember, from spelling tests to mini golf. Losing is not a concept I handle well.

Coach blows his whistle and Melody sets up again. She serves, this time hitting me in the head harder than before. I spin on my heels and press my fists against my hips. "What's your deal?"

"I don't know what you're talking about." Melody smirks. "I missed the net."

I take a step toward Melody, prepared to let her know that what happened at lunch today was a one-off. If I wasn't so thrown by how Logan treated me, that belittling conversation wouldn't have gotten as far as it did.

I hate a bully almost as much as I hate cancer. Cancer is a bully. It picks on your cells. Takes over your body. And when the medicine isn't strong enough, you die. I can't do anything about cancer, but I can take a bully down.

And I'm good at it.

Coach blows his whistle twice and the loud ring echoes in the silent gymnasium. Seems like everyone stopped to watch us. "Focus, ladies."

I pop my neck and turn back toward the net. Let that bitch hit me one more time. *Thump.* The volleyball smacks the back of my head again, and the snickering behind me sets my blood on fire.

I turn and lunge at Melody before she has a chance to figure out what's happening. She lets out a high-pitched, blood-curdling scream as I grab a fistful of over-processed hair and drag her to the ground. Melody is tiny, maybe one hundred and ten pounds, soaking wet. Even if she could throw a decent punch— which I doubt— she wouldn't stand a chance.

Coach blows his whistle again, hollering at us as the back of Melody's head smacks against the shellacked wood floor of the gymnasium. He snakes his arm around my chest, securing me in a school-approved choke hold. I've been in my fair share of fights at my old school. This may be Florida, but I doubt the protocols are *that* different from state to state. I hold my hands up in surrender, letting Melody's hair go, but taking a fistful of dyed strands with me.

Once I'm considered to be de-escalated, Coach has me escorted to the school guidance counselor, Miss Cherrybroom.

Cherrybroom stands outside of her office waiting, perfectly manicured nails curled into a fist at her hips. I walk through her open door and chuckle because her office is everything you'd expect a high school guidance counselor's office to be: plain and intimidating with a touch of warmth. You know, to remind the unruly that she's in charge but still understanding.

Cherrybroom opens my school file as she settles in behind her desk. "Danika Winters."

My manila folder is thick, having been forced into guidance sessions in California, every emotional outburst, every tear, every fist thrown was documented. I was considered high-risk because I was relocated from my friends, with a terminal mother... Blah, blah, blah.

"It's your first day and you're already getting into a fight." A sigh escapes Cherrybroom's thin coral lips, "I guess this is my fault. I should have scheduled to meet with you this morning,"

I shift in the oversized plush chair. "No. You should switch my classes. Melody is the devil."

"Seems like you've always been a fighter." Cherrybroom ignores my request. She flips through my file, silently skimming through each page. "Until the spring of last year. The fighting stopped, even while you were a victim of bullying."

Her big eyes widen as she mumbles, "Oh, my" under her breath. I know what she sees. I don't need her to remind me of what I've been through. I clear my throat and Cherrybroom abruptly shuts my overstuffed manila folder. "Your last counselor was very...uh...detailed in her notes."

"But not in her actions," I whisper.

"Hmm?"

"Look, ma'am, Melody doesn't like me for whatever reason and she's made it clear that I'm on her radar. I want out of that class."

Cherrybroom's thin lips press into a line and I can tell she's not going to give me what I need. *Just like my last counselor.* "Miss Winters, I'm not sure how they did things at your old school but here at St. A's, students don't make demands."

"With all due respect, ma'am, you've glanced at my file. Last year was terrible." My smartwatch vibrates, alerting me that my heart rate is well above normal for a resting rate. I bet it is. Just thinking about last year makes my skin crawl. "You don't want to intentionally subject me to additional bullying and risk me hurting myself or others as an act of retaliation. Do you?"

Cherrybroom raises one perfectly shaped, penciled-in eyebrow at me. "Do you honestly think changing one class is going to make any difference?"

"Did you really just ask me that?" Yes. One class, one bully can change everything. If she were any good at her job she'd know this.

Cherrybroom sighs and sags back into her seat. "No. I guess I didn't. Let me see what I can do."

Chapter 3

I glance down at my new schedule, a small smile tugging at my lips. Cherrybroom moved P.E. to second period, swapping it with math. She's probably right—switching one class won't stop Melody if she's determined to make my life miserable, but the less time I spend near her, the fewer chances she gets to torment me.

"Hey!" I shout as the paper is snatched from my fingers.

Logan glances at my new class list, a frown falling across his face and even then he's still beautiful. Beautiful but hateful. I bite the corner of my bottom lip. These feelings he's stirring up are going to break me if I don't get them under control. *I do not like him. I do not like him. I do not like him...*

"Are you stalking me?"

"Says the guy who sought me out and stole my paper." I reach for my schedule but Logan holds it in the air, just out of my reach. Black ink of a tattoo peeks from beneath the long sleeve on his left arm, which instantly knocks Logan's hotness down from nine to one. I hate tattoos.

Do I, though?

"You switched your roster to be in two of my classes," He continues, that dark gaze of his lifting to meet mine.

I stop jumping and set my hands on my hips. A crowd is forming around us and I refuse to be their circus monkey. "Why are you being such a dick? This isn't like you."

Logan shoves the paper at my chest, knocking me back a step and against the locker. He leans in close, whispering, "I swear to god, Danika, if you breathe one word about that night, I'll end you."

"What night?"

"Exactly." He pushes away and strolls down the hallway, grabbing the redheaded girl from P.E. by the hand as he goes. She's more than happy to follow, skipping like she's just won the lottery.

I swallow hard and try to remember that somewhere deep, *deep inside,* Logan is the kid I used to be friends with. Whatever he thinks I know has him wound up.

"What was that about?" Sarah asks, looking over her shoulder as Logan pulls the redhead into an empty classroom.

I shake my head. "I don't honestly know."

Sarah shrugs and links her arm to mine. "Men."

I STARE out the window on the ride back to my house. Sarah rambles about her day and the newest gossip. I've tuned her out, trying to scan my memories for whatever secret Logan thinks I know.

Sarah and I went to school together from kindergarten all the way through the eighth grade, as did more than half of the senior class. I didn't know Logan back in my elementary years. I mean, I knew him but didn't *know* him. That was when boys sat with boys and girls sat with girls. Except for Piper. When she came in the second grade, Cooper never gave her the chance to sit with us. He took Piper to her own table and it's been that way ever since.

I didn't take notice of Logan until halfway through the sixth grade. He was always the quiet, blend into the background type. That particular day both Piper and Cooper were absent. Sixth grade was when the cliques began to form, the same stupid cliques roaming our high school halls today. Logan sat by himself that day, not having any friends of his own that weren't Cooper's, and I felt bad for him.

That was the day we became friends.

We ate lunch together up until we graduated middle school, just the two of us, even though it made Sarah ridiculously jealous. But nothing we talked about back then stands out as grudge-worthy. I can't for the life of me figure out what he thinks that I know.

Sarah waves her hand in my face. "Earth to Danika."

"Huh?" I blink twice and realize we're sitting in my driveway. "Sorry. I guess I zoned out."

"Are you okay?"

"Yeah," I sigh. I shouldn't let whatever Logan's going through bother me, but I can't help it. I still have a soft spot for him.

Sarah looks at me skeptically. She was the only person that kept in touch after I moved and I was grateful for her friendship when I moved back last week. "I know Melody can be a royal cunt but give her time. She'll get used to you."

"I don't know. She seems to hate me."

"Don't take it personally. Melody hates everyone, herself included."

I force a smile and Sarah squeezes my arm. "Hang in there. It'll get better. First days are always the worst."

We both turn our heads at the roar of Logan's engine as he skids into his driveway. He gets out, slams his car door, and glares our way. Logan flips us the bird and then hurries up the front steps into his house.

Sarah lets out a breath at the same time as I do. "I'm sorry you guys are neighbors."

"Me too." I chuckle, but it's in no way happy. I realized we'd moved next door to each other yesterday. Logan was wheeling his trashcan to the road and I had just set mine out. I smiled and waved, recognizing him immediately. He glared and flipped me the bird, like he did a moment ago. Embarrassed, I ducked my head and went back into the house as fast as my feet would carry me.

"I thought you guys used to be friends. What happened?"

I shake my head, wondering if this was to be our new normal. "I have no clue."

P.E. and math. Why did Danika have to switch to my P.E. and math class yesterday? She's everywhere. My lunch table, my neighbor, my hallways, and now my classes. But worst of all, she's in my head. I can't stop thinking about her pretty little lips and what they could spill.

"Fuck!" I beat my fists against the steering wheel. I need to get this situation under control. I almost wonder if I could sit down and just talk to Danika. She used to be sweet and reasonable. But she's been gone a long time, and people change. Hell, I have.

I punch the steering wheel and the horn sounds in the parking lot, turning a few heads my way. Fuck 'em all. If anyone has a problem, they can come and tell me to my face. Otherwise, they can keep their judgmental thoughts to themselves.

Someone knocks on my window, making my racing heart jump. I look up, and who is it? Danika fucking Winters. I push the button on my door and roll down the window. "What?"

"Are you okay?"

I stare at Danika like she's stupid because she has to be. Or maybe she hasn't figured out yet that she's an unwelcome pest that needs to be exterminated. But the reality is that I don't want to make Danika's life any harder than it's already been.

If things were different, I'd pull Danika into my arms and ask how life in California was. I truly want to know how she's doing without her mom. She was my first real friend. The only person who had nothing to gain by being near me. No popularity by association—not that I was the popular one. No lurid acts. No leverage for one thing or another. The sad fact is, if I let her, she would *still* be the only person like that.

"I'm fucking fine," I growl, rolling the window up.

Danika stands upright, shakes her head, and leaves. Good. I don't like having her around. I'm too conflicted, torn between picking up where we left off and intimidating her to make sure she keeps her mouth shut.

I lean forward, rest my forehead against the steering wheel, and take a breath. I need to calm down before I do something stupid.

My passenger door opens and I squeeze my eyes shut, immediately recognizing the rosewater fragrance that is uniquely Danika. "Are you so stupid that you can't take the hint?"

Danika closes the door, her scent smothering all air space. "Probably, but something's up with you, Logan. I don't care that it's been a few years, people don't change this much. What happened?"

"You know what fucking happened!" I snap my gaze up to meet hers. Why is she doing this? Why is she forcing me to say what she already knows? How could California have hardened her so much?

I grip the handle of my door and get out. She can stay inside and suffocate on her rosewater air for all I care. "Fuck. You."

I LEAN against my locker and scroll through my phone, my thumb hovering over my Dad's number. Should I tell him the Winters are back? I'm sure if he knew he would pay them a visit and remind Mr. Winters of what's on the line. Mr. Winters, Dad, Sheriff Tomlinson, and I have a lot to lose if my secret comes out.

I change my mind and slip my phone back into my pocket. I can handle this myself. It would be my luck Dad would have a tail because of one of his clients and everything would come out if he visited the Winters' house anyway.

Across the hall, Melody sticks her foot out, tripping Danika as she passes on the way to class from her locker. The books and notebook she holds spill to the floor and she falls to her knees.

I stick an unlit cigarette between my lips and chew on the filter. My initial instinct is to run to Danika and help her to her feet, but I stay put. This is what I wanted. Melody will make Danika's life miserable, I'll add my own touch of cruelty to the mix, and she'll be too scared to defy me when I eventually offer her *protection*.

Danika climbs to her knees and reaches for the book nearest to her. Melody raises her red-soled heel to Danika's back and pushes her down. "Let's get one thing straight, *California*. Logan is mine. Everyone here knows it, and now you do too. If I catch you even looking at him again, you'll be sorry."

Danika clenches her fists and pushes onto her knees again, but Melody kicks her back down.

Damn it, Melody. That's enough.

Danika groans but covers the sound with a dark chuckle. "Have you told Logan you don't want to share anymore? He seemed pretty happy to have me in his car this morning. Even happier after I left."

I smirk and light the end of my cigarette. I didn't see that coming. Danika's newfound edge could be problematic to my plan, but damn it if her suggestion that we hooked up this morning isn't hot.

"You little bitch!" Melody raises her foot to kick Danika in the back again, but this time, Danika is ready.

She rolls onto her side and shoves the sole of her Converse sneaker into the leg Melody is balancing on. Melody goes down with a shriek and Danika climbs on top of the self-crowned queen, pinning Melody's hands to the ground with her knees.

"Get off me, you little wench!" Melody screams.

Danika sits on Melody's hips, an amused smirk playing on her face. People heading to class stop in the hallway and stare. Danika is a dead girl walking, everyone knows it, but watching someone take down the queen is a sight to see.

"You're fucking dead. Deader than dead. You think Piper has it bad, just wait. I'm gonna—"

Danika draws back and punches Melody in the mouth. "We could have been friends, but no. You had to be an effing." *Punch.* "Bully." *Punch.* "And I hate." *Punch.* "Bullies!"

I take a drag of my cigarette. It's half spent, wasted while watching my girl kick some ass, and damn if it isn't a turn on. I exhale and chuckle at the thought bouncing around in my head. *I bet she's just as feisty in bed.*

Gunner snakes his arms around Danika's waist and lifts her off of Melody, who's a bloody mess crying on the floor. "Easy there, doll face," he says, rubbing his hands on Danika's arms.

She's breathing heavily, likely coming down from the adrenaline rush that comes from a good fight. Gunner pulls her into a hug and I have the sudden urge to smash his face in. I like this fire in my chest. It's better than the nervousness Danika inspires or the numbness I usually feel. I know what to do with fire.

I toss what's left of my cigarette at their feet and walk off. He needs to know that Danika is mine.

And no one touches my shit.

Chapter 5

Logan wasn't in my P.E. class this morning like I assumed he would be, but surprisingly Piper was. We didn't talk—I've noticed she, like Logan, rarely speaks to anyone—but she did smile at me. So, that was cool.

I didn't necessarily punch Melody in the face because she's mean to Piper too. Although, I'd have no problem doing it again if she needed me to. I did it because Melody is a bully and someone needs to knock her down to size. Piper's name just happened to be the last straw.

By the time lunch period arrives, nearly everyone is whispering about what happened in the hallway. Melody went home, probably too embarrassed to show her bloodied face, but that doesn't mean the people at her table are any less vicious. Her friends, most of whose names I haven't figured out yet, glare at me as I set my tray next to Sarah. Even my only friend seems keen on not looking at me, intently poking her soufflé with a spoon.

The only person who appears remotely happy to see me this afternoon is Gunner. "Hey, doll face."

I smile up at him, not particularly fond of the pet name but happy to be making a friend. "Hey, Gunner. What's up?"

"Do you want to go down to Riverside with me tonight? Check out the stars and whatnot?"

I remember Riverside. Even back in the eighth grade, it was a known hookup spot. I guess some things don't change.

I smile politely, prepared to let Gunner down. I'm not that kind of girl. I've had boyfriends before. Made out with them. Explored a few of the bases even. But I've never gotten a home run, and believe me I could have. Giving someone my virginity is a gift I can never get back. I'm not against premarital sex. I just haven't found someone I like enough to do that with yet.

And I'm nowhere near ready to play ball with a guy I just met, even if he is cute.

Before I can decline, a football spirals through the air and hits Gunner in the back. He grimaces and turns, looking for his assailant. Everyone at the table seems as shocked as I am, but Gunner quickly finds who he's looking for and excuses himself.

No sooner than he's gone, Rachel says, "You can't sit here tomorrow."

Tad and some guy whose name I can't remember smirk. I half expect Sarah to stick up for me, but she's too busy dissecting her dessert. I get it. I've put her between a rock and a hard place. We may be old friends, but in the eyes of everyone here, I'm new and now, more so than ever, a target. If she has to choose between our friendship and surviving this year unscathed, I understand why she'd pick the latter, but it doesn't bother me any less.

Even though my feelings are hurt, my poker face is untouchable. I stab a tiny red tomato from the pathetic excuse of a salad our school has today and lift it to my mouth. "I'll sit where I want."

"Let me rephrase," Rachel folds her hands on the table. "You won't want to sit here tomorrow. Melody is a snake, constantly ready to attack. You didn't just poke her, you tried to cut off her head. The retaliation won't be pretty."

"I appreciate the warning, but I can take care of myself."

Rachel shakes her head. "It's your funeral."

I TWIST the cap off my coke and sit at Melody's table again. I know I should pick somewhere else to sit. Anywhere else, but people have dodged me all week. It's like I have a grenade strapped to my back and everyone is trying to avoid the explosion. It's fine. I've made my bed and now I have to lay in it. I will say two good things have come out of the fight on Tuesday:

1. Melody is no longer a raging cunt. While it is clear she doesn't like me, for the moment, she's not actively making my life a living hell. Dodged a bullet there.
2. Logan's no longer being a jerk. Probably because he's not around. The only time I've seen him in the hallway this week was when his face was attached to someone else's, and he's been at Piper's table during lunch.

I can't pretend I'm not disappointed. I wanted us to be friends again. Friends would quiet the relentless pull I feel toward him. Friends would soothe the ache in my hands, the urge to reach for him. Friends would make everything easier.

But we're not friends. Not enemies, either—just something in between.

Gunner, the guy who's been shamelessly flirting with me all week and the only one who seems happy I'm still here, winks before turning back to his conversation with Jake Brito. My stomach growls, a sharp reminder that the measly bowl of oatmeal I had this morning wasn't nearly enough. But the cafeteria's vegan options are pathetic, and I refuse to start brown-bagging my meals.

"Oh look, you're back again," Melody's manicured nails curl into a fist under her cheek as she leans on the table. I'm waiting for the shoe to drop, but Melody isn't stupid. She's probably already plotting her revenge, buying her sweet time and trying to make me sweat in the process.

It's not working.

"So, new girl," Tad slides off the top of the table and into the open space next to me. I don't like Tad. Outside of lunch I avoid him at all costs because he's got an icky vibe I can't shake.

"It's Danika," Gunner interrupts, defensively.

I smile up at him. Gunner is classically handsome with a jawline that gives Gene Kelly a run for his money. He's walked me to class and made it more than obvious that he likes me, but Gunner doesn't make my heart race the way it does when Logan's near. In fact, the only reason I'm even giving him a chance is to wash my infatuation with Logan away.

I steal a glance across the room to Piper's table. From what I've gathered Logan's brother, Cooper, still eats lunch with Piper every day. But seeing as Cooper was suspended for fighting again, Logan has taken over the job this week. He smiles and steals a cheese-smothered french fry from her tray. Piper rolls her eyes, feigning indifference and tucks her earbuds in. I bet this is what it's like for them at home. Fun. Playful. The complete opposite of how Logan is at school.

"So, what do you think?" Gunner asks, pulling my attention back to the table.

I blink twice, searching my brain for some trace of the conversation I tuned out, but I've got nothing. Once again, I got lost in my thoughts staring at Logan. I need to stop doing that. Thank God he's been skipping the classes we have together, I'd be royally screwed if he were there. "Huh?"

"The party tomorrow night. Want to go with me?" Gunner asks again.

Truthfully, I hate parties. Drinking isn't my thing, although, for the sake of appearances, I'll usually nurse a beer or two. Also, most parties bring drama and I'd rather not deal with any of it. But Gunner's hopeful eyes stare down at me and I don't want to disappoint him, especially if he's going to help me get over my infatuation with Logan. "I'd love to."

Gunner grins. "Awesome. I'll pick you up at nine."

Before I can react, he leans down and kisses me. His fingers weave through my curls, his lips warm and sure. His tongue brushes mine, soft and insistent, and I let it happen.

Our first kiss.

The bell rings, signaling the end of lunch, and he pulls back. I press my lips into a tight smile, letting him think I enjoyed the embrace when really, I'm confused.

He fingers one of my barrel curls and asks, "Want me to walk you to class?"

I shake my head and tell a tiny white lie. "I've got to go to the bathroom, but I'll catch you later."

"Okay. Bye, doll face." Gunner turns, leaving me in the now empty cafeteria to sort through my thoughts.

Our kiss was nice, but it wasn't earth-shattering. It felt safe, like kissing someone you've been with for years. There were no sparks or butterflies.

It was just a kiss.

I gather the trash my so-called friends left on the table, turn toward the nearest bin—then stop short.

Logan is standing by the door. Watching me.

And just like that, the world tilts.

y stomach lurches as Logan crosses the room, each step deliberate, radiating confidence that makes my pulse stutter. His gaze is a wildfire, scorching over me with an intensity I don't know how to handle —don't know if I *want* to handle. I toss my trash, freeing my hands in case I need to push him away. *Or pull him closer.*

"So, you're one of Gunner's playthings now?" His voice is low, dark, dripping with something dangerously close to jealousy.

I huff a laugh, more amused than offended. "You ignore me for *how* many days, and that's your opening line?" I tilt my head, watching him like a predator sizing up prey. He thinks we're playing cat and mouse, but he hasn't realized—I'm the cat. "Shame. I thought you had more bite than that."

A sinful smirk curls at his lips, as tempting as it is infuriating. "You know, once you spread those thick thighs of yours, Gunner will be done with you."

"Screw you."

The second bell sounds, signaling that anyone from this

point forward will be marked late. I should turn and run to my next class, then beg my teacher for forgiveness because I had lady issues. Instead, I hold my ground and cross my arms. Even if Logan's words are cruel, I can't help but want to hear what he has to say next.

"No thanks. I make it a point not to play anywhere Gunner has been. Or Tad for that matter." Logan pauses, his brooding gaze scorching my insides. "Jake at least wears a condom."

Even if that deep, gravelly voice of his sends shivers down my spine, the thought of him assuming I'd sleep with Gunner makes my stomach twist.

I turn to leave, done with his broodiness, but his hand wraps around my elbow. The sudden contact knocks the air from my lungs, leaving me lightheaded. My fingers fumble behind me for the table, gripping the edge as my knees threaten to give out.

"You can't trust him, Danika." Logan's voice is raw, edged with something dangerously close to desperation. His grip tightens just enough to make me *feel* it. "Gunner is a snake— just like Melody."

"Like you're any better? You've been nothing but a jerk to me ever since I came back."

Logan groans and kicks the trash can, denting the red metal cage around it. "You're nothing but a new skirt and the first person to nail you—"

I draw back and punch Logan in the nose. His head snaps back and the sound of his bones crushing is the only noise in the empty cafeteria. I've hit plenty of people since moving to California, probably too many, but each time it was justified. I always felt better afterward, but for some reason with Logan I feel guilty.

Logan wipes the blood dripping down his upper lip with the back of his hand and attempts to snap his nose back into place, only it's slightly more crooked than before.

All the tension falls from my shoulders when I step toward him. I did this. I should fix it. "Sit. Let me help."

Logan folds his arms and stands his ground. Dark circles have already begun to form under his eyes and the guilt of what I've done swallows me whole. He may be a jerk, but something made him this way. Maybe if I can figure out what it is and show him that I'm not the enemy, he'll turn back into the sweet boy I used to know. "Please."

With a huff, Logan complies.

Having a dad as a doctor, I've picked up a few skills. How to set a dislocated shoulder, CPR, how to stitch a wound, how to set a broken nose, and where the important places are to stab someone (or, in my case, hit) when in danger. Basically, Dad wanted to make sure that when I went off to college, I could fuck someone up and then fix what I broke.

"Slide down and rest the back of your head on the table. I don't want you flinching."

Logan follows my instructions without a word, his gaze locked on me as I kneel beside him. I place my thumbs along the bridge of his nose, but the angle feels all wrong—awkward, unsteady. I won't be able to set the bones properly like this.

Without thinking, I swing my leg over his waist, settling onto his lap. His hands find my hips instantly, strong and sure. I know it's just reflex, but that doesn't stop the jolt of electricity that shoots through me. My pulse pounds, each beat echoing in the space between us.

I close my eyes and let the high that comes with Logan's touch take over. I lean closer, my stomach pressing against the solid plane of his chest, and Logan's fingers tighten, digging into my ass. A sharp ache blooms beneath my bra, my nipples pebbling in response.

My eyes snap open, a rush of reality slamming into me. *Focus.* Clearing my throat, I reposition my thumbs along the sides of his nose and apply steady pressure. A sharp crack fills the air as the bones slide back into place.

"Done," I murmur, though my body tells me otherwise.

I linger in Logan's lap longer than I should, but he doesn't seem to mind. My body hums with the possibility, a dangerous curiosity unfurling in my chest. *What would it feel like to kiss him?* To give in to the heat simmering between us, to finally satisfy the pull that tightens every nerve when he's near.

This thing between us—it's impossible to define. A magnetic push and pull. An electric shock straight to the heart. A thrill laced with fear. It's all of that and more, and I crave it in ways I don't understand.

My hands slide down the sharp angles of his jaw, fingers locking around the back of his neck. My hair tumbles forward, a curtain of rosewater and longing shielding us from the rest of the world. He has to know what I want. Logan isn't the kind of guy to hesitate. He kisses everyone with a vagina.

So why not me?

I wet my lips, hoping he'll take the invitation. The moment stretches, thick and charged.

Then, without warning, Logan shoves me off him.

I hit the floor, stunned, my breath catching as I stare up at him. Tears prick my eyes—not from pain, but from something far worse. *Humiliation.*

He doesn't say a word. He just stands, turns, and walks out —like none of it meant anything at all.

"I've got it!" I call from my room, giving my hair one last spritz of extra-hold hairspray. I forgot how brutal Florida's humidity is—one step outside and my curls will start unraveling unless I drown them in product. I'm not ready, but time's up.

I rush down the stairs, determined to reach the door before my dad does. The last thing I need is for him to corner Gunner in the living room for an interrogation. Things between us aren't serious, but even if they were, I'd do everything in my power to avoid *that* conversation.

"Going out. Bye, Dad!" I say in one breath, yanking the door open and slipping outside.

Gunner stands there, running a hand through his golden-blond hair, eyes sweeping over me. He licks his lips, gaze lingering on my cropped *Doors* band tee and high-waisted jeans. I know most girls will be wearing something tight and skimpy with sky-high heels, but that's never been me. There's nothing wrong with dressing that way—it's just not my style.

"You look gorgeous." His voice is low, appreciative, as he steps in close, fingers curling around my waist.

Before I can react, his hand slides to the back of my neck, pulling me flush against him. His lips crash into mine, his tongue parting my mouth, claiming me. It's nothing like the slow, tentative kiss we shared in the cafeteria. This one is rougher, heavier—drenched in expectation.

And ultimately, disappointment.

I exhale when we break apart, searching for the spark that should be there. My heart beats steadily, unshaken, my stomach unmoved. Not even a flicker of excitement.

Gunner smirks. "I feel it too."

I force a smile, guilt gnawing at my insides. He thinks my exhale was one of pleasure—of *wow*—when really, it was a sigh of *oh*. Maybe all I need is time. But Logan's sneering voice from this afternoon creeps into my head, the way he practically spat out the word *playmate.*

I can't help but wonder... how many girls has Gunner been with? And how long do they usually stick around?

I swallow hard and meet his gaze. "Listen, Gunner, I need us to take things slow."

"I figured you weren't like the rest," he purrs, tucking my wayward strands behind my ears. "Why do you think I waited so long to kiss you?"

Three days isn't a long time, especially when you've just met, but arguing my opinion is pointless. As long as Gunner understands what slow means, we'll be fine.

Gunner drapes an arm over my shoulder and opens the car door for me. Logan is wrong. Gunner is sweet, patient, *normal.* The kind of guy I *should* be dating—not the broken ones with baggage who can't understand why I'm not ready to give my V-card to them.

We drive with our fingers laced over the gearshift, his thumb tracing slow circles on my skin. The engine purrs as he speeds down the highway, the car smooth, expensive, *fast*. I've never been in anything like it. By the time we pull up to the party, my stomach is still lodged somewhere in my throat. I use the ten seconds it takes for him to round the car and open my door to settle my nerves.

Even though it's only nine-thirty, the place is packed—cars crammed in the driveway and across the grass. Gunner pushes through the front door without knocking, because no one would hear it over the pounding bass anyway. He leads me straight to the patio, where the keg is already surrounded by half-drunk bodies. Pouring me a drink, he flashes a grin as he downs his own in one go.

Before I can take more than a sip, one of his football buddies calls his name. They launch into an endless conversation about next week's game, their words dissolving into a mess of stats and strategy that mean nothing to me.

Football was never a thing in my house. The only time it made an appearance on our TV was Super Bowl Sunday—for the commercials. But for a while, in sixth grade, it became *our* thing. Logan and me. Football, then milkshakes. What started as me wanting to make sure he had a friend turned into something I actually looked forward to.

But standing here now, listening to this conversation drone on, I can't take another second. I slip away unnoticed, cutting through the house and into the kitchen. My beer goes straight down the sink.

That's when Logan walks in.

He's not alone. A busty brunette clings to his side, and just like that, I hate her. Not for anything she's done, but because she has *his* attention. And I hate myself even more for wanting it.

He leans against the counter, pulling her in for a kiss that should've stayed behind closed doors. His dark eyes snap open mid-makeout, locking onto mine as I shamelessly watch.

I fold my arms and lean against the counter, feigning boredom. His dark gaze finally breaks from mine as he whispers something in the girl's ear. She nods and walks out of the kitchen, but not before he smacks her ass. for good measure.

I roll my eyes, pretending to be put off by the extra show of PDA when really my body is humming. "You're disgusting."

Logan crosses the kitchen, grabbing a soda from the fridge. He dumps half of it down the sink and tops it off with whatever's in his flask. "You're just jealous."

"Not even." I push off the counter and stand beside him. Even with two black eyes, Logan looks amazing, but I'll never tell him. His ego is larger than Harry Styles' and I have no desire to feed it.

"You know," I say, tilting my head, "I've never seen you do *anything* besides make out with a girl."

Logan smirks, lips curling around the rim of his drink. "Sorry if I don't make it a point to entertain you, but what I do behind closed doors is my business."

"Do you even *take* anyone behind closed doors? Or are you just happy putting on a show for whoever's watching?"

His smirk deepens. "Why do you care so much?"

Because I'm jealous. Because I hate that I *want* to be one of those girls.

"I don't," I lie, shrugging. "I just think your reputation is all smoke and mirrors."

Logan studies me for a beat, then tilts his head. "Would watching appease you?"

I raise a brow, calling his bluff. "I don't know. Maybe."

"Fine." Logan grabs my arm. "Let's go."

My pulse races as Logan drags me out of the kitchen and down the hallway to the living room. *What have I gotten myself into?*

He whistles and damn near every girl in the room looks our way. Logan points at a blonde from my math class and wiggles his finger for her to follow us into the hall bathroom. He shoves me in first, then holds the door for his new plaything.

I cross my arms and glare. The thought of this girl satisfying him in a way I can't twist my insides. I don't like it. "Do you even know this chick's name?"

He looks at her and raises an eyebrow.

"Emily," she says, her voice dripping with lust.

Logan unzips his pants but keeps his gaze on me. "On your knees, Emily."

The girl excitedly fists his cock then slips it in her mouth. I try to focus on Logan's face, but Emily's noisy slurping is hard to ignore. My gaze drifts to her bobbing head. I've never watched porn, let alone seen it live. The experience is uncomfortable and yet oddly arousing.

"What?" Logan guffaws, probably noticing the flush on my cheeks.

I shake my head, too embarrassed to admit what's happening to my body. I read a lot. The steamy romances I like talk about how girls are dripping wet, soaking their panties. I always thought it was an exaggeration. Totally understand what they're talking about now. "Nothing. I just thought it would be bigger."

"It's bigger than anything you've ever played with."

I smirk, feeling my cheeks burn hotter, and roll my eyes. "Either Emily here is the world's worst blowjob giver, or you're having a hard time concentrating." I stick up my pinky and wiggle it. "Little-Logan having performance issues?"

Logan grabs Emily by the hair and lifts her to her feet. "Out."

She wipes her mouth with the back of her hand and then slips out the door without a word. My heart breaks for Emily because no girl should be treated this way.

Logan follows her to the door and turns the lock on the handle. I don't know what's different about Emily and me, but I don't think he wants us interrupted. The air crackling around us fills with tension as he steps in front of me. The ebon of his irises disappears, swallowed by his large black pupils, and something about the way he looks at me makes it hard to breathe.

Logan is inches away, his exposed cock pressing against my leg, sending a rush of warmth through me. I fight the urge to lick my lips because I don't want to give Logan the impression that I want him, even if I do.

I've kissed my fair share of people and done some heavy petting, but this base is one I don't have much experience with. because I've only seen three penises in my life.

My first was uncircumcised and absolutely terrifying.

The next was so veiny it looked like a road map.

And the other was pencil-thin and crooked.

Logan's is thick, long, and smooth with a full mushroom tip. If I were ever to consider licking any of the now four penises I've seen, it would be his.

"You seem awfully critical of Emily's blowjob skills. Care to show me what you've got?" Logan's lips kiss the spot just beneath my ear.

I swallow hard, not confident in my skills, but I don't want to seem intimidated, either. I reach between us and wrap my fingers around Logan's silky shaft. I squeeze just hard enough to milk a quiet moan from his lips and move my hand across its length once.

Then twice.

Logan's eyes drift shut and my body hums, begging for him to touch me. Desire pelts through me like an unforgiving rain. It's overwhelming. I let not-so-little-Logan fall from my grip and step around him to the bathroom door.

I stop in the doorway and look over my shoulder as I say, "Put yourself away. That thing isn't even worth talking about."

oosebumps prickle across my skin as I press my back against the cold bathroom door, trying to ignore the images flashing through my mind. Logan's taking his time, and for that, I'm grateful. I don't want to think about what he's doing in there, but I highly doubt he's just taking a piss. Heat creeps up my neck. Is *he thinking about me?*

"Hey," Gunner's voice jolts me back to reality.

"Oh, hey." I force a casual smile and pretend I wasn't thinking about Logan's massive dick—again. The space between my legs tingles, betraying me and sending a rush of heat to my cheeks.

I glance up at Gunner, feigning innocence. Nope, no dirty thoughts here. My mind is pure as freshly fallen snow. *Liar.*

"Where'd you go?"

I jerk my thumb over my shoulder, keeping it casual. "Bathroom."

Please don't come out right now.

"Oh. Okay." Gunner takes my hand, his grip warm and

steady, and tugs me deeper into the house—down to the basement.

I let out a quiet sigh of relief, grateful Logan is still...doing what he's doing and try not to wonder how long *that* usually takes.

The handrail to the basement glows under a string of blue holiday lights, casting an electric haze over the staircase. I never knew Florida houses could have basements—I always thought the low water table made them impossible. But apparently, when you have more money than God, anything is possible. Including this: a fully transformed black-light dance party, complete with a DJ spinning beats that vibrate through the walls.

Gunner digs in the front pocket of his shorts and pulls out a small plastic baggie with two white pills inside. "Want one?"

I force a smile that's sure to look like a grimace. I don't do drugs, never been curious enough to try. I haven't even smoked pot and it's legal in California. My friends did all kinds of stuff when we partied, but after years of saying *no* they didn't waste their breath offering. "What is it?"

"E." Gunner places one pill on his tongue and swallows, expecting me to do the same.

I shake my head. I've never tried ecstasy before and don't plan on my first time being with some guy I barely know, even if he does like me. Gunner tucks the pill back in the baggie and slips it in his pocket again. "Your loss. Come on."

He pulls me into the center of the dance floor, where Sarah, Melody, Rachel, Tad, and Jake are already lost in the music. Sarah reaches for me, tugging me into a hug before leaning in to yell over the pulsing bass, "I'm sorry."

"It's okay," I yell back because it's pointless to have this conversation now. Sarah hasn't been the best friend these past few days. Sure, she's still picked me up and brought me home from school, but that's as far as her kindness went. We didn't talk in the car, let alone on campus. If not for her semi-welcoming smile at lunch, I'd think driving me was a chore and we weren't friends anymore. "Let's talk tomorrow."

Gunner steps behind me, his hands firm on my waist as he pulls me against him, ending my conversation with Sarah. Our bodies move like one as we fall in rhythm to the music.

Too many songs later, I'm out of breath. I stop moving as the music changes over and look around. Sarah is still going strong, dancing with some chick in my math class, Jake and Rachel are practically screwing each other on the dance floor, Tad's locking lips with a brunette I've never seen, and Melody and Gunner are nowhere in sight. *When did they disappear?*

I step around people, slowly making my way to the stairs to the main floor. The living room feels a hundred degrees cooler, making my skin break out in goosebumps again. I amble through the house and find my way back to the kitchen. I'm dying of thirst but have no desire for beer or anything of that nature.

"The keg is outside," Logan says while I open the cabinet nearest me.

My stomach comes to life, flipping and jumping at the sound of his voice. I thought he'd left after the bathroom debacle, but I guess he stayed. It dawns on me that we're the only ones in the kitchen. Everyone else is either outside on the patio or down in the basement, which makes me oddly uncomfortable, especially now that I've seen his dick.

I swallow the knot in my throat and turn around, pretending to be unfazed by Logan's presence when, really, I feel my pulse everywhere, toes included. "I wanted a glass of water."

Logan strides around the kitchen island like he owns the place, heading straight for the fridge. I know he doesn't, but whoever does must throw a lot of parties—everyone here moves like they belong. He swings the door open, grabs a bottle of water from the rack, and tosses it to me.

"Here."

Despite my best efforts, I'm at war with myself whenever Logan is near. The rational part of me knows exactly what he is—trouble. A player. A punk. The last thing I need in my life.

But then my heart skips, my stomach flips, and every nerve in my body betrays me, leaving me tangled in a mess of bad ideas and even worse decisions.

I catch the water with ease, twisting off the cap and taking a slow sip. The cool liquid soothes my parched throat, but it does little to ease the heat simmering beneath my skin. I'm warmer than I realized—though I suspect it has less to do with the party and everything to do with Logan. "Is this your form of an apology for acting like a jerk all week?"

Logan ignores my question and hops onto the kitchen island, his long fingers gripping the edge of the counter. The ink on his arm flexes with the movement, the dark lines shifting over taut muscle.

Maybe it's because of what happened in the bathroom, or maybe I'm finally losing the fight against my feelings, but I need him to say something. Anything. A nagging fear settles in my chest—if we can't figure out how to communicate now, this will never be more than a fleeting moment, a reckless mix of pride and lust.

I take a breath. "What's your tattoo of?"

Logan smirks and extends his forearm. Twisting my fingers through his, I trace the intricate design of an octopus, its curling tentacles wrapping around his skin like it's trying to hold onto him. He shudders beneath my touch but doesn't pull away.

My fingers drift across his palm, and he closes his hand around mine, his grip firm yet careful. I glance up, locking onto his amber eyes—their rich depths encircled by the faint ring of his contacts. The air between us thickens, every breath charged with something unspoken.

He feels this. There's no way this is one-sided.

"I'm surprised your mom let you get this."

Logan pulls his hand back and grips the edge of the counter again. His jaw tenses and I get the feeling his family dynamic isn't picture-perfect anymore.

"Saw your boyfriend a little while ago," he says, his voice unreadable.

I bristle at the assumption. Just because Gunner and I kissed doesn't mean we're together. Relationships aren't something I take lightly. Committing to someone means more than just stolen moments and heated glances—it's a step I don't take unless I'm sure. And boyfriends? They always expect more than just kissing.

"He's not my boyfriend," I say, keeping my voice even.

Logan's lips curl into something between a smirk and a sneer. "That's good because Gunner and Melody are upstairs fucking each other's brains out right now," he says, his voice a temerarious purr.

I clench my jaw to keep it from falling open. I can't be mad at Gunner. Not really. But I kind of want to be. Just a few hours ago, I had Logan's dick in my hand and at lunch I would have kissed him in a heartbeat if he would have let me.

And even though Gunner and I aren't together, the thought of him buried inside Melody makes my stomach churn.

"Hey, doll face," Gunner says, strolling into the kitchen like he doesn't have a care in the world, with Melody a few steps behind him. He pulls me into a backward hug, his arms locking around my waist. The scent of beer and an overuse of cologne floods my senses. "Where'd you disappear to? I've been looking everywhere for you."

I cross my arms, Logan's words still fresh in my mind. Gunner is supposed to be the nice guy. And nice guys don't cheat. But it's not cheating if we're not dating, I remind myself.

"You're the one who disappeared, Gunner. Not me," I say coolly.

Gunner steps in front of me, tilting my chin up with his thumb, forcing me to meet his gaze. His usually bright blue eyes are bloodshot, his pupils dilated—probably from whatever pill he took earlier. I swallow hard, wishing I felt something more than frustration.

"I had to take a piss," he says, voice smooth as honey. "When I got back, you were gone."

My gut tells me not to believe him, that something more happened than what he's letting on. But my head tells me to take a breath. Calm down. And think logically.

"What about Melody?" I ask, testing him.

"What about her?" He shrugs. "She's Logan's girl."

I thought Melody was overreacting the other day in the hallway. I don't regret beating the shit out of her—she started it —but if she really is Logan's girlfriend, then she had every right to be pissed at me... and every other girl he's cheated with.

Logan drops his chin to his chest and shakes his head.

As if on cue, Melody slinks toward him, stepping between his legs like she belongs there. She slides her hands onto his thighs, her fingers creeping dangerously close to his crotch and the same fire I felt around Emily ignites in my veins.

I don't want Melody touching him.

I don't want anybody touching him.

Logan grunts and shoves her back a step. "Quit."

My imagination runs rampant, torturing me with images of a naked Melody writhing beneath Logan. Her sweat-glistened body arching as Logan buries himself between her legs. The image flickers into motion; only Melody is no longer beneath Logan. I am.

I clear my throat and look at the floor, trying to shake the thoughts loose. "I should get home. Dad will ground me if I break curfew."

It's a lie—I don't even *have* a curfew—but Gunner doesn't know that. I just need to get out of here, take a shower, and figure out what I'm doing before someone gets hurt. *Before I* get hurt.

"Okay, doll face. Let's go." Gunner dips his head and presses his lips to my crown. He looks at me with bedroom eyes and I have a feeling that his definition of taking things slow and mine are completely different. I could maybe consider going a *little* farther than kissing if I felt something, anything, when we are together, but I don't.

"No. Stay with your friends. It's not your fault I have an early curfew tonight. I'll catch an Uber or something."

"I'll take you," Logan says, sliding off the counter.

Melody cups his cheek, desperate for his attention, but he doesn't so much as glance at her. He just pushes her hand away, his eyes locked on me.

Gunner pulls my hair to the side and sinks his teeth into my neck. My breath hitches, heart lurching at the unexpected contact. My body reacts before my brain catches up. And as thrilled as I am to finally *feel* something for him, the whole situation feels... dirty. Like a show of dominance between two predators.

Gunner tightens his grip around me and chuckles darkly. "Tell me, why would Danika go anywhere with *you?*"

Logan stares, gaze locked onto the spot where Gunner's mouth met my skin. His jaw tenses, his fingers curling at his sides. He opens his mouth to say something, but I cut him off.

Because I can see exactly where this is headed.

I step forward, out of Gunner's grasp, and brush my fingers over my neck.

"Actually, Logan," I say, voice steady. "That would be great."

Chapter 9

"So, you and Melody are a thing, huh?"

I twist the seatbelt between my fingers, the silence in the car stretching unbearably thin. Logan hasn't said a word since we left the party ten minutes ago, and it's killing me. I take a ragged breath, forcing my lungs to expand even though it feels like they're being squeezed by a rubber band.

He grunts and squeezes his steering wheel, the leather creaking beneath his grip. "Yes and no."

I shift one leg under me and turn in the seat to face him. Even under a blanket of darkness, the air between us is thick—whether from the conversation or just the weight of being near him, I'm not sure. "Care to explain?"

"Not really."

I shake my head. This isn't the Logan I used to know. He would never string girls along or show such little respect for someone as to cheat on them. "I need you to try, Logan. I can't do whatever this is we're doing anymore if you don't."

He glances over, his eyes locking onto mine for a moment

before flicking back to the road. We're almost home, and I know once we pull into that driveway, this conversation will end. "What is it you think we are, Danika?"

My chin drops to my chest as I exhale heavily. **I don't know.** And maybe that's the problem. My body shakes with nervous trembles, so I hug myself, rubbing my arms as if I'm cold. I pretend, for both our sakes. But of course, Logan notices—he always does—and without a word, he turns up the heat.

We pull into the Harris' driveway and park beside Cooper's Jeep. Surprisingly, Logan doesn't bolt out of the car. He reclines his seat and stares at the headliner, brows bunched together. After a long stretch of silence, he says, "I hate Melody."

"Then why are you with her?"

He laces his fingers behind his head and closes his eyes, his shirt stretching across his chest. "We're not. I've never touched Melody and never will, but she's insisted we were together since sophomore year."

I snort. "Bitch sounds crazy."

Logan chuckles and turns his head. He opens his eyes and, even in the dark, I can see the way his pupils have swallowed that beautiful brown. "She's a level of crazy that puts Jessica from *Love is Blind* season one to shame."

"You watched that?" I ask, a grin taking over my face.

"Don't judge me." He smirks and looks back up at the roof. "Anyway, last year, I stopped fighting her on it. She wanted the title without the benefits? Fine. I could still hook up with whoever I wanted, and she got to say she was my...whatever. It's never been a problem."

I tuck my hair behind my ears, just to have something to do with my hands. I still can't decide if what they're doing is cheating, but I guess it doesn't matter, so I change the subject. "Does this mean you're officially done being a jerk? Because I missed you, Logan."

His silhouette shifts, and I think he nods, but it's hard to tell in the dark. After a few more moments of silence, I reach for the door handle. But before I can open it, his voice cuts through the quiet, short-circuiting my brain.

"I'm sorry," he says and I freeze. He exhales roughly, gripping his keys. "I thought if I made you afraid of me, I could intimidate you into keeping quiet."

"Oh, Logan." I exhale loudly and lean back against the cushion of the seat. "I honestly have no clue what secret it is you think I know, but even if I did, I wouldn't tell anyone. You should know me better than that."

"Good. It was killing me being such a jerk to you." Logan looks down at his hands and fidgets with his car keys. "What do you see in him?"

"Who?"

"Gunner," he says, his voice rough and gravely. There's a pain in the way he says Gunner's name, maybe even a little jealousy, too, but I don't read into it. The last thing I need is to over-analyze our conversations and start fixating on every detail. Not gonna cross that crazy line.

I shrug. "He's cute, I guess, and nice."

Logan snorts. "That fucker is far from nice."

"Says the man who has been nothing but a jerk to me all week."

Silence fills the space until he says, "You could do better."

My heart stutters. I lick my lips, pulse pounding in my ears. **"With who? You?"**

The words slip out before I can stop them. And now I can't breathe.

How did I get here? How am I sitting in Logan's car, asking a hypothetical question I'm *dying* to know the answer to? What happens if he says yes? Do I end things with Gunner? Would Logan end his weird arrangement with Melody for me? My head spins, thoughts tripping over each other.

I take a slow, deliberate breath. I need to calm down. For all

I know, Logan will just laugh—play it off like a joke—and we'll go back to being friends. Like we used to be.

The flick of a flame from a lighter illuminates Logan's face, highlighting the sharp angles of his jaw. The man truly is beautiful. Something inside him is broken, that's clear as day, but he's beautiful, nonetheless.

He inhales deeply, holding the cigarette between his fingers. "Maybe," he exhales, smoke curling around his lips. "But I'm no good for you."

I left my phone in Logan's car. I keep telling myself it was an accident, but deep down, I know better. I want to finish our conversation. After Logan's declaration, he bolted, practically running into the house. I stayed in the car for a full minute, alone in the dark, replaying one single word in my mind.

Maybe.

Now, I stand on the porch of the Harris home, the white wooden door open behind the screen. Don't these guys know how dangerous it is to keep their home wide open this time of night? Then again, there are only two cars in the driveway. Maybe they're waiting for Mrs. Harris to get home.

"Logan!" Cooper's voice rings out from inside the house, sharp with panic.

The hair on the back of my neck stands. There are only so many reasons someone's voice carries that much fear and pain at the same time.

None of them are good.

I lean to the left, trying to see inside. Whatever is

happening is a family matter. I should leave, but my feet won't move.

Logan rushes out of what I assume is his bedroom and freezes in the hallway. From where I stand, even from twenty feet away, I see the color drain from his face.

"Call 911, Logan. Hurry!" his brother cries. "Don't do this to me, Piper. Come on, baby, stay with me."

Logan doesn't move.

My heart pounds as I wait for him to do something—anything—but he's a statue.

I yank open the screen door and sprint inside. "What's the—"

The words die in my throat. My stomach drops to my feet.

Cooper is on the bathroom floor, cradling Piper in his lap. Her head lolls against his chest, eyes closed. Pajama shorts and a shirt cling to her limp body, the ends of her dark hair splayed across her fair skin—skin that's too pale.

Cooper trembles, his arms wrapped around her as if he can hold her soul inside her body. A bloody handprint stains the wall where he must have reached for the towel now pressed against her wrists. Crimson water overflows the tub, staining the porcelain red, pooling on the ceramic tiles beneath them.

Cooper looks up at me with tear-stained cheeks. "I don't know what to do." He glances down at Piper and kisses the crown of her head, then whispers. "Please don't leave me."

"Stay there. You're doing great," I tell him, forcing strength into my voice. My fight-or-flight instincts kick in, only I'm not fighting for my life—I'm fighting for hers. My dad's medical advice and a million episodes of Grey's Anatomy come rushing back. *We can do this. We can save her.* "Just keep pressure on the cuts."

I scan the room, taking in every detail in a fraction of a second. There is a lot of blood. I know the bathtub water makes it look like Piper lost more than she actually did, but it's such a deep red and there's just as much on the floor. It's hard to say if anyone will get here in time, but I keep this to myself. Cooper's already panicking, whispering prayers of hope into Piper's ear. I won't add to his panic.

I step over to Logan. He's pale-faced, wide-eyed, just staring. "Logan?"

No response. I touch his arm and shake him a little, ignoring the fire in my veins. I need to sit down and have a come-to-Jesus meeting with my body. We—my heart, my head, my stomach, and just for shits and giggles, I'm going to say my vagina too—we all need to understand that Logan is bad news. He will obliterate us. Hell, he's already destroying us and we aren't fully friends at this point. *Yet.*

"Logan?" Still nothing. He's in shock and I need him to focus. I slap him across the face and bite back a smile, enjoying my hand on his skin more than I should. Especially considering the circumstances.

His brown eyes blink down at me, dazed, like he's just realizing I'm in his house.

"Where is your phone?" I vaguely remember why I'm here, because my phone is still in his car, but Logan's is closer and time is of the essence.

"It's...it's...in...mmm...mmy..." his thumb hitches over his shoulder.

I don't wait for Logan to finish. I step around him and run into his bedroom. Any other time I'd appreciate how clean it is or take in the little things that make Logan who he is to try and better understand the person he's become, but this isn't a social call. This is life or death. Literally.

I snatch his phone off his desk and run back into the hall. "What's your password?"

"0916," Cooper yells.

The screen unlocks to a photo of Logan, Cooper and Piper at a birthday party as kids. She's in the middle, wearing a bright yellow bathing suit. It's a beautiful picture. One I want to know more about, but again...not the time.

"911, what's your emergency?" the speaker on his phone booms.

I step around Logan and stand at the bathroom entrance. "Hi. Um, I'm at my friend's house, and she just tried to kill herself. There's blood everywhere. My other friend is trying to stop the bleeding but she's lost a lot. We need someone here stat."

"Take a breath, ma'am. Have you applied pressure to the wounds?"

I suck in a breath, my lungs burning as I exhale, not realizing I had said all that in one mouthful. "Yes."

"Good. I have someone on their way. Is she breathing?"

I look to Cooper, who's staring at me wide-eyed. Either he doesn't know or she's not. Both options aren't good. I step deeper into the bathroom, my shoes leaving bloody water footprints on white tiles that hadn't yet been stained. I rest my hand on Piper's chest and wait. The rise and fall of her lungs is shallow, and almost unnoticeable, but it's there. "Yes."

"Good. Stay with me. Tell me something about her?"

I look to Cooper again. He's shaking. Poor guy is still freaking out, but at least he's stopped crying. I hate it when men cry. Not because it kills their masculinity, but because for a man to allow himself to be that vulnerable, the pain he's feeling must be so great that it just explodes out of him.

I glance up and over to Logan. He's trembling, still stuck like a statue in an earthquake in the hallway. I bring my gaze back to Cooper. I reach out and touch his shoulder; he flinches but looks up at me. "Cooper? Tell me something about Piper. Anything."

He blinks twice, sucking in a ragged breath. "Um...she's allergic to cats."

I try to smile and nod in encouragement, but it's hard.

Seeing Piper like this brings up a horde of memories of my mom. Seeing Piper like this dredges up memories I'd rather forget. My mom didn't die by her own hand, but the cancer took her all the same. Death is death. Whether it happens by your own hand, someone else's, or sheer dumb luck, death leaves a veil of darkness in her wake. Some veils are just harder to see through than others. I close my eyes and swallow, pushing the memories of all the tubes and wires away.

"Indian River EMT!" The screen door swings open. A paramedic rushes in first, medical bag in hand, followed by two others with a gurney. He stops in the doorway for a moment, taking in the bloody mess then kneels beside Cooper.

I step out of the way and into the hall again. Logan's still unaware of his surroundings, his gaze stuck on Piper as if the image disconnected from his brain. I grab him by the arm and pull him into his bedroom, out of the path of the paramedics. Everything that happens next is a blur of motions. Before I can decode the medical jargon, Piper is lifted onto the gurney and wheeled out the door. Cooper stands in the hallway looking between his traumatized brother and dying sister.

"Go," I tell him. "I've got Logan. Take care of her."

Cooper nods without hesitation and runs after them, the front door slamming shut behind him.

Logan snaps out of his daze. His head turns slowly, his brown eyes dark and stormy, locking onto me with a force that nearly knocks me back.

"Get the fuck out."

"Excuse me?"

Logan doesn't reply. Instead, he turns and slams his bedroom door so hard the pictures in the hall rattle. I stand there utterly in shock. I've just helped with one of the most traumatic experiences any of us has been through, and he's kicking me out? *What the hell?* Not forty-five minutes ago we had a breakthrough out in his car. We are becoming friends again, I think, and this is how I'm thanked. Fine!

Screw you, Logan!

I may be struggling with whether I want to be just friends or something more, but he jumps between enemies and potential lovers faster than Disney princesses fall in love.

I stomp down the hallway, too pissed to notice the trail of blood leading to the front door, and slip. I fall to the ground, more frustrated than I was before because this is all his fault. If Logan hadn't told me to leave, my favorite jeans wouldn't be ruined and my ass wouldn't be sore

I scramble to my feet and march back to Logan's bedroom door, fully prepared to barge inside and ream him a new asshole, but it's locked. *I Miss You* by Blink182 seeps through the walls on full blast, and my world stops.

All the frustration inside me melts away with the second verse. I lean against the door separating us, tears on the brink of escape from the realization that Logan thinks Piper is already gone.

Please, please, let Piper make it.

I wipe my eyes with the back of my hand and suck in a shaking breath. I can't break down, not yet. I told Cooper I'd take care of Logan and that's what I'm going to do.

I open the bathroom door and look around at the mess. There's blood everywhere: the shower walls, the floor, the towel bar from where Cooper probably pulled himself up, and trailing through the house to the front door. Logan's phone lies in the middle of it all, abandoned. I bend down and pick it up. Using the part of the hanging towel not stained red, I wipe the screen off and unlock it again.

The same picture greets me, only this time it seems sadder. They were such cute kids. So innocent with their whole lives ahead of them. I swallow the knot in my throat and open the recent call log. Someone's got to tell his mom.

"Logan, sweetie, you never call. Is everything alright?" Mrs. Harris's voice comes through, slightly muffled by music in the background. She sounds happy. Carefree.

My stomach knots.

This is going to ruin her night.

"Uhh..." No. Everything's not okay. "Hi, Mrs. Harris. It's Danika, your neighbor."

"Oh," she says, not bothering to hide the surprise in her voice. "Hello, dear."

Neither Logan nor Cooper show up to school on Monday. I'm not surprised, but I really wish I'd remembered to grab my phone. Being without it sucks. I don't have social media, but two days without my e-reading app has been hell. And more than anything, I want to know how Logan is doing. How Piper is doing.

There's some chatter about all three of them being out, but mostly, everyone is fixated on Friday's football game. So, the Harris drama fell into the background.

After school, I sit near the kitchen window, earning a handful of curious glances from Dad as I impatiently wait for someone—anyone—from the Harris household to come home. I stare at my open book, rereading the same sentence for what feels like an eternity, when finally, around dark, Cooper pulls into his driveway.

I jump up so fast my chair clatters to the floor. Not bothering to close the door behind me, I sprint across the grass. Cooper notices me as his Jeep beeps locked and practically collapses on the bottom step of his porch, elbows on his knees.

I sit beside him. "How is she?"

"Alive." Bloodshot eyes meet mine, and my stomach twists. Cooper looks rough. Dark circles, an unshaven jaw, an exhaustion that makes him look five years older than he did last week. He hasn't slept much. Maybe hasn't showered either. "Thanks to you."

I don't want to think about what could've happened had I not been there that night. Instead, I pull Cooper into a hug, like I so desperately want to do for Logan. But Logan has shut down, retreating into himself the way he used to when we were kids. I'd hoped that with all the changes he'd made while I was gone, he might have changed that, too. No such luck.

"No, Coop," I murmur. "That was all you. You saved Piper."

Cooper sniffles and pulls back. We share an awkward smile before he lets out a weak chuckle. "I'm gonna shower. I stink."

I nod, hoping he's not offended by the truth. But Cooper just laughs, shaking his head. "See you around, Danika."

TUESDAY MORNING, Logan's car is in its usual spot, but he's nowhere to be found. I need an update on Piper. And my phone. I've never gone this long without it. It's not like I expect some life-altering call from California—everyone there was washed from my hands the day we left—but having it feels like a security blanket.

At lunch, Sarah drops into the seat beside me and slides my phone across the table. "Here. I was wondering why you were ignoring me. I texted you like a million times, but I guess Logan had this the whole time. Also, in case you were wondering, I took a personal day yesterday."

I anxiously take my phone from her hand and double-tap the screen. Unsurprisingly, it's dead. It doesn't matter. I'm just glad to have it back. "Thanks. How was he?"

Sarah tilts her head to the side and looks at me skeptically. I haven't told anyone about what's going on in the Harris home. It's not my place and the way people treat Piper, I think the truth would do more damage than the rumors.

"Uh... Logan is fine. Why?"

I shrug and play it cool, pretending like I'm not losing sleep over what's happening next door. "No reason. Logan just hasn't been home much lately."

Before Sarah can press, a shrill voice cuts through the cafeteria.

"You little slut!"

I barely register Melody stomping toward me before she throws her soda in my face.

"What the hell, Melody?" Sarah shrieks, grabbing everyone's napkins from the table. She hands me one and I wipe my face while she dabs my chest. We seem to realize, at the same time, that our efforts are useless and toss the soggy napkins on the table. My shirt is soaked. And worse, it's sheer.

"How did you do it?" Melody demands.

"I'll be right back," Sarah says, leaving me to defend myself. "I think I have an extra jacket in my locker you can cover up with."

The thought is nice, but Sarah is half my size and has mosquito-bite-boobs. There's no way in hell I'll be able to get her jacket on *and* zipped. I cross my sticky arms over my now-see-through shirt and glare at Melody. "Do. What?"

"Logan!" She screeches, slamming her hands on the table. "He broke up with me and it's all your fault."

A smirk tugs at my lips. Even though Logan's avoiding me, he's still thinking about our conversation from the other night. And that makes my stomach flutter. "Did you honestly think it was gonna last between you two?"

Melody's face burns red as I pluck a tater tot from Rachel's tray and pop it into my mouth. Not exactly vegan, but the horrified look on Melody's face is worth it. "You're obviously not satisfying Logan if he's seeking pleasure from everyone but you."

"I'm gonna kill you!" Melody screams, lunging across the table with claws out. She shoves me, sending me crashing to the floor. Pain flares up my spine as my back hits the shellacked wood floor of the cafeteria. I raise my arms, covering my face from her pathetic attempt at a fight.

People gather around us, toes of colorful heels and brown shoes the only thing I see beside me. Melody slaps at my head, occasionally scratching me with her lilac acrylic claws. They hurt, but they don't break the skin.

I'm down for only a few moments when the attacks begin to lose momentum. I grab her wrist and yank it against her stomach, gripping her shirt with my other hand. I shift my weight, flipping us over in one fluid motion and my fist connects with her face.

People around us laugh and I notice a strange smell. I leap up, realizing Melody's pissed herself, and jump back. This is the kind of humiliation you don't recover from. I feel bad, but the bitch shouldn't start what she can't finish.

The tiny hairs on the back of my neck stand on edge and I whirl around, looking for the cause. I catch a glimpse of dark hair near the corner of the cafeteria. I immediately know it's him and push my way through the circle of people around me.

"Logan!" I shout, but he's gone so fast I wonder if I truly saw him.

On Wednesday, Cooper comes back to school, which is concerning because he looks as bad, if not worse than he did on Monday. We sit together at lunch. For the most part, we don't talk. But eventually, he opens up and says that Piper is okay and, fingers crossed, will be back to school on Friday.

Wednesday is also the first time I see Logan. He's at his usual lunch table, glaring the whole time I'm with Cooper. I want nothing more than to strut across the cafeteria and force him to speak to me, but Logan is prideful. Having just publicly broken up with Melody, I doubt he'll take my demands lightly. I take a breath and force myself to be patient. Logan can't ignore me forever.

I won't let him.

I hate hospitals. They smell like blood and chemicals, but for Piper I put aside my own issues and be the brother she needs because today we're bringing her home. All three of us—Mom, Cooper, and me—united to show her we're family and we've got her back.

Tomorrow she'll attempt to resume a normal life: back to school, working a few nights with Cooper at the Red Onion, and maybe even a party or two if Cooper will let her. It'll be hard to pretend like nothing happened in front of everyone, but Piper will put a fake face on and get through it because she has no other option.

I unlock my car and turn my gaze to the white BMW pulling into Danika's driveway. A chill slithers down my spine, it's eerily similar to someone else's I used to know. My feet stick to the ground as the man gets out of his car. I try to inhale, but the pressure in my chest increases.

My mind has done this to me a million times over, but that doesn't make seeing him feel any less real. Grey eyes meet mine, and the man gives a two-finger salute, like we're old friends. I don't return the gesture, physically can't, even though I want nothing more than to flip him the bird. It's not until he's disappeared inside the Winters house that my feet find the will to move.

I should get in the car. I should drive to the hospital. I'm supposed to be there in twenty minutes and be supportive of my sister. She's going through so much more than I am right now.

Instead, I run into the house. My stomach lurches into my throat and I barely make it to the kitchen trash can in time before yellow acid expels itself.

"Fuck," I whisper, closing my eyes, hoping to wipe that smug smile from my brain. But all I see are memories. All I feel is the nonexistent hand on my shoulder squeezing, lingering longer than necessary. My stomach churns again, but there's nothing left to expel. I dry heave over the trash can again for five minutes and then sag onto the floor.

This can't be happening. Not again.

My gaze follows Danika as she bypasses Sarah and heads straight for Piper's table. Rumors about where Piper has been have floated around since she got back. Most people think she was in rehab for a drug overdose while others assumed she was hooking on a street corner. If only they realized how much worse the truth was.

Danika sitting at that table could potentially send the gossip mill into overload. Piper's everyday rumors were too much to handle, she doesn't need new ones added into the mix. And I don't want to risk anything tipping her over the edge again.

Where the fuck did Cooper go? He usually handles this shit.

I storm across the cafeteria and grab Danika's arm as she

sets her tray on the table, turning her to face me. I'm on edge, sleep-deprived, and out of smokes. I don't have the patience to play nice because she wants to be St. Galentine today.

"What the fuck are you doing?" My voice is low, but the bite is unmistakable.

Danika barely flinches. If anything, she looks relieved. Like she was waiting for this. For me. "I was wondering when you'd acknowledge me again." She reaches out, fingertips grazing my arm, her touch too light, too soft. "How are you?"

I jerk free of her grasp and glare. This isn't a social call. I'm not here to talk about me or my feelings. I'm fine. In fact, I'm great. Fucking great. "Leave Piper alone, Danika."

That pretty little smile falls and Danika's arms cross over her chest. "You can't tell me who to be friends with, Logan. I was coming over here to tell Piper about a book I thought she might like. It's about—"

"I don't give two shits what the goddamn book is about!" I snap, catching the attention of more than a few people in the cafeteria. I don't want to take my frustrations out on Danika, but she's here and they're uncontrollably spilling out of me. I need a drink, and a smoke, and quite frankly to get laid. I haven't touched anyone since Emily at Jake's party, and maybe that's the problem. Maybe I need something—someone—to ground me. To make this spiral stop.

"Logan." Cooper's voice cuts through the fog, his hand a heavy weight on my shoulder.

Memories flicker like scenes from a movie across my mind, and I fight the urge to throw up again. I haven't eaten, haven't slept since yesterday. I can't. Everything around me unearths a buried demon and I'm more agitated than a rabbit on crack.

I shrug Cooper off, my jaw locking. All I wanted was to protect Piper, but when I play the hero it's not good enough. Somehow, I fuck it up. I fuck everything up because I'm not the golden boy. I can't throw the perfect spiral, or get on the honor roll, or do anything right because I'm. Not. Cooper.

I don't know why I keep thinking things will change. They've been this way ever since I can remember. He can talk some sense into Danika and warn her to keep her distance. It's not like anyone ever listens to me anyway.

"You fucking deal with her then. I'm done."

Chapter 14

My fingertips kiss the grass while I wait for Robby—the second-string quarterback— to start the play. He's taking his time, which pisses me off. It's the first game of the season and we're getting our asses handed to us. I've done my part and taken down everyone in my way with excessive force, but it hasn't helped. Anxious energy buzzes under my skin and it's driving me crazy. I need to do something, anything, to make them go away.

It's not helping that all night Gunner's made witty comments, adding fuel to the flames in my veins. I've tried to ignore him because Danika is somewhere in the stands, being a supportive girlfriend. But I also know that her gaze periodically follows me, and having her here brings back a nervousness I haven't felt in years.

"You've got a thing for Danika. Don't you?" Gunner taunts from beside me.

I ignore him and focus on the sound of our fans. Our team might suck, but the parents who pay out the ass for their kids to attend St. A's show up to our games religiously despite our historical losing streak.

"We both know she's out there," Gunner continues, purposely pushing my buttons. The dude's got a fucking death wish I'd be happy to satisfy, but I'm trying really *really* hard to keep my shit together. "And tonight I'm finally going to score."

"Hike!" Robby yells, catching the ball as I turn and throw all of my body weight into Gunner.

We topple to the ground, but I get the upper hand and straddle Gunner's waist. I yank his helmet off and my fist connects to his face with a sharp, precise blow. From the amount of red gushing, I'd say his nose is broken.

I let Gunner shove me off because I want a fight, not a massacre. We've got maybe sixty seconds before the referee blows his whistle and I plan to make the most of it.

Gunner grins, blood dripping and pooling in his mouth. He looks like a sadistic clown, one that haunts your dreams and carves up kittens or some shit. I fucking hate clowns. He swings and throws a left hook to my ribs. The pain spreads through my body like ink in water, slithering its way into every nook and cranny of my soul.

I let him land another shot to my center and even though I'm sure he's cracked one of my ribs, I can finally breathe. The anxious energy fizzles away and I'm left with the calm I've been searching for all day.

Fighting is the only reason I bother to come out onto the dyed green grass anymore. Although, it's usually our opponents I go after. For the record, I hate football, and I have ever since the homecoming game in my freshman year. That was the first game our dad missed. He may have been an abusive ass most of my life, but I still craved his approval. Fucked up, I know. But what can I say? I'm a kid with daddy issues.

That was also the day I completely fell off mom's radar. I saw her in the stands. I. Saw. Her. But she was too consumed with her phone, stressing over Piper returning to her bio-mom's place.

Mom didn't see me score the winning touchdown.

She didn't see the tackle that dislocated my shoulder.

She didn't notice when I came home with a bag of ice taped to me.

She *did* notice Cooper's black eye and tended to him like he was a fucking newborn baby.

That game was when I realized I never really liked the sport. I played because it was the only time my parents acknowledged my existence as more than a nuisance, until they didn't. I was pissed and unlike Cooper, I couldn't walk around campus beating the shit out of people.

But on the field, I can do whatever I want with little to no consequence.

The referee blows his whistle, flagging us with a fifteen-yard penalty for unsportsmanlike conduct. Coach Riley yanks me back by the shoulder pads while Assistant Coach Greene does the same to Gunner. They escort us off the field, like two pissed off parents, and leave us on the sidelines.

"Sit your ass down, Harris, and don't fucking move!" Spit flies from Coach Riley's mouth, spraying his hand and the finger in my face.

I spit a wad of blood-tinged saliva on the neon-green grass beside the bench. It would be fun to change the bulbs in the stadium lights to black lights. I bet the field would light up brighter than a Christmas tree with all the chemicals they spray.

"We're going to lose the game because of you," Gunner growls from the other side of the bench. He grabs his blue and white helmet and throws it near the water station. Unlike me, he actually cares enough to try his best each game. Too bad for him his best isn't worth a damn.

"No. We're going to lose because Cooper didn't bother to

show up and you can't block for shit." I look over my shoulder at the people in the stands.

Even though we're losing thirteen to three, the crowd screams enthusiastically as the play continues without us. The majority of the first row in the stands is full of cleat chasers, anxious to be tonight's newest playmate. They don't care which teammate they leave with as long as they show up to the after-party in our arms.

I lock eyes with a pretty brunette with long pigtails and short shorts. She reminds me of Danika back in the eighth grade: awkward and top-heavy. I give her a small, upwards nod and she and her friends squeal with excitement. Not caring if Coach gets pissed, I strut over to the girl.

The girl grips the rail separating us and looks down at me. Her shirt has 96, my number, scrawled on it in glitter blue paint; something else my best friend used to do back in the day. Tonight, Danika's probably wearing Gunner's number and it sets me on fire again. I've never been the jealous type, but Danika is changing me. I just haven't figured out if it's for better or for worse yet.

"Hey, Logan," she purrs.

I don't bother asking for the girl's name. I don't care what it is. In an hour, maybe less, she'll be washing me of my infatuation with my neighbor. But for now, she'll serve a different purpose. "Got a smoke?"

The girl's smile falls for a fraction of a second before someone hands her a cigarette. "I do now."

She places the cigarette between her cherry-red lips and lights it, taking a drag for herself before passing it to me. I grab the cigarette from her but don't actually want it. My ribs are throbbing now that the adrenaline has worn off. I have a feeling that smoking will take this pain from tolerable to unbearable.

The girl beams down at me. "Are you going to Jake's party tonight?"

"Move!" my least favorite voice says, pushing her way through the bundle of women crowding the rail. I fight a smile, because I know without a doubt Danika is here for me. Not Gunner. It doesn't matter that I piss her off and push her away, she always comes back.

"Are you insane?" Danika yells.

I shrug, taking a drag off the cigarette in my hand. I was right. Breathing hurts like a bitch. I drop the cigarette beside me and vaguely wonder if the chemicals on the grass are flammable. Normally, the thought would be amusing, but with Danika in the stands I don't want to take any chances and step on the wasted cigarette until the cherry goes out.

My red-lipped plaything glowers. "Back off, bitch, I was here first."

"Shut the fuck up, Lydia," Danika replies, and I vaguely remember that is the girl's name. "I have no problem throwing you over this rail to get you out of my way."

Lydia crosses her arms and raises one perfectly plucked eyebrow. "I'd like to see you try."

Danika smirks, stepping towards Lydia who flinches. As thrilling as it is watching her fight over me, I don't want Lydia any closer than she already is.

"Dani!" I call out, using her middle school nickname to snap her focus back to me. "Shouldn't you be checking on your boyfriend?"

"He's not my boyfriend."

"Awe, babe. You came to check on me," Gunner says coming up behind me, oblivious. "This is why I love you."

Lydia and her friends gasp. As far as I know, Gunner has never said those words to anyone, let alone publicly. It's a big moment for Gunner's reputation, and one-hundred percent a shitty, selfish way to drop the L-bomb. I hope Danika can see this for what it is—a move to get down her pants. There's no way this dickwad fell in love in three weeks.

Me on the other hand...nope. *Not going there.*

Danika's face drains of color. She looks like she might be sick but forces a smile that lands somewhere between a grimace and a wince. "Gunner—"

"I thought I told you sorry sacks of shit not to move!" Coach Riley's voice cuts through the moment, sparing Danika from what was about to be a very public, very humiliating conversation. "Get your asses back to the bench before I ban you from next week's game!"

Chapter 15

At half-time, the stadium plunges into darkness, the scoreboard's faint glow the only light on the field. I welcome the shadows. They let me hide—from the spotlight, from the moment, from Gunner's grand confession. Because love? Yeah, I'm so not ready to deal with that.

The people around me aren't as comfortable. A collective murmur rises: *What's going on? Is this supposed to happen?*

Then, suddenly, the lights flare back on, and AJ Mitchell's *Slow Dance* blares through the speakers. As if on cue, St. A's players pair up and start swaying, actually slow dancing on the field. Laughter ripples through the stands because it's ridiculous—like a scene straight out of a cheesy teen romcom. But the worst part hasn't hit yet.

Gunner, microphone in hand, smirks as he locks eyes with me. Then, he starts to sing. "*If you stay for a minute, girl, I'll never let you down...*"

"What the fuck is this shit?" Coach Riley yells, throwing his clipboard to the ground.

I cover my face with my hands, peeking through my fingers. I don't know what's happening, but it's so embarrassingly sweet I can't help but smile. Gunner, to his credit, can actually sing. And he's going all in—dancing like he's starring in *High School Musical*, fully committed to the performance. He takes a slow step toward me and I look over my shoulders as the girls around me begin to jump and scream like he's a rock star. This is too much. Too ridiculously much.

By the time the chorus ends, Gunner is directly below me. The music fades, and then—oh god. He drops to one knee.

Another collective gasp echoes through the crowd.

"Danika," he says, grinning up at me. "I know it's not prom, so this could very well be the first of three proposals. But will you go to homecoming with me next week?"

Hands touch my arms and shoulders. The girls around me lean closer, probably hoping to be the first to hear my answer. Homecoming is a big deal—a milestone in whatever *this* is between us. And this? This is the sweetest thing anyone has ever done for me.

I nod, my voice refusing to cooperate.

The girls around me scream in excitement and the song starts to play again. Coach Riley throws his hands in the air, frustrated, and storms off the field. The referee blows his whistle, calling the game and people file out of the stands. Gunner stays on the grass. Staring. Waiting.

When the crowd thins, he jumps the barrier between the field and the bleachers and races up the steps. He spreads his arms, grinning like he just won the Super Bowl, when he's only a few feet away and pulls me in, then spins me around. When he sets me down, he kisses me—deep, passionate, the kind of kiss that belongs in a Nicholas Sparks movie.

It should be perfect.

But my stomach twists.

Something is *wrong*.

As beautiful as this moment is, my stomach twists. Everything feels wrong. I should be melting into Gunner's arms, soaring sky-high with elation. Instead, my feet are weighted to the ground and I'm drowning in regret.

Every fiber of my being screams that I should have said *no*.

Chapter 16

"**R**achel's going with Jake, you're going with Gunner, Melody's going with some trust fund college freshman and I'm going to be the loser all alone at the Homecoming dance tomorrow night," Sarah whines, sifting through a rack of dresses at a store I can't even begin to afford. She pulls a short, feathery blue one off the rack and holds it in front of her.

I shake my head. "You'll look like a peacock."

"But I'll be the best damn looking peacock at that dance," she laughs and then puts the gown back, her search continuing.

I pretend to sift through dresses. Even though Dad would probably let me splurge on a new one, things are still pretty tight. We're living off his credit cards until his first check comes, which should be any day, but I don't want to add any extra stress. My closet has a handful of fancy gowns no one on this coast has seen. I'll wear one of those.

Sarah puts her hands on her hips and looks around, her lips pressed into a tight line. "Why does everything have to be so hideous?"

"Because you have unrealistic expectations for what this mall has to offer." The tiny shopping complex this town calls a mall is half empty, barely surviving with a few chain stores and a handful of small-business ones. It's a miracle the building hasn't gone bankrupt, considering how many empty storefronts there are.

Sarah sighs with a chuckle. "You're right. We should head down to West Palm. Their mall is way better than ours."

"How far is it?"

She twists her cherry red lips, thinking. "Maybe forty-five minutes. If we hurry, we can probably make it back in time for tonight's game."

I won't be buying anything there either, but what the hell? Tonight's game is bound to be packed. No one will notice if I'm not there. "I can miss one game."

"You don't think Gunner will be mad? They're doing the whole homecoming court thing tonight."

I shrug. Gunner isn't who I'd be worried about, it's Logan. Even though we haven't been on the best terms since I've been back, there is still an unspoken agreement that I'll be at every game. But we aren't close like we used to be, and most days, he acts like I don't exist. Truthfully, I shouldn't even be thinking about him, and yet here I am. "Does it matter? I'm not on the homecoming court."

"Oh, before we leave, I want to check out Merlot's. The new limited edition Louis Vuitton bag is due out any day, and I've gotta have it," Sarah says, strutting over to the tiny store.

"Oh. My. God. Sarah? Is that you?" Melody's voice rings like nails on a chalkboard as soon as we walk inside. My insides cringe at the exaggerated show of excitement she's putting on. I don't understand why people have to be fake. The girls in California at my old school were the worst; friend to your face but foe to your back. Melody would have fit in perfectly there.

Sarah throws me an apologetic glance before pasting on a

forced smile and turning to face Melody and Rachel. Adjusting the strap of her oversized bag, she says, "Melody, what are you doing here?"

Melody leans in for a faux kiss on Sarah's cheek, her eyes locked on me the entire time. I narrow mine, ready for a battle of wits if necessary—though, with Melody, it'd be more of a massacre than a battle. She's about as sharp as a bag of cotton balls.

"Rumor had it my favorite Harris was wandering around somewhere. So, Rachel and I thought we'd do a little shopping."

I roll my eyes and drift toward a display of purses I can't afford, pretending to find one that I like. I need a job. Better yet, I need a new school—one where social status isn't determined by the price tag on your handbag because if I'm being honest, I care what people think of me. I want to be liked by my classmates. I want to look back at my senior year and smile. I can't say that for last year.

"EEEK!" Melody squeals. "It's here!" She looks around and spots the only employee on the floor. "Ma'am! Ma'am! This isn't a social hour over there. You're on duty and I want that purse."

The sales associate—clearly irritated—plasters on a customer service smile and steps toward us. "How can I help you, ladies?"

"Are you *dense*?" Melody snaps, jabbing a manicured finger toward the display. "That purse was released last week. I *want* it."

The woman's forced grin turns into a sly smile as she says, "I'm sorry, but all the ones we have were sold as pre-orders, and at this time, the company isn't releasing any more. Perhaps try eBay."

"Well un-preorder one and give it to me!" Melody demands with a stomp of her foot.

"I'm sorry Miss, but that's not possible. If there's anything else I can get you please let me know." The sales lady turns her back to us and saunters back to the counter.

"That bitch has more," Melody insists, digging through her purse for her phone. "She just doesn't want to sell one to me. Wait until Daddy hears about this. He'll have her job, and she'll be sorry."

"For crying out loud, Melody. Not everything is about you." The words are out before I can stop them. From the looks on everyone's faces, I *definitely* said that out loud. Oops. Oh well.

Melody squares her shoulders and stalks toward me. "Excuse me, bitch?"

I set down the purse I was pretending to like and turn to face her. She's practically vibrating with rage, and I have to fight back a smirk. Getting under her skin is *too* easy. I fight a smile, loving how riled up she is, and amble over to the jewelry display. "I'm just saying that's not how retail stores work. If the woman had one available, she'd sell it to you. You shouldn't try to mess with someone's livelihood just because you didn't get your way."

Melody's nostrils flare. "Listen here, you little—"

She stops mid-sentence, eyes flicking past me. I follow her gaze—and just great. Of all the people in this town, in all the stores in this mall, Logan Harris walks into *this* one.

Melody instantly switches gears. "Oh. Em. Gee. Logan!" she squeals, voice dripping in fake sweetness. "What are you doing here?"

Every muscle in my body tenses as Logan moves closer. He's ignored me all week, but unlike before, he's not avoiding me. If anything, it's the opposite—I see him everywhere, always with a different girl, always kissing her like he's starving. Hands in her hair. Fingers gripping her waist.

The memory alone makes my cheeks heat.

Logan doesn't even acknowledge Melody. He walks straight past us, heading for the counter. He and the saleslady have a quiet conversation and she disappears into the back. Moments later, she returns with a bag—probably containing *the* pre-ordered purse. Logan hands over his credit card without hesitation.

Obviously frustrated that nothing in this store is going her way, Melody turns her attention back to me. "That's a pretty necklace, Danika. Are you going to buy it?"

I don't even bother checking the price tag. I already know it's too expensive. I put it back. "No."

Melody arches her brows at me, her lips curling into a sinister smirk. "Why? Is it too expensive for you? Maybe the thrift store down the block is more your speed."

"Anyway," Sarah interrupts, stepping between me and Melody, using her body as a shield against Melody's harsh words. "We should probably get going. If we're going to make it down to West Palm before rush hour."

Melody juts out her bottom lip, fake pouting. "Awe, is pretty little Danika too good to watch her boyfriend play football tonight?"

I hate her. If I were a lesser woman, I'd fire back and spit more nastiness in the air than Melody would know what to do with. But I was raised better and this is a testament to Melody's character, not mine. Instead, I tuck my long chocolate strands behind my ear and say, "Gunner is not my boyfriend."

"Of course he's not," She smirks triumphantly. "He doesn't do monogamy or have you not realized that yet?"

A rush of heat climbs up my neck. I don't even have to turn around to know Logan is close. My body already senses him. I close my eyes, breathing in the scent of his cologne, letting myself get carried away by how heavenly it is.

"You're not coming tonight?" He asks from behind me, his voice devoid of emotion because he couldn't care less what I do anymore. "You used to go to all of my games."

I turn slightly, meeting his gaze. "You used to be a better friend."

The words hit their mark. For a fraction of a second, something flickers in his eyes—something unreadable—but it's gone before I can place it.

Melody, still trying to piece together what's happening, points between us. "Is there something going on between you two?"

"No," Logan growls.

Then, without another word, he walks away—shoulder bumping mine as he passes.

The doorbell chimes, its familiar melody ringing through the house, and my stomach twists in response. When Dad asked who I was going to the homecoming dance with, I didn't lie. Gunner had asked me in the most over-the-top way imaginable, and even though I don't feel much for him, I couldn't bring myself to say no.

Dad, of course, still wants to pull the whole protective father act. If he had a group of intimidating friends and a small arsenal at his disposal, they'd be stationed by the door, ready to grill my date. But he doesn't have friends, I don't have a boyfriend, and deep down, we both know there's nothing to worry about tonight.

Still, the thought of Gunner standing outside, corsage in hand, sends my pulse racing. My last boyfriend refused to go to school functions—a pathetic attempt at rebelling against his parents. Every other dance, I went stag with a group of friends. While my date might not be my first choice, I'm still excited to experience tonight.

I race down the stairs, my royal blue Converse perfectly matched to my dress. Heels and I have never gotten along—I can barely walk in them, let alone dance. Unlike Sarah and probably every other girl tonight, I actually want to enjoy myself, not spend half the night complaining about my feet before giving up and going barefoot.

Dad, of course, is waiting like a snake in the grass to attack and beats me to the door. His broad frame fills the doorway, blocking any chance for me to see if Gunner went all out with a blazer and tie or kept it casual with just a button-down.

"You must be Gunner," Dad's voice is deeper than usual, thick with that classic overprotective-father intimidation. I roll my eyes. He may be big, but he's a total softie.

"No, sir."

My heart stutters, my breath catching as I process Logan's voice. What the hell is he doing here? I push up on my tiptoes, barely catching a glimpse of his dark hair over Dad's shoulder. Dad's arm extends as he shakes Logan's hand, giving him what I'm sure is a death grip to establish dominance. *Men.*

"I'm your neighbor, Logan," he says, hesitantly. They exchange a few hushed whispers then Logan asks, "Is Danika still here? I have something for her."

Dad exhales through his nose, clearly debating whether to be difficult, before stepping aside and settling onto the couch. Logan steps inside, his gaze sweeping over the room. There's no judgment in his eyes, but that doesn't stop the insecurity curling in my stomach.

Our home is simple—too simple compared to the sprawling estates in the neighborhood. Logan's house is a modern, two-story U-shape built around an enclosed pool. Ours? A single big square with an open-concept living room, dining area, and kitchen. There's a laundry room and a bathroom downstairs, with two bedrooms and two bathrooms upstairs. For the average person, it's nice. Here? It might as well be a shack.

Logan's gaze moves to me, tracing me from head to toe. His eyes catch on my sneakers for a beat, lips quirking like he's holding back a smile. "That doesn't look like anything our mall sells."

I twist my hips, letting the drop-waist skirt of my thigh-length A-line dress sway. Of all the dresses in my closet, this one is my favorite. "I'll take that as a compliment. You know, you're supposed to be going to a dance tonight and not a funeral. Right?"

Logan smirks and shrugs, shoving his hands in his pockets. We stand there in silence, the tension in the air building between us. Logan looks good, really good, in his black slacks and matching long-sleeved button-down shirt. I reach out and touch his tie, my fingers slipping down the smooth satin. "We match."

"I... uh... got you something," he stammers, pulling a small white box from his pocket.

I look at Logan, my brows pushed together in confusion, as he lifts the lid, exposing the gold necklace with a teardrop gem I was looking at yesterday. "How did you..."

"I saw you put it back on the display before Melody became a raging bitch," he says, handing me the box.

I trace the delicate gold chain, my fingers brushing the teardrop sapphire. The necklace is even prettier than I remember, and considering how expensive everything in that store was, I can only hope it's overpriced costume jewelry and not a real gemstone. Because that would be too much.

"But when?" I should probably say thank you, but no one's ever given me jewelry before. Everything I own is five-dollar costume stuff.

"After you left with Sarah." He shrugs again. "It's no big deal."

"No big deal?" I shake my head, then throw my arms around his neck. "Logan, this is huge! Thank you."

Logan drives me crazy. Half the time, I hate him. But in moments like this, when he's thoughtful in that quiet, Logan way, I remember why I don't.

His arms wrap around my waist, pulling me flush against him. I tilt my head up, and for the first time, I notice the ring of green around his irises, the flecks of gold that look like lightning.

And just like that, every fluttery, jittery, flippy emotion I've been battling wins, and I have the sudden urge to kiss him. I know it's wrong. Gunner is on his way in the limo he refused to let me chip in on, and here I am pining over Logan. *I'm going to hell.*

I slide my hand up Logan's neck, brushing my thumb against his cheek. I wet my lips, hoping he'll get the hint. This is Logan Harris—the notorious womanizer. If he doesn't read the neon sign I'm flashing at him, he needs to start wearing his glasses again.

Just as I see a glimmer of understanding cross Logan's face, my dad clears his throat, reminding me that we aren't alone. Hiding my disappointment, I tuck my hair behind my ears and take a step back. "Can you help me put it on?"

Logan nods, silent, and I hand him the necklace before turning around. The pillows of his fingers drift across my neck as he sweeps my hair to one side. I shiver and grab my long locks, twisting the curls simply to force my mind to focus on something besides the way I react to him.

"Done," Logan whispers.

His fingers skate across the back of my neck, drifting to my collarbone. I stand, still as a statue, until the warmth of his lips press against the crook of my neck. I gasp and look over my shoulder. He tilts his head, waiting for me to signal again that it's okay to kiss me, when a horn honks outside.

Beep! Beep!

Logan steps back the same second I do, but the guilt crashes over me in waves. The same guilt I felt on the football field. The same guilt that reminds me I should be excited to see Gunner.

Except I'm not.

I wish Logan were my date tonight.

I shake the thought away and force a smile. "You should come with us."

"Nah," Logan says, raking a hand through his intentionally messy hair. The look is too good—too damn good. "I don't like not having my car."

"Isn't half the fun of a dance getting drunk and not having to worry about driving?" Not that I have any intention of getting drunk tonight. I'm sure there will be beer or something in the limo and probably more at the after-party. I just don't plan on having more than two drinks tonight.

Logan leans against the door and crosses his arms, pulling his shirt tight across his chest. "Wouldn't know. I've never been to a dance before."

Damn, he's hot. How is it humanly possible for one person to look this good?

"Why are you going to this one?" I step around him, pushing the curtain aside to peer out the window. Our time is running out. The back passenger door of the stretch limo opens, and Gunner steps out. He looks handsome in his tailored suit, which probably costs twice as much as my dad's car payment, but Logan looks better. "Do you have a date?"

Logan takes my hand and nervous tingles climb my arm. I turn my gaze to him, letting myself get lost in his eyes that I swear just twinkled. He brings my palm to his lips, kissing the tender spot beneath my thumb.

"No," he murmurs. "But someone made it clear I've been a shitty friend. I'm going for you, Danika. Just in case something happens."

"It's a school dance. How much trouble can I get into?"

Logan chuckles darkly, and I can't help but wonder if he knows something I don't. "Guess we'll find out."

Chapter 18

I think St. A's has every dance at the Horizon Hotel. I thought I heard once that someone's aunt or something owns the place and gives the school a discount... or whatever. I don't actually know because the line I gave Danika about not having been to a dance wasn't bullshit.

I've never had a girlfriend, never wanted one, so the desire to go to one of these functions was nonexistent. But I'd go to the ends of the Earth for Danika. I may have avoided her and been a jerk the past few weeks, but that's only because I hate seeing her and Gunner together. I've tried to push her from my mind, to replace her with everyone I could sink my teeth in, but they always felt wrong.

Their hands don't set my skin on fire. Their lips never tasted right. And when they'd reach for my cock, I'd pull away. Danika was the last girl to touch me. I don't want anyone to erase what that felt like.

But having someone, anyone, in my arms when the urge to hold Danika takes over is better than being alone.

Danika leaves the safety of the rented ballroom and finds me outside, sitting on the railing that separates the beach from the hotel. I pull a cigarette from my shirt pocket and tuck it between my lips. I have no intention of lighting it, but chewing on the filter helps silence the incessant chatter in my head.

"I was wondering when you'd get here." Her tiny fingers grip the skirt of her dress so it doesn't fly in the breeze. I wish it would. I'd love to see her perky ass. I'm sure my imagination isn't doing it justice.

"Didn't think you'd notice the way Gunner is all over you."

Scratch that—I *will* light it. The thought of Gunner's hands wandering over Danika's backside while she does nothing but shake her head and giggle sends a wildfire raging through my veins.

I flick the spinner of my lighter and shield my cigarette with my free hand. When the cherry burns red, I inhale, letting the sting of smoke chip away at my soul. My ribs still hurt, but I'll take physical pain over this feeling any day. "Seems like you two are getting serious. He can't keep his hands off you."

"He's been ridiculously clingy." Danika rolls her lined eyes, butterfly lashes fluttering. "But I think I'm finally willing to admit there's nothing between Gunner and me."

"You thought there was?" I ask on an exhale, immediately taking another drag. The cigarette is helping. A drink would be better, but my flask is empty, and beggars can't be choosers.

"No, but I wanted there to be."

"And why's that?" I hold the smoke a little longer than usual. My lungs burn, screaming for clean air, but I need the cloud in my chest to smother the fire raging inside me. Anything to dull the ache. I had my chance in the cafeteria once—and I blew it. Case in point? Our lack of a kiss today.

"Because I was using him to forget about you," she half whispers.

What? The smoke catches in my throat, turning my exhale

into a coughing fit. My eyes sting as I pound a fist against my chest, struggling to breathe. But by the time I manage to pull in a full breath, Danika is gone—vanished back into the ballroom.

I drop the rest of my cigarette, crushing it under my heel before following her inside. I've never chased a girl before—literally or metaphorically—but tonight is a night of firsts. Then again, I've never met anyone who drives me insane the way Danika does.

"I don't want to," Danika says, her back to me, arms crossed..

"Come on, babe," Gunner replies in his slickest of voices. "It's got the best view. You'll love it up there."

"Look, I'm sorry if I've led you on, but I'm not going up to your room."

Gunner puts his hand on Danika's lower back and escorts her toward the refreshment table. She digs her heels into the ground, trying her best not to cause a scene while still holding her ground. "Let's get a drink and dance some more. We can talk about it later."

"Dani!" I shout, jogging across the room. She looks over her shoulder at me, eyebrows pushed together in confusion at the faux-panic in my voice. "Hey, I'm glad I found you. Your dad called. He said he couldn't get a hold of you. Something's wrong with your cat. You've got to get home."

"My cat?" She asks, scanning my face for clarification.

I lift my eyebrows and nod, hoping she'll catch on. Something clicks and she covers her mouth with her hands.

"Mr. Scratchems? Oh, my goodness." She turns to Gunner and rests her hand on his arm. "I'm so sorry, Gunner, but I have to go. Logan, can you give me a ride home?"

"Yeah, of course." I link my fingers with Danika's and pull her away from that prick. We weave through the ballroom, dodging partygoers, and burst through the double sliding doors of the hotel. Adrenaline courses through my veins, pumping with the same ferocity as it does in a fight.

When we reach my car, Danika leans against the black paint, laughter spilling from her lips. "Really? My cat? You know I'm allergic."

I shrug and pull a cigarette from my pocket. My heart pounds harder than usual—harder than it ever does when Danika is around. Thank fuck I stuck two in my pocket earlier. I don't light this one. Instead, I let it hang between my lips and swing my keys on my middle finger. "I need to tell you something."

Danika kicks one foot up against my door and looks up at the stars. "Oh, mercy. What now?"

If she were anyone else, I'd tell her to get her shoe off my car. But this girl... she could get away with murder. "Gunner had a running bet that he could get you up to his room and fuck you." The words feel like acid on my tongue. "I overheard some guys in the locker room talking about it after the game last night."

Danika turns her head to look at me, eyes wide. Her lips part, a question hanging on the edge of them she's not willing to ask. I hate that I caused her pain. Technically, Gunner is the one making her cry, but delivering the news hurts me almost as much as it hurts her.

"And Jake spiked the punch," I add, my voice tight. "which is why Gunner wanted you to have another drink."

"So, that's why you came," Danika whispers, her gaze falling to her shoes. She nibbles on her bottom lip, likely trying to bite back the wetness pooling in her eyes.

I step in front of her, planting my feet on either side of those scuffed royal blue Converse. Lifting her chin with two fingers, I force her to look at me. My heart thumps in my chest, my body vibrating in rhythm with each pulsating beat. Her big brown eyes look up at me, filled with water after the first round of tears trail down her cheek. She sniffles, fighting to keep control of her emotions.

I'm fighting too, only my battle is completely different. Danika's not just the first girl I've felt a connection with, she's the first person. Period. All my life I've been an outsider in my own home. The buy-one-get-one-free kid my parents never really wanted. The punching bag when Dad got drunk. The one left behind and forgotten on more than one occasion. The embarrassment with a stutter. And always, always, in Cooper's shadow.

But when I'm with Danika, everything fades to black.

It's goddamn terrifying.

"Have I told you how beautiful you look tonight?"

The corner of her lip lifts into a sad smile as she shakes her head.

This close it would be too easy to kiss her. To dip my head and finally taste those lips. Normally, I'd take advantage of her bruised heart and relish in the spoils of being a rebound. We'd have our fun, then go our separate ways. There's never any forethought or afterthought with girls.

But I've thought a lot about Danika.

I want more than one night with her.

So.

Much.

More.

"Want to get out of here?"

"I guess we should. After all, Mr. Scratchems is sick." She smiles again, and this time it's warm and appreciative. "What do you have in mind?"

"Jake's having another party tonight." That I planned on avoiding. "Or we could go back to my house and watch a movie."

Danika exhales softly, then reaches out, trailing her fingers down my chest, skimming over my shirt until they stop at my belly button. A shiver rolls through me. I drop my hands to her waist, hesitant, uncertain what she wants—what she expects. She's been nothing but a maze of mixed signals, and the last thing I want is to misread this moment.

She drops her head back against the passenger window and looks up to the night sky again. "Neither. I have a better idea."

Chapter 19

The parking lot's asphalt is rough beneath my bare feet, but I don't complain. It was my idea to leave our shoes in Logan's car and take a moonlit walk on the beach. When I proposed the idea, I expected Logan to laugh and shoot me down. Instead, he flashed that disarming smile of his and agreed.

We step back through the hotel lobby doors, earning a curious glance from the concierge. Logan winks, flashing that signature crooked smile, and just like that, the woman—who can't be older than twenty-something—turns the color of a fire engine. She ducks her head, pretending to focus on her computer, but her not-so-subtle glances give her away.

Logan holds the door to the pool deck open for me, and I shake my head, grinning.

"Please tell me I don't look like the lady from the lobby."

"Nah." He shoves his hands in his pockets. "You're way prettier."

"Way to lay it on thick."

He smirks and lights the cigarette that's been hanging from

his lips. He takes a drag, looking up at the sky on the exhale. The night is beautiful. Clear. Warm but with a comfortable breeze. One for the storybooks.

"I hate that you smoke."

"Really?" he asks, his dark hair reflecting in the moonlight.

I nod, giving no further explanation. I know lung cancer and lymphoma are two different diseases, but cancer is cancer. My mom lived a healthy life. Exercised regularly. Ate all of her fruits and vegetables. Avoided meat products. Only had one glass of wine a night, if that. She had a perfect bill of health when it took over and still she died.

Logan's purposefully putting a carcinogen in his body and asking for Death to come knocking. I can't sit back and watch someone I care about die again.

"Okay." He takes one last drag, then snuffs out the cigarette in a nearby ashtray. Exhaling a slow stream of smoke through his full lips, he says, "I'm done."

I look at him skeptically. "What do you mean you're done?"

He leans forward, resting his elbows on the metal railing that separates the beach from the hotel—the same spot I found him perched on half an hour ago. "I quit."

"No one just up and quits smoking." I lean against it, too, looking at the rolling quilt of black that kisses an equally dark horizon. "They use patches and gum and wean themselves."

"I only smoke to quiet my thoughts." Logan shifts beside me, and I feel his eyes on me, heavy and searching. His voice is softer when he adds, "But when you're around... everything isn't so loud."

I bite my lip, my gaze trailing the rolling tide. A picture-perfect moment for a picture-perfect ending. I have to be dreaming. Real life doesn't have moments like this. They're saved for movies and romance novels.

Logan grabs my elbow and takes a step closer. His hand, fire against my skin, sends a shiver rippling through me, and we both know I'm not cold. "I need you to do something for me."

"Oh, yeah? And what might that be?"

He tucks a loose strand of hair behind my ear, leaving a trail of electric tingles in his wake. "Promise we'll go to prom together."

I exhale slowly, turning back toward the water. "Logan..." I hesitate, fighting the hope blooming in my chest. Someone like him—someone who could have anyone—how can I believe he'll still want me in five months? If I let myself believe it now, and he changes his mind later, I'll be wrecked.

"How do you know you'll even want to be my date?" My voice is quiet and careful. "That's, like, five months from now."

"I went to homecoming *for* you, Danika. I want to go to prom *with* you. Please." Logan's big brown eyes twist my insides in the best of ways. I nod, not trusting my words, and he smiles. A true, genuine smile. "Good. Now, how's about we take that walk."

Logan threads his fingers through mine and holds my hand as we make our way down the steps to the beach. The sand is colder under my toes than I expected. I shiver and Logan, of course, notices. He unbuttons his long-sleeved shirt and drapes it over me. I slip my arms through and am blanketed with his scent.

Feeling the weight of his stare, I bite my lip and look down at the shells reflecting under the stars. "I didn't picture you for an undershirt kind of guy."

Logan shrugs and then stares out into the darkness. A comfortable silence falls between us as the roar of the waves meets the sand. For the first time, my thoughts are hushed and I'm able to enjoy our time together. I don't know how long we've been walking when he says, "Tell me about California."

The question forms a pit in my stomach. This is the first real moment Logan and I have had, and I don't want to ruin it by digging up the past. But I can't ignore it either. Not if I want us to keep moving forward.

I pull the sleeves of his shirt tight around me, hugging myself like it might somehow keep the memories at bay. "There's not much to tell. We went there. Mom died. We came back."

Logan stops walking and gently pulls me into his arms. Without hesitation, I wrap myself around him, pressing my face into his chest. His heart is racing nearly as fast as mine.

"Was it that bad?" he murmurs.

I nod, fighting the lump in my throat. Thinking about Mom always brings the pain rushing back, raw and unrelenting. She suffered so much, especially at the end, and I was powerless to help her.

"Can't start with the easy questions, can you?" I ask, my voice cracking.

The past few years weren't just bad. They were hell.

We moved into a house near the hospital so we could be close to Mom. Dad even took a job in the ER just to be nearby. The house was fine, but the neighborhood was a nightmare— six drive-by shootings, eight drug busts, and two pedophile stings in one year.

My high school wasn't any better. It was overcrowded, with not nearly enough resources. The teachers were tired. The kids were vicious. And I was the preppy Florida girl with a target on my back. I learned to fight out of necessity because the weak don't survive. My sophomore year was okay. People realized I wasn't a pushover and more or less left me alone. But junior year was the worst. Mom died. My boyfriend photoshopped my head on a naked body and sent the image to everyone because I wouldn't sleep with him. My friends abandoned me, and I was slut shamed for the rest of the year.

It sucked.

I was struggling enough without my mom, but to lose my

friends? My boyfriend? My reputation to protect me? It was too much.

I lost the will to fight those last few months, which only made the bullying worse.

My body trembles in Logan's arms as the memories crash over me, tears spilling before I can stop them. He holds me tighter, rubbing my back in slow, soothing circles. "Shhh," he whispers.

It's been so long since I've let myself cry like this. I didn't realize how much I was holding in. It feels good to finally let it go.

I exhale a shaky breath, then glance up at him, smirking through the lingering tears when a soft melody drifts from Logan's phone—piano keys filling the night air.

"Dance with me," he whispers.

Not waiting for my response, or for me to ask how he started the music, we sway under the moonlight. Logan holds me tight against his chest. When the chorus starts, he pushes me back, his hand in mine, and spins me around before pulling me in again. He keeps my hand in his and wraps the other around my waist, leading me with big steps around the sand in a horrible version of a waltz, or tango, or some fancy dance.

I look up to the sky, my self-pity tears turning to laughter. Logan spins me, and I trip over my feet before he pulls me in for a clumsy dip. The song sings the chorus again with what sounds like an actual church choir and Logan stills. He cups my cheeks, fingertips tucked into my hair, and tilts my head to look up at him. "I'm sorry for every moment before this one."

I shrug because what do I say to that? I forgive you? You can't forgive someone you were never mad at. "That was a beautiful song. What was it?"

A smile tugs at Logan's lips. "It's called *Because of You.*"

"I didn't peg you for a pop music kind of guy."

"Can't help what songs speak to the soul."

My lips fall open a fraction of an inch, catching Logan's attention. His gaze flickers down for the briefest second before he exhales, looking out toward the horizon instead. Silence falls between us again. This time isn't as comfortable as before, but it's not entirely uncomfortable either. It feels like there's more to be said, but not tonight. I yawn involuntarily and Logan's grin stretches even wider.

"Let's get you home."

I close my spiral notebook inside my Biology textbook and lean onto my side to grab my phone off the nightstand. I pause the music playing from my iTunes app and stare at the screen. I haven't given my number to anyone besides Sarah since moving back, not even Gunner, and can't for the life of me figure out who this is. I hope it's not written on a bathroom stall somewhere.

Me: No

Unknown number: Why not?

Me: Because I don't make a habit of going to people's houses I don't know.

Unknown Number: My bad. It's Logan

Interesting. We've hit the texting stage. I guess that means I can officially call us friends now.

> Me: Still a no.

My phone dings again, almost instantly. Instead of a verbal protest, Logan sends a GIF of Bugs Bunny with big pouty eyes, ears down, and tears rolling off his cheeks. I roll my eyes and toss my phone on the pillow beside me. I need a few more hours to myself or I'll never pass tomorrow's test. No sooner than I've flipped my textbook open again, another text comes through.

> Logan: I've got pizza.

So persistent.

> Me: I don't eat cheese. Sorry.

> Logan: You'll eat this one. I made it. Everything is vegan. Down to the crust.

I suck my bottom lip between my teeth and shake my head, heat climbing my neck. He made me a pizza. I guess a short break won't kill me. If I go over to Logan's now instead of after dinner, I might actually get a full night's rest. The late-night movie marathons we've had every night since homecoming have been great but tiring.

> Me: How did you even get my number?

> Logan: I bribed Sarah with naked pictures of Cooper

I laugh and lean against the headboard. I knew Sarah had a crush on Cooper in middle school. Didn't realize she *still* had one.

> Me: You're disgusting.

Logan: Come on, Dani. It's getting cold.

Me: Fine. Give me a minute.

Logan stands on his front porch waiting for me as I cross the grass from our yard into his. I run my hands down my faded skinny jeans as I get closer, unsure of why I'm nervous. It's just Logan. I didn't need to spend ten minutes finding the perfect outfit and then five minutes in the bathroom fixing my hair. But I want to look good for him.

Logan reaches for my hand and pulls me into a hug. You'd think we haven't seen each other all week by the way he's acting, but that's not the case.

Gunner hasn't been to school the past few days, which means I haven't had the opportunity to formally break up with him. Tad says he's home with strep throat. Rachel says mono, which is probably closer to the truth since Melody has been out sick, too. So, while he's been out, I've played the dutiful girlfriend.

Sitting at their lunch table.

Smiling and nodding when people ask if I've been to check on Gunner or if I miss him.

Buying my time until tomorrow night's game.

Gunner may be a jerk for taking a bet out on me, but he needs a real breakup—not rumors about Logan and I getting together behind his back. They have enough beef, and I don't plan on adding to it.

Logan, of course, is not happy but says he understands. More so because those rumors will hurt my reputation more than Gunner's. So, Logan has sat with Cooper and Piper every day this week. Skipped the classes we have together. And overall acted like I didn't exist in the hallways.

Just like before.

After school, though, is a completely different story. We've fallen into a routine, simply out of happenstance. I do my homework while Logan is at practice, cook dinner for Dad even though he's been working a swing shift this week, and I never know when he's coming home, and then when I can't stand to be away any longer, I knock on the Harris door.

But today is different. Today, my heart skips a little faster and beats a little harder because Logan sought me out. I'm one hundred percent sure I'm making more out of this than it is. Piper and Cooper are working tonight and Mrs. Harris is out. Logan is probably just bored and lonely and knew I'd be coming over at some point anyway.

Try telling my heart this.

I pull back from the hug that's teetering on uncomfortably long for two people who are supposed to be *just friends*, but Logan pulls me tighter against his chest for a second longer, then let's go.

"Come on." He rethreads his fingers with mine and pulls me into the house. I close the door behind me and let him lead us into the kitchen, where he pulls out a chair at the table for me, and then scoots me in once I'm seated. "Can I get you something to drink?"

When I don't immediately answer, he reaches for a glass from the cabinet and fills it with ice water, then sets it on the table in front of me. I stare at this cup, utterly confused. "Uh, Logan?"

"What's up?" he asks, placing two slices of pizza on a paper plate. It looks amazing—all the peppers, onions, and mushrooms layered over a pesto sauce. My stomach growls, almost silencing my thoughts.

Almost.

"What's going on?"

"Nothing." He grins. "Why?"

"You're being chivalrous. Are you feeling okay?"

Logan laughs and sets the plate in front of me. "I'm perfect."

He pauses to take a bite of his pizza, smiling against it. "Are you coming to tomorrow night's game?"

"Of course."

He nods, wiping his lips with the back of his hand. "Are you going to break up with Gunner before?"

Ah. I understand now. This is bribery. He thinks a good meal will sway me to stay strong when Gunner returns to school tomorrow. Logan never had anything to worry about, but it's fun making him sweat. I roll my eyes. "Probably."

I CLOSE MY EYES, listening to Logan's heart thrumming wildly despite his slow, steady breaths. Pretty sure if it were a race, our hearts would tie for first because mine's beating just as fast. My finger paints an invisible squiggly line on his chest, above his shirt. I look up at his perfect face, admiring the strong curves of his jaw and how long his lashes are. I smile, knowing he can't see me with his eyes closed, and move my squiggly line further down his chest to the top of his abs, then back up his sternum.

"I have a question."

"Ask away." His voice vibrates through his chest, sounding even deeper than it normally does.

"Have you ever had a girlfriend?"

Logan's body shakes with a silent laugh, rocking me on top of him. "Define girlfriend."

There's no way Melody was his only girlfriend. She doesn't even count! I push up onto my arm and look down at him. "How is that possible?"

He tucks my hair behind my ear and smiles up at me. I love when he does that. "I never wanted one. I could get the benefits without the commitment. I didn't see the point."

I slide back down, resting my head on the pillow this time

instead of his chest. "That's gross. I don't even want to think about how many girls you've been with."

Logan shifts upward. He tucks his knuckle under my chin and turns me to look at him. "I can tell you I've never done this with anyone."

"What? Talk?"

My mind starts running, flickering a stream of faceless girls in compromising positions before my eyes. Logan huffs through his nose, a shadow falling across his face. He tucks his hands behind his head and stares at the TV. "I talked plenty as a kid. It just took too damn long for anyone to listen."

That's a loaded statement. Probably tied to the mystery secret he thought I knew. The more I think about it, the more his words ripple through me. The hurt hidden behind them echoes in the room. "What happened, Logan?"

He shakes his head. "Nothing. What I meant was that I've never let a girl in my bed before. I've never laid beside them and not made a move. Those girls may have had my body, but you've got something more."

"What's that?" My pulse races so fast it's teetering on the edge of a heart attack. Please say heart; tell me you love me because my feelings for you are so intense, I don't know what else they could be.

"Doesn't matter. You're not ready for it." He puts an arm around me and pulls me back onto his chest.

I didn't mean to fall asleep in Logan's bed, it just happened. One minute, we're watching a documentary on HBO about McDonald's, and the next thing I know, Logan's alarm is going off. It was the best night's sleep I've had in months, but I know if Dad catches me, he's going to lose it.

I sneak through the kitchen door and close it slowly. Carefully. It's 5:15. Dad gets up at six like clockwork, no matter how late he goes to bed. If I tip-toe upstairs and slip under the covers, he'll never know I was gone all night.

I pad through the dark kitchen, fearful that turning the light on will somehow magically wake him early because, of course, that would be my luck.

"And where have you been, young lady?"

I jump and cover my racing heart with my hand. The light above the dining room table flicks on, casting shadows on his face. Dad's sitting there, newspaper open on the hardwood table, coffee in hand. Amusement dances across his face. I've never snuck out before or back in for that matter. At least, to his knowledge, I haven't.

"Holy hell, Dad," I exhale, pressing a hand to my chest. "You scared the crap out of me."

He chuckles, clearly enjoying this more than I am. "Imagine how I felt walking into your room this morning, only to find your bed just as empty as when I went to sleep."

I slide into the chair across from him and steal a sip of his coffee. It's a dark roast with cream and no sugar. Not my personal favorite, but it was Mom's. "You're awfully calm."

"Well, I figured this was coming. You and Logan were close before we left. When he showed up Saturday with that neck-lace," he points to the sapphire I've yet to take off. "I knew all bets were off."

I wipe the sleep from my eyes with my palms, then run my fingers down my cheeks. It's too early for this conversation. I don't know what to say. So, Dad speaks for me. "What *is* going on between you two?"

I set his mug back on the table and slide it across the hard-wood surface. Mom would have a fit if she were still here. She hated water rings or condensation from cups on her antique table. But Mom's not here anymore. I frown, the constant reminder dampening my morning. "Nothing. We're just friends."

Dad crosses his arms and clucks his tongue. "Uh-huh. Just friends, my ass." He smirks. "So, you've become friends who have sleepovers?"

"I don't see what the big deal is. If I'd fallen asleep at Sarah's, this wouldn't be an issue."

"Sarah can't get you pregnant."

"And neither can Logan."

"Really?" Dad asks, rubbing the day-old scruff he's yet to shave. "Care to explain? Because last time I checked, a penis was a super straw meant for making babies."

"Oh, God! Dad! Really?" I bury my face in my hands. We are not having the sex talk. Not now. Not ever.

He laughs.

"Logan is the last person in the world I'd pick to do that dance with." I shudder and pretend to gag for good measure, but the idea isn't as repulsive as Dad's phrasing makes it. I bite my lip, letting my thoughts run rampant. I might just let Logan have sex with me. Maybe. If we get into a relationship and we wait a while. *Maybe.*

"If you say so, kiddo. Just wear a condom. I'm too young to be a grandpa." The corners of his lips lift again before he takes another sip of coffee.

"Dad!" I shake my head. "I can't even with you. I'm going upstairs to get ready for school."

"Need a ride?"

"No thanks. Sarah's taking me." I stand, pushing in my chair. I really do need to get ready. I told Sarah I wanted to get to school early. The sooner I find Gunner, the sooner I can get our breakup over with.

"Your birthday is coming up. We should go get that car I promised you."

"When do you want to go?" I'm sure it'll be something used, but a car is a car. I love Sarah, but it would be nice not to rely on her.

"I'm off today. Want to head over to the dealership after school?"

"Sure, but I need to be back at the school by seven."

"Oh yeah? Why is that?" Dad chuckles, already knowing the answer. *Of course, he remembers.*

I roll my eyes, my face heating. "You already know why."

I TWIRL a lock of hair between my fingers, anxiously watching the cafeteria door. I haven't seen Gunner all morning, but I know he's here. Somewhere. Unfortunately, so is Melody. She's bound to be wherever he is. Apparently, they both magically got over their illnesses at the same time.

If I were a betting girl, I'd wager that Melody is going after Gunner because she thinks I stole Logan from her. Who knows, maybe inadvertently I did, but as far as I'm concerned, she can have him.

Finally, after what feels like forever, Gunner walks into the cafeteria, surrounded by his usual posse. I practically jump off the bench seat and run over to them. Gunner takes my enthusiasm as excitement to see him. His grin stretches from ear to ear. "

Hey, doll face. Miss me?" He wraps his big arms around me and leans in for a kiss.

I turn my head and give him my cheek. The thought of where that mouth has been this past week makes me sick. "Of course. Are you feeling better?"

Gunner releases me and gives an upward nod to someone behind me. "Definitely. I'm ready to kick ass at tonight's game. You'll be there, right? The last game wasn't the same without my favorite cheerleader in the stands."

"About that." I lace my fingers with his and take a step backward. "Can we talk? Alone."

Tad elbows Gunner, smirking like a kid with his first dirty magazine, and Gunner has the same stupid grin on his face. I'm sure they're thinking we are going to have some steamy reunion. He's going to be disappointed. "Of course, babe."

I lead Gunner out into the hallway, where he immediately pushes me against the lockers. His hands run from my waist down to my hips, his lips hovering near my neck. "God, I missed you."

"Gunner, stop." I push my palm against Gunner's chest, but he doesn't move. He presses his mouth against the exposed skin, sucking and biting. I pinch my shoulder up, hoping it'll force his face away, but he doesn't move. "Gunner, please."

Suddenly, he's yanked back by the collar.

"What he hell?" Gunner stumbles, glaring.

"She said stop, asshole," Logan growls, shoving him away.

I suck both my lips between my teeth and fight a smile. My Logan. Always here to save the day.

Gunner trips over his feet and chuckles darkly, a malicious grin on his face. "What is it with you and this chick?"

"Leave him out of this," I say, reaching for Gunner's arm.

Gunner jerks out of my reach and presses his brows together. He must finally realize what's about to happen. "Him? You're worried about him? I was the one assaulted."

"Don't be such a baby," Logan quips.

I smirk, then force the corners of my lips down. My mother raised me better than to laugh when someone is hurting. I take a second to compose myself, then say, "Look, Gunner, this thing between us. It's over."

"Are you fucking kidding me, Danika? I told you I loved you. I got us a beautiful hotel room that you skipped out on, had planned a romantic breakfast, that you also missed, and you're the one dumping me?" He shakes his head. "I don't think so."

I cross my arms out of habit but keep my tone steady. Calm. "You can't refuse to break up, Gunner. That's not how relationships work."

"Did you guys ever officially start dating?" Logan interjects with a shit-eating grin.

"Why the fuck are you still here?" Gunner roars.

Logan squares his shoulders. "Because I know you. I know you're a sadistic prick and I don't trust you alone with Danika."

These two are going to end up fighting and getting kicked out of tonight's game if I don't do something. I don't think Logan will care, but Gunner will be crushed. I set my hand on Logan's arm, ignoring the electricity traveling between us. "I'll be okay. Just give us a minute."

Logan grits his teeth and begrudgingly nods. "I'll be right there." He points to the cafeteria doors. More for Gunner's understanding than mine. "Watching."

"It's him, isn't it?' Gunner asks, the fight in his tone gone. His shoulders roll forward and I finally feel something for him. Pity. I've never seen him look so defeated. I hate that I'm the one who's breaking him.

I shrug. "Yes and no."

"Damn it, Danika. I had you first." Gunner turns and punches the locker.

"And you took a bet out on me, Gunner!" I say, letting my frustration seep into my tone. I set my hands on my hips. "How could you?"

He runs his tongue over his teeth and looks down at his feet. Not even attempting to deny it.

"Logan and I have history. He and I will always be...us. But he wasn't the deciding factor. You were."

Gunner raises his gaze to meet mine and I'm surprised to see his eyes a little glossy. "I'm sorry."

"It's too late for sorries, Gunner."

I take my helmet off and throw it on the ground earning me another flag from the referee. I don't know what's going on tonight, but we're sucking.

Bad.

Cooper wasn't allowed to play because he was suspended for fighting. Again. Tad's got butterfingers, dropping every ball. And I don't know where Gunner's head is. As for the rest of the team, they're busting their asses, but that doesn't mean they don't suck any less. We haven't lost this badly since my freshman year.

I bend down and pick my helmet up as Coach Riley pulls me off the green. I don't even care anymore. There's no way we're going to win without a miracle. Losing this game means we're out of the playoffs. Our season is essentially done and it's only just started. *Fuck me.*

Grabbing a cup of water from the dispenser, I sit on the bench, dump the contents on my head, and then toss the Styrofoam behind me. It's the middle of October and still hot as balls outside. If not for the pretty little brunette sitting at the edge of the bench behind me, legs crossed, arms tucked by her side, looking more uncomfortable than a sinner in church, I wouldn't bother to be here. I would have walked off and left already, but I want Danika to see me at least try and save this game. I know tonight can't be easy for her.

Coach throws his clipboard on the ground and motions for me to go back on the field. I sigh and shake my head. I'm done. I don't care about this team but I go back out anyway, only to get my ass handed to me. The game ended and, as expected, we lost. Coach doesn't even bother to follow us into the locker room. He probably realizes that anything he could say would be a waste of breath.

I take my helmet off and stare at the stands, watching the crowd clear out. Searching for where that pretty shade of brown went, but I don't see Danika anywhere.

"She left me. She'll leave you too," Gunner says behind me.

I grip the face mask of my helmet and ignore him. Danika's out there somewhere. I saw her once tonight. She wouldn't leave without saying goodbye, especially now we're taking our relationship to the next step. I haven't actually talked to her about it yet, but I'm almost positive she'll say yes.

"Fucking whores are all the same," he mumbles.

I turn, lift my helmet, and smack Gunner across the back of the head with it. He stumbles a step to the side, then turns and lunges at me. His shoulder hits me in the stomach, and I'm knocked to the ground. He climbs on top of me, and the only thing I can do is tuck my elbows in and lift my arms to cover my face.

Gunner's got a mean right hook and lands more than one punch to my ribs. I stay on the ground, taking the beating. Waiting for him to wear himself out because he has the upper hand. Then I'll make my move.

Indistinct voices blur into the teacher from *Charlie Brown*. "Wah-wah-Wah." Someone pulls Gunner off of me.

Someone else, a parent maybe, lifts me to my feet. A light shines in my eyes, blinding me, moving from left to right. Left to right. The light clicks off as a hand taps my cheek.

"You're good," he says.

The spots in my vision clear and I grimace. "Thanks, Dr. Winters."

I place my hands on my hips and glare up at a freshly showered Gunner as he emerges from the locker room. I've replayed the fight on the field in my head a thousand times. It looked like Logan snapped, but I know him. At least, I think I still do. Logan's thrown me a few curveballs these past few weeks, but every now and then I catch a glimmer of the boy he used to be and that boy wouldn't attack someone unless provoked.

"What did you do?"

Gunner drops his arms, giving up on the notion that I'll run into them. Why he ever thought that in the first place is beyond me. That blow to the head must have messed with his memory because we aren't together anymore. "What makes you think I did anything? Logan's the one who started it."

I follow as he walks past me to the school parking lot. The only cars left are that of the players and possibly the coaches. Everyone else has already left for the night either to go home or to Jake's house for his weekly after party. One I have no desire to attend.

"Bullshit. What did you say to him?"

Gunner throws his hands in the air and spins on his heels to face me. "Jesus, Danika. I didn't do anything. Why can't you get it through your thick skull, Logan's fucking nuts, just like Piper."

I smack Gunner across the face so hard that my hand stings.

Why do that? Why bring Piper into this? No one knows the hell she's gone through this year, and the rumors people have spread are nasty. Arrested for prostitution. Drug binge. Whoring around for her Mama's rent. Someone even said she was probably dead and then laughed. Laughed! I don't understand how my classmates can be so cruel.

"If you ever do that again," Gunner growls, stepping into my personal space. "You'll regret it."

Dad always warned me: if you fight like a man, be prepared to be hit like a man. From the look in Gunner's eyes, I have the sneaking suspicion he's resisting the urge to retaliate. I cross my arms and glare, unfazed by his warning. I can take a punch just as good as I throw one. "Don't threaten me, Gunner."

We stare at each other, neither one of us wanting to back down. For him, it's pride, but for me it's principal. I won't be bullied into submission, and I damn sure won't stand for him badmouthing Piper in front of me. Logan was right all along. Gunner is a snake in the grass.

Gunner grabs my wrist, breaking our standoff. His hands are ice against my skin. I dig my heels into the ground and jerk my hand, but he holds tight. "What the hell, Gunner? Let me go."

Gunner's grip is firm, never breaking, no matter how many times I try to shake free. He pulls me toward his car and a tickle of panic climbs my spine. I've never seen this side of him before. He pops his trunk with his key fob and drops his duffle bag inside, then closes it—all with one hand. Letting go of my wrist, he shoves my forward. "Get in."

I touch the tender skin of my wrist, becoming even more heated as I realize it's going to bruise. "No."

"Hey!" Logan yells, dropping his duffle bag and sprinting across the blacktop. "What the hell is going on here?"

"None of your business, Harris." Gunner flicks his hand at Logan, shooing him away. "Go home to that whore of yours. Danika and I have business to attend to."

Logan ignores the dig at Piper and looks at me, eyes locked on mine. His gaze trails down to my wrist, watching me attempt to soothe the dull ache. "Dani, are you okay?"

I nod, butterflies swarming at the use of my middle school nickname. I love hearing it leave his lips. Maybe it's the adrenaline of the situation messing with my emotions. Or maybe I've finally given up fighting myself, but every feeling I'd forgotten comes flooding back faster than I can process. The pain of telling Logan about my mom's cancer. The tears I thought would swallow me whole when I said goodbye before our move. The excitement I'd feel watching him play football. The twists in my stomach when he'd touch me, even accidentally.

I've had a crush on Logan all along and didn't realize it.

That's why the pull to be near him has always been so strong.

Why no matter how rude Logan has been to me, I've forgiven him.

It was always him.

"Danika," Gunner says, emphasizing the *ka* in my name, "and I were just leaving."

"No, we weren't," I snap, taking a step to my left. I don't know what it is that makes Gunner feel he has the right to control me, but I'm over it. We aren't together, but even if we were I wouldn't allow him to treat me like this.

Logan holds out his hand to me, "Come on, Dani."

Gunner steps forward and shoves Logan in the chest. "What is your deal with this chick?"

Logan barely moves an inch. He grits his teeth, cheeks pulsating. I've seen this look a thousand times; Logan is pissed. Back when we were kids, he'd walk away from a jerk like Gunner. But now that I've seen what Logan is capable of, how the fire inside him takes over, I know without a doubt there will be bloodshed. Again.

Gunner smirks, probably feeling like he's the man on top or something. He's an idiot. With every passing second, I realize how much I've misjudged him. My desire to wash away my feelings for Logan made me blind when the truth was staring me in the face.

Gunner grabs my wrist again and Logan snaps. He rushes Gunner, knocking me to the ground in the process. My bare knees scrape against the asphalt but, overall, I'm okay. I scoot back and climb to my feet as the boys wrestle each other. Gunner gets the upper hand, sitting on top of Logan and punches him in the face. Logan puts his arms up defensively and lets Gunner wail on him again.

I know what he's doing, he's wearing Gunner out, but that doesn't mean Logan isn't suffering in the process.

I stand on the sidelines, anxious energy bubbling under my skin. It kills me. Watching Logan get the snot beat out of him, knowing I could do something to help. Gunner lands another punch, splitting Logan's lip, and I can't take it any longer. I run up and kick Gunner in the side of his head, knocking him off of Logan.

"Fucking, bitch!" Gunner yells, rubbing his ear.

Logan rolls onto his side and then pushes himself up. Each movement is slow and controlled. I know he's hurting. There's no way he didn't break *something* tonight. "Don't fucking talk to her like that."

"Whatever," Gunner says, rising to his feet. "No skirt is worth this much trouble. Keep the bitch."

Logan takes a step forward, but I grab his arm. I appreciate the notion, but one fight just ended. We don't need another and, truthfully, I don't know if he'll survive it. Gunner's face is bloodied, nose twisted, lip split, but he looks like he feels a million times better than Logan.

Gunner steps into his car, slams the door, and then peels out. Logan stands by my side until Gunner's no longer on school grounds. He turns to me, taking my cheeks in his hands and says, "Are you okay?"

"Me?" I laugh nervously. Outside of a sore wrist, I'm fine. "How about you?"

I run the pad of my thumb across Logan's lip, smearing the blood to see how deep the cut is. It looks superficial, but it's hard to tell in the dark. I wrap my arms around his waist and pull him into a hug. My heart's racing. I was never scared—not for one minute—but I'm trembling. Adrenaline does crazy things to your body.

Logan grunts under his breath. I drop my arms and step back, narrowing my eyes on his beautiful, bloody face. "What's wrong?"

"Nothing." Logan turns and walks toward his abandoned duffle bag. His steps are slower, his spine rigid, tilting his torso to the left.

"Logan," I warn, following close behind.

"It's nothing, Danika, I'm fine." He bends down to pick up his bag, fighting a groan in the process.

I poke Logan's side with my finger and he sucks in a breath, lips pressing into a tight line. "Uh-huh. Sure you are. I think my dad is still here if you want him to check you out again."

"I'm good." Logan insists, ignoring his pain and my frustration.

I swear, it's his mission in life to agitate me in every way possible. As much as I hate the storm he creates inside me, I can't stay away.

I shake my head, letting out a sigh of disappointment. "You're so stubborn."

"You wouldn't have me any other way." Logan nudges me with his elbow. "Are you coming to Jake's party with me tonight?"

I wrinkle my nose. That's probably the most unappealing idea I've heard all day. "Pretty sure that's where Gunner's headed."

"Fuck Gunner. Besides, I want to show up with you on my arm and let everyone know you're mine."

Logan wants to show me off? On the outside, I'm calm. Collected. Inside, I'm doing the happy dance. "When did that happen? Last I checked, we were just friends."

Logan grabs me by the waist and pulls me into him. He looks down at me, beautiful brown eyes locked on mine. Tonight, they're the color of whiskey, and I'm already drunk on them. "You were always mine, Danika. You always will be."

Jake's party is in full swing by the time we arrive. I have to park in the street because every available space leading up to the house is full. I slip my hand into Danika's, allowing our fingers to tangle together. She looks at me with a sideways glance, failing at fighting a smile, but doesn't pull away. I hold them tighter, letting the electricity traveling up my arm take over.

I didn't realize how much I wanted this. Now that I have Danika, I'm never letting her go.

When we reach Jake', I open the door, letting her walk in first and then place my hand on her lower back once we're both inside. The music is loud, blasting through the whole house surround sound.

I lean closer, her rosewater perfume wafting my senses. "Want something to drink?"

Danika nods and I lead her into the kitchen. I head for the fridge and grab a can of soda from the bottom drawer, prepared to tackle tonight like I do every party—on the edge sober. "What do you want?"

"Can I just have a soda?" Her eyes scan the group of people behind me. I'm sure she's looking for Gunner, probably to stay as far away as possible.

"Of course. You don't want a mixed drink or anything?" I pop the seal and split the coke between two red plastic cups.

Danika shakes her head. "No. I don't really like drinking, but don't let me stop you. I can drive tonight if need be."

I smirk and hand Danika her cup. "I hardly ever drink at these things."

"Bullshit."

"Tis true." I take a sip to hide the smile on my lips. I've never told anyone my secret. I've gotten good at pretending to be drunk: rarely pouring a drink in front of anyone that wasn't from my soda-filled flask, locking onto someone's lips when pressured to do a keg stand, and disappearing altogether in the middle of the night. That last trick is my favorite. I hole up in a room, with my Netflix app, and people assume I'm there with a chick. "Everything you've been told about me is a lie."

Sure, I usually end up having a combined drink or two by the end of the night, but it's never enough to affect me. I can't remember the last time I even had a buzz at a party.

Danika tilts her head like she knows I'm full of shit. "So, your reputation for sleeping with anyone who will spread her legs for you is malarkey, too?"

I set a bottle of whiskey on the counter, for show, then hand Danika her cup. "I'm not saying I'm a saint, but the number of women I've had sex with is probably much lower than you think."

"Bullhonkey."

I chuckle. This girl is too cute. Like cupcakes and unicorns cute. I didn't just say that. *What the fuck is happening to me?* "Do you just make words up in place of cursing? Or was that an actual word?"

"That is an actual word, but I do try my hardest not to cuss. Although, sometimes, I massively fail."

"Why? It's just a word. No one cares if you have a dirty mouth."

Danika's smile falls, a glimmer of sadness dancing in her eyes. "My mom said ladies should be respectful."

Some chick I hooked up with last year crosses into the kitchen. She glances at us curiously and pours herself a drink. I roll my eyes and lean against the counter; I can do this. I can keep my reputation and the girl. "Your mom is living in the past."

"My mom's dead."

Shit. I knew that. Way to be insensitive. I run my hand over my face and exhale loudly. "Sorry. My dad isn't around anymore much. He's not dead, but sometimes I wish he was."

"Don't say that, Logan. People can atone for their mistakes, but they can't come back from the dead."

"Logan!" Melody squeals, barging into the kitchen.

She throws her arms around me and plants a sloppy kiss on my lips. She tries to force her tongue in my mouth, but I clench my teeth and push her off. Melody still hasn't gotten the hint that we're through. I've been nice, I've been mean, I've blatantly ignored the girl, and it has yet to penetrate her thick skull. "Melody, you're drunk."

"Like that's ever stopped you before." She wiggles her eyebrows.

I shake my head. This can't paint me in a good light, but Danika just leans against the counter, an amused smirk playing on her lips. Melody follows my gaze, realizing for the first time that we aren't alone in the kitchen. "Ugh. I lost fifty dollars because of you, bitch."

Danika grits her teeth and then smiles. I think one of the

reasons I like her so much is that I've never heard her say a mean thing about someone, even if they deserved it. She's the kill-them-with-kindness type. "Sorry, I'm not a slut, Melody."

"Whatever, I know Sarah told you about the bet. There's no way anyone would turn down sex with Gunner. He's a fucking god in bed." Melody takes hold of my wrist and tries to pull me out of the kitchen. "Come on, we're playing dirty spin the bottle."

I plant my feet firmly on the tile. The last place I want to go is upstairs, to what we call the chambers and play *that* game. I'm hanging on by a thread with Danika tonight. If I get paired with anybody *but* her, this ship is sunk. "I don't think so."

Melody groans. "Since when does Logan Harris turn down an easy hook up? Is it because little Miss Goody-two-shoes wasn't invited? Fine, she can come too."

"I don't think—"

"Sounds fun," Danika interrupts.

I shake my head, silently pleading with Danika not to play. There's a reason this game is dirty. You spin the bottle and pair up with whoever it lands on—boy or girl— and if it lands in the middle of two people, you get both. After everyone has a partner or two, the moderator, usually Melody, locks everyone in a room for ten minutes. The chambers. They lock from the outside and there's no leaving until time's up.

"Huh. You'll do this, but not Gunner." Melody shakes her head.

"Why do you care so much?" Danika asks, her black Converse climbing the stairs in front of me.

"I don't. I just hate losing." Melody grabs Danika's hand, knowing I'll follow.

Upstairs, Melody sits Danika between two guys from the football team who eye her like she's fresh meat. The game is by invitation only. Rarely do we get new people because Melody holds all the power. Danika being here tonight brings the game to a new level and the thought of anyone touching her makes me sick to my stomach. *This sucks. I've got to do something.*

"Alright," Melody says, setting the decorated bottle in the middle of the circle. There's twelve of us, six guys and six girls. I'm seated across from Danika, mentally calculating the amount of force I need to spin the bottle so it lands on her. "Who wants to go first."

"Me." I lean onto my knees before anyone else can grab the bottle.

I pick it up, making sure its weight hasn't changed, then set it back on the ground. I line the bottle up with Carly, who is four people to the left of Danika, and spin. The bottle circles three times before reaching terminal velocity, then slows, and finally stops on Danika. For everyone else, this is a game of luck, but for me it's science.

The one thing I'm better than Cooper at.

A few girls groan as I stand and extend my hand to Danika. I escort her to the upstairs couch and sit beside her as we wait for everyone to pair up. When the final couple is sorted, Danika tenses beside me.

Melody jingles the bedroom keys in the air and everyone matriculates toward her like cattle to their master. "You know what time it is. Remember, don't do anything I wouldn't do."

The couples follow in a mess of a line behind Melody as she locks them two by two in their chamber. When it's our turn, Melody glares down the hall at us. Danika stands, head held high, and walks to the door Melody waits at. She looks calm, but I can tell with each sway of her ponytail that Danika is nervous.

Hell, I'm nervous.

"I don't know how you paired with her," Melody growls at me, "but whatever you did with the bottle, you can't do it again. Hand-picking your partner isn't allowed."

"I don't know what you're talking about," I say as Melody

shoves Danika into the room and slams the door behind me. I flip the light on, assuming it'll make Danika more comfortable, as the click of a lock signals our time has begun.

Danika wiggles the doorknob and then sighs. "Who has doors that lock from the outside? What kind of medieval shit are Jake's parents into?"

I rub the back of my neck. For the first time since losing my virginity in this game, I'm nervous. "Well, that depends on who you ask. Officially, they are small business owners."

"And unofficially?" Danika asks, taking a turn around the room.

"Porn."

She runs her fingers across the bedsheet and looks over her shoulder at me. "Shut up."

Those butterfly lashes bat and my mouth goes dry. I lick my lips and clear my throat. "Rumor has it, this house used to be a brothel. They bought it twenty years ago, updated all the appliances and whatever else needed updating, but kept the kinky stuff."

"You lie."

"Only if what I've been told are lies. Jake doesn't talk about it."

She turns to the window and pushes the blinds open with one finger. This room looks out at the pool, at the chaos of the party. "Where is he anyway? I'd be pissed if people were having a party in my house and I wasn't home."

"I'm sure Jake's around somewhere, but he doesn't care." He's just happy not to be alone, but Jake's family secrets are his to tell. And while I know Danika won't say anything, I keep my mouth shut.

"Huh." She says, sitting on the bed. "So, what now? What would you do if I wasn't me?"

Her big brown eyes lock on mine, the vulnerability in them undeniable and a turn-on. I shrug. "Anything you'd let me do.

Most girls have no inhibitions when they agree to play the game."

Someone's cries of pleasure penetrate the wall. Danika tenses again and I can't help but wonder how far she's gone. I assumed California parties put our parties to shame. I mean, it's fucking California, but right now, Danika seems so innocent. So virginal. "We don't have to do anything you don't want to."

Danika sighs and lays back on the bed, the hem of her dress riding up almost to her hips. Most people wear jeans and a T-shirt to the games, but tonight, she wore a short black flower-print dress to match her shoes.

I walk over and sit on the bed beside her. I lean onto my side, propping myself up with one arm, and brush the hair away from her cheek. "Talk to me, Danika. You were the one who told me I shouldn't bottle my feelings up. Remember?"

She rolls to face me, the warmth of her breath dancing against my skin. I stare into her eyes, fighting with myself to stay in control.

"I know. It's just...this is too hard."

"What is?"

"Fighting what I feel for you. It's exhausting to pretend that I don't like you, but I'm terrified to give in."

"Why?" Why fight anymore? She's mine. I'm hers. What is holding her back?

"Because I know you'll break my heart."

I can't promise she won't cry because of me. And I can't promise to always be there for her because a promise like that is too big, but I can promise that she's the only one I want to try this with.

I can't be just friends with this woman. I need to know what her skin feels like on mine and once we cross this bridge, I don't want friends with benefits. Friends share, and the thought of sharing Danika sets me on fire. I've already had to share her lips with Gunner, and it ate me alive every time I saw them together.

No. If we're going to do this, it's going to be done right. But I don't say anything. I keep my thoughts to myself because I don't want to scare Danika away.

Instead, I cup her cheek. She looks up at me with those bedroom eyes, silently begging for my lips, but I wait. This is a moment I can't get back. It needs to be savored, and etched in my memory because I've never been so nervous to be this close to someone before.

Danika closes her eyes, growing impatient with me, and presses her mouth to mine. Her lips are as soft as petals, parting to allow my tongue in. I feel her suck in a breath and hold it as I slip my fingers into the base of her ponytail. I pull her on top of me and her legs straddle my waist. There's nothing but a few thin layers of fabric between us, and it's torture.

I want this woman more than I've wanted anyone in my life.

Danika curls her fingers around my neck. Her nails press into my skin, sending a small surge of energy straight to my pants. My cock twitches and by the way her hips move against mine, I think she can feel it.

"Well, well, well."

Danika and I hear at the same time. She pulls away and sits up, her chest excitedly rising and falling as she tries to catch her breath. I prop up on my elbows and glare.

Melody stands with her arms crossed in the doorway. "I guess little Miss Goody-two-shoes isn't so innocent after all. Time's up."

Chapter 26

Holy fireworks explosions!

No, not fireworks.

F-ing grenades.

Fireworks are beautiful but loud, leaving their observers awestruck. Grenades shock and destroy everything in their path and I have been destroyed.

I knew kissing Logan would have an effect on me, but I wasn't prepared for this carnal need to take over. I wanted him. Needed to feel him everywhere. Even now, as I slide off his lap, I can feel his hard length rub against my silk panties. It sends a tingle to my core.

I smooth the wrinkles from my skirt and pull the tie from my hair. I run my finger across my scalp down to my roots, releasing what can only be called love knots. Logan threads his hand with mine and those same tingles spread up my arm and to my core again. I bite my lip and wish I stopped fighting my feelings sooner.

I half expect the other playmates—oh! I get it now, Gunner's playmates—to clap when we emerge but the hallway is silent. Empty. Everyone has gone their own way, like their hookup never happened.

Melody hits me with her shoulder as I pass through the doorway and whispers, "Slut."

I ignore her and look over the banister as Logan and I descend the stairs, seeing the party with new eyes. I get it now. The people dancing together and making out in corners are chasing this tingling euphoria. And those who disappear into bedrooms, they're trying to satisfy the needy ache that comes with those tingles.

Logan takes me straight to the kitchen. Just as before he gets two plastic cups and a can of soda, splitting it between us. I take a sip, but it doesn't satisfy the new thirst I have. I set my drink on the counter and say, "Let's dance."

He shakes his head. "My dancing skills are strictly reserved for moonlight serenades with the girl who owns my heart. I'll watch you though."

I pout because I don't want to dance with just anyone. I want to dance with Logan. I step closer and put my hand on his chest. His heart beats violently. I smile because mine's doing the same thing. I look up into his eyes, too drunk on the moment to relish his words and lick my lips.

Logan sets his drink on the counter behind him and then wraps his arm around my waist, eliminating the space between us. His head dips and his mouth presses against mine, his tongue sweeping in with a vicious hunger. Logan's kiss is pure perfection, this one even better than the first, if that's possible.

I've got this terrifying yet thrilling feeling that nothing between us will be the same after tonight.

Logan pulls back and I rest my head on his chest. I close my eyes, savoring this moment because nothing has ever felt so sweet. Mom was right. She warned that when I finally gave in to the pull, it would change me forever.

It has.

"Okay." The word rumbles in his chest.

I look up and grin. "Okay, what?"

"One dance."

Logan

"I know your secret," Sarah strolls beside me in a pair of jeans and a red shirt. It's not her usual outfit, but she looks good. I'd compliment her, but I don't want Danika to think I'm a jerk and hitting on her friend.

I walk back into the kitchen again and toss Danika and my old cups in the trash. People are sketchy. There's no telling what may have been slipped into our sodas while left unattended. But because I have an audience now, I grab the bottle of whiskey stashed in the cabinet above the fridge and pour in just enough to flavor my soda. I know I shouldn't care what Sarah thinks of me, but I do. All it takes is one person to ruin the reputation I've built for myself.

"Oh, yeah?" I bring the rim of my red plastic cup to my lips and take a sip. "And what secret might that be?"

Sarah leans into me, nudging my arm with hers. "That you have a crush on Danika. Don't worry. I won't tell." She smirks. "Although, for the record, I'm pretty sure she likes you, too."

I chuckle into my cup. Sarah is a day late and a dollar short with that news. "Like anyone would care."

"You and I both know you're full of shit." She punches my shoulder. Normally, her weak hit wouldn't even phase me, but I've taken a few beatings tonight. I'm working hard to keep Danika in the dark, but I'm sore. "A lot of people would care, particularly the girls you've been screwing."

I smirk but hide it with another sip of my drink. We both know I haven't been playing the field like I usually do. Hell, everyone knows. If not for the random sophomores claiming to have hooked up with me to boost their reputations, my name wouldn't even be a whisper this semester.

"Guys!" Rachel pushes through the crowd in a panic. She looks around, her gaze bouncing from one face to the next around us before settling on Sarah. "Have you seen Danika?"

The tiny hairs on the back of my neck stand on end. My stomach churns at the tremble in Rachel's voice.

How long have Sarah and I been in the kitchen for? Two, maybe three songs? Nothing that bad could happen in fifteen minutes.

Then again, if I know my *friends*, they're probably pissed having lost the bet, and I know Melody is out for blood. It's not the money they would be mad about, they have more than enough to go around. It's the principle of losing.

Sarah shakes her head, not the least bit concerned. "I'm sure she's around here somewhere. Why? What's up?"

Rachel bites her lip. A tiny wrinkle forms between her brows and on an exhale, she says, "Melody convinced me to have Danika try my drink, only it was spiked, and now I can't find her."

"You did what?" I rush into the living room again, pushing people out of the way. Being a head taller, I have a better view of the room than the girls, but I don't see Danika anywhere. "Where was the last place you saw her?"

"We were dancing, but then someone bumped into me and spilled their beer on my shirt. I went to the bathroom to clean myself up and when I got back, she was gone."

"Goddamnit, Rachel! How could you let this happen?" Sarah yells over the music.

Rachel shakes her head, tears running down her cheeks. "It was supposed to be funny. Danika's so serious all the time. Melody thought we should loosen her up." She looks at me. "I feel really bad. I'm sorry."

I clench my hands, crushing the red cup and spilling my

drink. I take a deep breath and try to keep myself from snapping. This isn't Rachel's fault, not completely. Getting angry won't help. I need to find Danika, get her someplace safe, then deal with those assholes later. "How long ago was this?"

Rachel shrugs. "Maybe five minutes. I think."

A lot can happen in five minutes, but considering they were just downstairs, I'm hopeful. "Rachel, check this floor. Look in every corner and at every couch you can find. Then start checking cars. "Sarah, this house has six bathrooms. Two downstairs and four upstairs. You check those. If she is not there, help Rachel by looking in car windows. I'm going to check the chambers."

"Logan, it's a party. They're probably locked." Sarah says, hesitantly. She's never been invited to play the game. She doesn't know the house like I do.

"I'd bet my left nut they're not."

Chapter 27

My heart drums in my chest when I reach the first closed door. I suck in a breath and reach for the knob. Considering I know the rooms lock from the outside, I'm not surprised when it twists. I step into the room without a care in the world that there's a couple getting it on. The dude tunneling into the chick from behind barely blinks when I walk around the side of the bed. His fingers shove the face of a girl into the pillows, her red hair twisted in his palm. *Not Danika.*

I turn and storm out, not bothering to shut the door behind me, and run to the next chamber. The one Danika and I were in. This door is locked from the inside. Something possible but only if you have the key.

My stomach twists and a feeling of dread courses through me. I lift my foot and kick the white door, leaving a dirty footprint on its pristine paint. The frame makes a cracking sound but doesn't budge. I kick the door again, and this time it swings back, thumping against the wall.

"What the fuck!" A female voice shrieks.

I recognize it immediately, wishing I hadn't. The soda in my gut twists with bile and lurches into my throat when I see her. Danika lies, passed out in the center of an elaborate four-poster bed. Gunner stops tugging at Danika's panties, leaving them loose around her thighs and gives an upward nod.

Melody finishes tying Danika's wrists to the headboard, a smug look on her face. "You're fixing that door before Jake finds out what you've done. He's going to be pissed if you don't."

I walk further into her room, my blood boiling hotter with each step. Danika groans her head rolling to the side. It takes every bit of self-control I have not to beat Gunner's face in, but I need to know what all they've done to her.

I play it cool, looking around the room with an uninterested expression that's *really* hard to hold.

"Want in?" Gunner asks, completely unaware of how fucked up this situation is.

I always knew he was a low-life prick. I just never realized how low he was before tonight. "What the hell are you two doing?"

Melody giggles. Her annoying fake schoolgirl laugh grates my nerves. It's always bothered me, but tonight it's intensified. "Just having a little fun."

"Dude, it's not like you aren't going to tag her anyway," Gunner says, unbuckling his belt. "What's the problem? We're just getting a head start."

"You're my fucking problem!" Is this what he does? Drugs girls who refuse to sleep with him? I shove Gunner's arm and push him back a step. "This isn't cool, Gunner. You could go to jail for this shit!"

Melody snickers and steps off the bed. She saunters to her dresser and grabs her phone, her thumbs incessantly tapping at the screen. "It's not our first rodeo, Logan. Relax."

I grit my teeth and point a finger at her face. If she were a dude, I'd break her nose. "I swear to fucking God, Melody. If you so much as turn that camera on, I'll bury you in so much legal shit your rich daddy won't be able to afford that Ivy League tuition you're shooting for."

Melody crosses her arms, a sour look on her face. "I'd like to see you try."

I smirk. My dad may be a piece of shit who beat on me when he was drunk, but he's one of the best lawyers in town. "Watch me."

"I've been half-ass decent about the Danika shit you've put me through," Gunner warns. "But threaten Melody again and we're done."

"We were done the moment you laid your hands on my girl."

Gunner takes a step toward me, chest puffed. If he wants a fight, fine. He's got one. What's another ass kicking on a night like tonight? I clench my fists, waiting for him to make the first move—Dad told Cooper it's always self-defense if you don't strike first—when someone screams.

"Shit," Gunner mumbles as Sarah runs into the room. He leaves without another word and I let him because all I want to do is get Danika out of here. I'll make him pay for what he's done. Just not tonight.

"Oh my God! Logan!" Sarah looks at me with tears in her eyes. Her shaking fingers trail across Dani's cheek. She frantically pulls at the ties on Danika's wrists, struggling to free her.

"I don't see what the big deal is," Melody drawls from the corner, cocking a hip and folding her arms. A smirk tugs at her lips. "The bitch needed to loosen up."

Sarah finally frees Danika's wrists and pulls her limp body into her lap. Sarah turns to Melody with fire in her eyes. I've never seen Sarah mad before. She usually lets everything slide but I'm glad to see she has a backbone. "What about you?"

"What about me?" Melody snarks.

"Should I drug you and let you nearly get raped so you can

stop being a raging bitch? Because if that's how I can get you to loosen up, then by all means, tell me where your stash is." Sarah hitches her thumb over her shoulder and glances at the door. "Or should I chase down Gunner again? I'm sure he's got a few roofies left in his pocket and a hard dick. He can loosen you right up."

"Watch yourself, Sarah," Melody says through gritted teeth. She steps forward, attempting to establish dominance, but I see her for what she really is. A scared little girl. "Keep talking like that and you'll be dead to me."

Sarah chuckles darkly. "If this is who you've become this year, I don't want anything to do with you. Call me when you remember how to be a semi-decent human being. Until then, stay the hell away from me and Danika."

I shimmy Danika's black lace panties up her thighs, ignoring how sexy they are because everything about this situation is wrong. When she's decent again, I slip my hands under her back and legs and lift her into my arms. She groans and rolls her head into my chest. "Uh, a little help."

"Oh. Sorry. What can I do?" Sarah asks.

"Move her arms. They're throwing me off balance. I don't want to fall down the stairs." I don't think I would, but I'm tired and sore and not taking any chances.

Descending the stairs, the party is still in full swing. No one seems to notice I'm carrying an unconscious Danika or if they do, they don't care, which speaks volumes about the people here. We make it outside and Sarah opens the passenger door to my car. I bend down, setting Danika in as gingerly as possible, then close the door. "You should probably text Rachel."

"Oh! Right." Sarah pulls her phone out and shoots a quick message. Her phone pings almost instantly with what I'm assuming is a reply. "Rachel wants me to drive her home. She doesn't feel safe staying the night with Melody tonight."

"I don't blame her."

Sarah chews her bottom lip, mulling over her words before texting Rachel back. Hesitantly, she looks up at me. "I don't know how I feel about leaving you alone with Danika in the state that she's in."

"It's fine. I'll take care of her."

Sarah stares at me for a moment then nods. I'm not a bad guy. Despite my reputation of being a drunk playboy, there's not much anyone can say about me that's bad. "You know her dad can't see her like this. He'll freak."

I've seen how Dr. Winters handles intense situations. He's the voice of reason, but I doubt he would be so calm when it comes to Danika. "I figured as much."

"So, what are you going to do? Rachel's meeting me here in a few minutes and I don't want to leave until I know your plan."

I reach out and set my hand on Sarah's shoulder. I appreciate her concern, but I've got this. Outside of her own home, there's nowhere safer in the world tonight than with me. I lean down and stare into her eyes. "Trust me when I say, we Harris men, we take care of our girls."

ooper sits on the front steps, waiting for us when I pull into the driveway. He stands with a frown as I get Danika out of the car. When I reach the house, he opens the front door and follows me inside. "Is she okay?"

"Probably not." I wait for him to open my bedroom door, then let him enter first so he can pull the comforter back. I lay Danika down and pull the blanket up to her shoulders, then stare down at her. I like the way she looks curled up in my bed. Too bad the circumstances aren't different. That one night we fell asleep together was amazing.

"Where are you going to sleep?" he asks me.

Danika's mouth falls open, a soft snoring sound leaving her lips. I'd say she looks peaceful, but that's a lie. I grab one of the pillows and toss it to the floor near the end of the bed. "Here. I want to be close in case she has a reaction or something. I don't know what Melody and Gunner gave her."

Cooper chuckles, shaking his head in amusement. "Taking a page out of my playbook, brother."

Not gonna acknowledge that. I pull my shirt off and toss it in the corner of the room where yesterday's clothes wait to be washed. "How is Piper doing?"

He shrugs. "As good as can be. She hasn't spoken to me yet, but I know she will. Eventually." Silence falls between us. Cooper stares at Danika while I change out of my jeans and into a pair of basketball shorts.

"What?" I ask, noticing a small smile on his lips. Cooper gets this stupid, goofy expression when it comes to Piper. Looking at Danika, he's got the same one.

"Do you love her?"

"Do you?" I'm not talking about Danika. Cooper barely knows her. I'm talking about Piper because I have never seen someone fight so hard for another person. The shit thing is, Piper doesn't even realize Cooper's been fighting her battles for years. Too bad he's stuck so far in the friend zone. There's no coming out without a miracle.

"That's a stupid question."

"But she's fucked up, Coop. Don't get me wrong, I love Piper like a sister, I just don't think falling for someone so broken can be healthy for you."

Cooper smirks. "We're all broken, Logan. You. Me. Her." He tilts his chin at Danika. "Falling in love is finding that person who's willing to pick up your pieces and help put them where they belong."

I step into the hallway and grab a blanket from the closet. I don't have time to think about love. I don't *want* to think about love. This thing with Danika and I just started. Love isn't in the cards. Not yet.

"You're getting way too philosophical for me." I drop the blanket at my feet, by the pillow, and look at the door. "I'm going to bed."

~

"Logan?" Danika asks, her voice hoarse from sleep. She groans and rolls to the side of the bed, looking for me.

"It's okay. I'm here." I grab the wastebasket and set it beside the bed in case she pukes. I've never needed to roofie a girl to get her to sleep with me. I don't have any experience with this drug, but Google says the aftereffects are similar to a hangover only worse.

I know hangovers.

"Why am I in your bed?" Her face pinches together in pain and she groans again. "Holy crap, my head is killing me."

Under other circumstances, hearing a curse word slip from those pretty little lips would be cute, but Danika looks like she's on her deathbed. I reach out and touch her cheek. "Can I get you anything?"

"Could you—" she tries until a lurching sound eats her words.

I lift the trashcan to Danika's face just in time because what's left in her stomach empties. I grab her hair with my free hand, holding it back and out of the way like I've seen people doing in movies. I don't usually do this. When a girl starts throwing up, that's my cue to leave, but the thought of abandoning Danika when she's at her weakest doesn't even cross my mind.

She wipes her mouth with the back of her hand and rolls onto her back. "What happened to me last night?" she asks pain in her voice.

"You were drugged."

There's a long stretch of silence as Danika processes my words. I'm sure she's trying her hardest to remember the night. "How?"

"Rachel tricked you into drinking a spiked drink, but it was Melody's idea."

Tears pull in Danika's eyes as she rolls onto the pillow. Her sobs aren't violent, like I expect. They're soft, like that of someone who has been through this before. My heart squeezes at the thought and I hope I'm wrong.

"Hey, hey," I tell her, rubbing small circles on her back. "It's okay."

Danika sniffles and peeks over the pillow at me. "How is it okay? How is any of this okay, Logan? I—" But before she can finish her sentence, she crawls to the side of the bed and throws up again.

When she collapses on the mattress I say, "I'll be right back."

I leave her in my room, lights off, and head to the kitchen for a glass of water. On the way back I grab a rag and wet it in the bathroom sink for her head. The thought of grabbing crackers crosses my mind but I doubt she's hungry.

When I get back into the room, Danika is out cold again. I set the water on the bedside table and place the rag on her forehead. This whole situation sucks. I'd turned the mess Gunner created last night around and then he and Melody had to go and ruin everything. I should be mad at Rachel too. After all, she was the one who actually drugged Danika, but if she hadn't told us what was going on Danika would be a lot worse off. So, I guess she's somewhat pardoned.

Danika's phone dings for the hundredth time. Her dad has left a million messages. By the looks of things, she wasn't supposed to be out all night.

No one has ever worried about me the way he does her. I remember the first weekend I stayed out and didn't tell anyone where I was. I expected to get my ass reamed when I came home that Monday, but it was like my parents didn't even notice I was gone.

I was twelve.

Fucking twelve!

When I finally did make it home, the only thing Mom was pissed about was that I didn't take the trash out that morning and we missed the pickup. I should go next door and tell Mr. Winters what happened. He's a caring parent, unlike mine.

With a heavy hand, I knock on the mahogany door at 202 Willow Street. My knuckles beat against the grain with equal parts determination and fear. *I can do this.*

Mr. Winters peers at me through the windowpanes with a curious eye. He opens the door, hands on his hips, an amused yet cautious grin on his lips. "Tell me why you're at my door, and where my daughter is."

"I..." My voice cracks.

I clear my throat and try to push down the nerves creating a knot inside me. I stand up straighter and roll my shoulders back. I've never had a girlfriend, and even though Danika and I are only treading those waters, seeing Mr. Winters today feels a heck of a lot different than it did last night. All of this is new territory for me and on top of it, I have to be the bearer of bad news.

"I saw your texts to Danika and wanted to inform you she's okay."

Mr. Winters steps onto the welcome mat, forcing me back a step. He's a lot more intimidating this morning too, but I get it. We're talking about Danika. I'd cut through any and everyone in my way to get to her, too. "And how do you know about my texts?"

"Because I saw her phone."

Mr. Winters lips press together in a firm line. His patience with me grows thin, as do most adults... sooner or later. "Logan, I'm going to ask this as nicely as possible but please don't mistake my docile manner for weakness. I will end you if I have to."

I swallow hard, feeling the severity of his words. I'm not a pushover by any means, but something about Mr. Winters tells me he knows no one would notice if I disappeared, let alone care. "Why do you have my daughter's phone?"

I take a deep breath, wanting to get all of this out as fast as possible. "Because some asshats drugged Danika last night and her friend Sarah and I saved her before anything bad could happen. She's sleeping the drug off in my room, but she's throwing up a lot, and I'm worried because I don't know what's normal and what's not when it comes to roofies because I've never drugged anyone before, and swear I don't plan on it."

"Damnit, Logan, you should have led with that." Mr. Winters pushes past me and runs across his front yard to mine. Without waiting for me to catch up, he pushes the door open and walks into my house. "Danika!"

"She's this way." I lead him to my room, ignoring a nosey Piper peeking through a crack in her door. It's the first I've seen of her since she got home. I need to check on her and apologize for not going to the hospital. But right now, Danika comes first.

"Shit," Mr. Winters mumbles, kneeling by the bed.

Danika's olive skin is a sickly yellow color and from the doorway I can see she's soaked the bed from either sweat, piss, or vomit. Whatever it is, I'll clean it up.

Mr. Winters presses two fingers to Danika's wrist and looks at his watch, the wrinkle between his dark brows growing deeper with each passing second. He pushes his daughter's hair from her face and stares. "Her pulse is strong."

I sigh, relieved at the good news. She looks so terrible, I was worried. I step forward and set my hand on Mr. Winters' shoulder.

He looks up at me, curiosity dancing in his eyes, and I say, "Don't worry, Mr. Winters. I'll take care of her."

Chapter 30

"You scared me, baby girl," Dad says as I walk through the door.

My head still pounds, though not as viciously as when I first woke up. I can't believe I slept the entire day away—in Logan's bed, no less. Everything after our kiss in Jake's kitchen is a tangled blur, memories stitched together in disjointed flashes. The party itself? The ride to Logan's house? Nothing but black.

Today is a different kind of haze—snapshots of Logan at my side, a bucket nearby. At some point, I showered. I can almost see myself under the water's spray, steam curling around me as I try to piece everything together. But who put me there? How I got dressed? Gone. Just...gone.

Dad's big arms wrap around me, holding me tight like they did the day Mom died. "For a second, I thought I was going to lose you too."

"I'm sorry," I whisper, my voice cracking. I want to cry again, but there aren't any tears left. I can't imagine how hard seeing me in that state must have been. First, Mom withered away.

Then I was broken and weak, so much more than I've ever been. And, despite how hard it must have been, he left me at Logan's to rest and build my strength.

Dad is the strongest man I know.

Dad smoothes my hair and places a kiss on my forehead like he's done countless times when everything fell apart. "Shhh. You're alright and that's all that matters."

I nod and sniffle, pulling away from his embrace. Guilt reminds me that I spent too many days crying last year. It doesn't matter that *my* mom died or that school had become my personal hell, he was suffering too. Dad never got the chance to grieve because he was too busy taking care of me.

I'm nearly eighteen, now. He shouldn't have to keep drying my tears. "I should get changed and bring Logan back his clothes."

Dad nods, noticing for the first time that I'm wearing a much too big for me Machine Gun Kelly band Tee and a pair of basketball shorts. Upstairs, I take another shower. There's something comforting about using my own soaps and shampoos. Although, when I rinsed the vomit off at Logan's earlier, Piper's shampoo smelled oddly similar.

I wrap myself in a towel and stare at my reflection. Everything about me looks the same. Same long dark hair. Same brown eyes. Same olive skin, but I feel different.

When my ex-boyfriend Austin circulated the naked photos that he fabricated of me around school, I felt broken. Defeated. Powerless because no one took my side. No one cared to listen when I said the pictures were fake or that he was lying. All of that, paired with my mom's death, and I spiraled into a dark place.

Not as dark as Piper, but close.

Thinking back to everything that happened last night, my so-called friends stripped me of my power again. Gunner used me to win a bet. Then he and Melody drugged me, physically making me powerless for what I can only assume was retaliation. The same sickening veil of darkness falls over me again, and I feel myself spiraling.

By the time Monday comes, everyone will have their own version of what happened yesterday. I'll probably be bullied again and have a repeat of last year. I close my eyes and press my forehead against the glass. *Why does this keep happening to me?*

My eyes snap open when someone knocks on my bedroom door. "Just a minute!"

I hurry to my closet, slip a loose pink shirt over my head, and then reach for a pair of pajama shorts. Even though I slept most of the day, I'm still tired. I feel the downward cycle repeating. I was tired a lot last year.

Someone knocks again, just as I finish pulling my shorts over my hips. I open the door, and Logan stands there, hands in the pockets of his board shorts, which surprisingly are plaid tan color and not black. Even more surprising is his solid white shirt.

"Hey," I say, blatantly staring. My heart flips and some of the darkness fades away. "What are you doing here?"

"I know I need to give you space. You've been through some fucked up shit the last twenty-four hours, but I took your dress to the dry cleaner. I didn't know what to do with it, and my dad's friend owns the place. So, he met me there when I told him it was an emergency." Logan extends a yellow claim ticket for me to grab. "It'll be ready for you to pick up after school tomorrow."

"Oh." I take the slip of paper and turn in to my room. I set it on my desk beside the box labeled books that's still waiting to be unpacked. "Thanks."

Logan stands in the doorway and looks around. It's funny how, just a few days ago, I was lying in his bed for the first time watching a movie and now he's here. I feel like we've come full circle, only the happy, fun part of our budding friendship was skipped. Instead, we've been plunged into a rough patch. The kind of roughness new *whatevers* don't survive, no matter how tantalizing the spark is between them.

Logan rubs the back of his neck. "So, about tomorrow..."

"What about tomorrow?"

"I went out on a limb and texted Sarah." He runs a hand through his perfectly disheveled hair. "I told her I was taking you to school. After everything that went down, I don't trust anyone right now and I want to keep you safe."

"I can count on one hand the amount of people I trust right now," I whisper.

Logan, Cooper, Piper, and Dad.

That's it.

Even though Sarah helped Logan last night, she still placed a bet against me. Or on me. I really don't know. It's confusing. What I do know is that friends don't make bets about other friends behind their backs.

"Thanks," I tell him, my voice cracking like my exterior. "But Dad bought me a car last night. I can drive myself."

Logan extends his arms, inviting me in for a hug. I step into the embrace and let his warmth blanket me. I close my eyes and for a moment everything feels like it'll be okay. The weight of what happened last year isn't smothering me, and my anxiety about tomorrow fades away. Here in my room, it's just me and him.

Logan presses his lips to my temple, bringing back the butterflies I felt last night. "Then we can take your car, but I'm not letting you show up to school alone."

y alarm isn't set to go off for another thirty minutes, but I lay awake in my bed, memories of last year swallowing me whole. I never told Dad how bad the bullying got. As a guy, he wouldn't understand and as an adult he *really* wouldn't understand.

The torture I was put through wasn't limited to the school walls. Austin, my ex, and his friends—friends that used to be my friends—bombarded my social media with degrading memes, comments, and pictures. Those, of course, fueled the inferno around me. I tried to stay strong, always putting on a mask of armor whenever anyone was around but, eventually, even the toughest of armors crack.

Dad knocks at my door, probably to tell me he's leaving. He likes to get to his office early. Why? I have no clue, but it's been this way for as long as I can remember. As the door creeps open, I pull the covers over my head and roll onto my side, turning my back to him.

He sighs, and then the edge of my bed dips. "You look tired."

My heart beats a little faster. The veil of darkness weighing me down lifts a little but then comes down harder than ever. "What are you doing here, Logan?"

His hand finds my back and he rubs small circles over the blanket. I close my eyes, enjoying the sensation. "I talked to your dad this morning. He's worried about you."

I sit up, pushing the blanket behind me in the process and glare at him. "Why are you being so nice all of a sudden? Everything about you changed at homecoming. Is there a bet or something you're in on, too? Because if so, just tell your friends you won and leave me alone!"

I throw myself back onto my pillow and reach for my blanket to hide under again. I know I'm lashing out, but I'm hurt and angry and drowning in memories. I should skip today and maybe the next few days, at least until I'm able to build my armor again. If Gunner or Melody see me like this, they'll know they've won. Usually, I don't give up without a fight, but right now I don't have any fight left in me.

Logan yanks the blanket off my body and tosses it on the floor. He grabs my shoulder and rolls me onto my back. I turn my head, refusing to look at him, but he takes my chin between his fingers and forces me to stare at his pretty face. "You're really going to make me say it, aren't you?"

My chin wobbles and I clench my teeth to keep control of my emotions. All I've done the last twenty-four hours is cry. I didn't think I had any tears left. Apparently, I do.

"I like you, Danika. I like you a lot. I want us," Logan wiggles his finger between us, "to be a thing. A real, we're together exclusively, thing."

"That's called a relationship."

"Fine. Cool. Whatever it is, I want it with you. I was going to say something last night, but then everything got fucked up." Logan lets go of my chin and takes my hands, pulling me into a sitting position. "Now, I need you to get up and get dressed.

We're going to face these assholes together. Whatever happens today, I've got your back."

I want to smile, to throw my arms around Logan and tell him how much it means to me that he's here, but I don't feel happy. I'm scared. "I don't want anyone to see me."

Logan exhales loudly, but he doesn't sound frustrated. I'm sure he's used to this kind of moodiness with Piper. She gets it. She's on the same slippery slope I was on last year, the same one I feel myself falling down now. Only Piper's deeper down the rabbit hole than I ever was.

Logan slides off my bed and walks into my closet. When he comes out a minute later, he sets my only pair of school pants, my black Chucks, and the shirt he sent me home with yesterday on my bed. "Get dressed. I'll be back in ten minutes and then we're going to school. If you skip today, these fuckers will know they've gotten to you, and then they'll never stop."

Ten minutes later, my front door swings open. It should bother me how Logan effortlessly waltzes into my home, but I don't have the energy to care. He tosses a black hoodie at me and says, "Put this on."

Slipping it over my head, I'm surrounded by Logan's scent and the spicy, heady smell lifts me a little further out of my darkness.

Logan takes me by the elbow and pulls me into his arms. We stand there for what feels like an eternity, the only sounds are our breaths and beating hearts.

"I like you, Danika," he says, the deep rumble of his voice vibrating in his chest. "I can't say that about many people and I think we can both agree that there's something epic happening between us. As much as I don't want to be just friends with you, we can go back to that if it's what you need. Whatever you decide, I'm not going anywhere."

Logan crouches down and rests his hands on my knees, which are pulled close to my chest. I look at his thick fingers, feeling their warmth penetrate my skin through my pants, then look up into his eyes.

Today, Logan wears his glasses for the first time in public since the eighth grade. It's an attempt to divert the expected chatter from me to him, which might work since he's transitioned from bad boy with an attitude to sexy nerd overnight.

Personally, I like the glasses. While his current pair is much more stylish than the thick-framed freebies he used to wear, just seeing him in glasses adds an extra level of comfort I wasn't expecting.

That signature crooked smile greets me as Logan flips his palms over and he waits for me to be ready. "Come on, babe."

Once I am, he pulls me to my feet and immediately wraps his arms around my shoulders. A group of people approach, merely trying to get into the school building, and I freeze. We should have parked further away.

Logan pulls the hood over my head, covering most of my

face, then whispers, "Anytime you start to freak out, just remember, Tad takes it in the ass."

I laugh and shove Logan in the chest, stepping back from his embrace. I need a second. Between my flipping butterflies and nervous bats, I think I might puke. Surprisingly, Logan doesn't notice my distress. He's too focused on my mouth.

"There's that pretty smile." He takes my hand in his and escorts me into the building. I press close to his arm, hyper-aware of the weight of a dozen curious eyes on us.

People whisper as we walk the halls together, but Logan ignores everyone. When we pass Gunner and Melody, Logan puts his arm around my shoulders. I close my eyes, turning my face into his chest. I'm not ready to face them. Not yet.

Reaching my first class, I force myself out of Logan's arms. Having him as my personal security blanket has been a godsend. If only I could hide in his embrace all day.

I look through the windowpane in the metal door of class-room 1C. My classmates laugh and talk like Saturday never happened. I grasp onto the sliver of hope that the jerkfaces who hurt me kept their mouths shut, but I'm not holding my breath.

Logan presses his lips to my temple and whispers, "You don't have any classes with them this morning. It'll be okay." I nod against his mouth and he continues, "I'll be here waiting for you when class gets out."

The first bell rings and Logan leaves me, turning down the hallway. I knew he'd eventually have to go, but I didn't expect my anxiety to skyrocket once he did.

I walk through the row of desks, head down, and take a seat all the way in the back. Outside of a few curious glances, no one says anything to or about me, which is a relief, but that doesn't mean people aren't talking. I saw how fast rumors spread about Piper. I'm not out of the woods yet.

As promised, when class ends, Logan stands in the hallway, waiting. He puts his arm around my shoulder again, attracting more looks than I've had all morning. Although, that was his plan—take everyone's eyes off me. I guess it would have worked better if we weren't attached at the hip, but I'll take the curious stares if it means feeling safe.

I survive my next two classes because of Logan. He's thought of everything. Dad provided medical excuses, requiring both of us to sit out at PE all week, which Logan hand-delivered to Coach Riley. Being the jerk that he is, Coach pulled his cell phone out of his pocket and called my dad. Just to verify the notes were real.

They were.

As for Biology, Logan had a note for that class, too. Apparently, there was a death in my family, so I did not complete the weekend reading and was not ready for today's quiz. I spent the class period silently reading the chapters while everyone else tested.

Walking out of class, I don't have to search for Logan. I don't know how he does it, but he's always at my door, waiting for the bell to ring.

Waiting for me.

I smile, feeling a little more like myself, taking my place under his arm. For a split second, I forget what's next in my schedule. I feel like a girl should in the arms of the guy she's crushing on. Happy.

That bubble bursts as soon as I see the double doors leading into the cafeteria. The veil of darkness that had just begun to lift falls over me again and I think I'm going to be sick.

"Do you want to go through the line and get food?" he asks as we approach the cafeteria.

I shake my head and my stomach knots because I'm officially out of time. I have to face Melody and Gunner. I have two options: pretend nothing happened or call them out, which could either lead to a fight or an emotional breakdown. All of my options suck.

My feet are heavy and each step is a struggle. Logan puts his hand on my lower back to guide me into the cafeteria. At this point, blending in with the crowd, I'm probably imagining the eyes on me. Real or not, I feel them and don't like the attention. I shove my hands into the hoodie's pocket and clench my fist until the ache from my nails alleviates the ache in my chest.

I hold my breath as we draw nearer. Melody smirks, whispering something in Gunner's ear, eliciting a laugh from him. Gunner sits on the table and taps his thumbs against his phone, actively avoiding me. At this point, in their eyes, I don't exist.

I'm okay with that.

Logan passes our usual table and makes a beeline to Piper's, which is disconcerting. I'm pretty sure everyone who hadn't noticed me before is staring now because sitting with Piper is the equivalent of committing social suicide. If you're not a Harris, you just don't do it.

I'm doing it.

"How are you holding up?" Cooper asks.

While I don't eat meat, I still appreciate the smell of good food. Cooper's shepherd's pie smells halfway appealing, which makes me realize I should probably eat something. All I've had the last twenty-four hours is a slice of toast, but I can't eat. I think I'll be sick if I do.

"I don't know. I expected to be tormented about what went down this weekend, but everyone's been eerily quiet."

"I'll be right back," Logan says, leaving me at the table with Cooper and Piper. The nervous flipping in my gut amplifies, but not to the extent it was this morning. Logan wouldn't have left if I wasn't in good hands.

"You're fucking dead!" I hear Logan shout as something knocks a trash can over. *More like someone.*

"Shit," Cooper mutters, jumping up. I spin in my seat and search the room for Logan. Following Cooper with my gaze, it doesn't take me long to find him standing by our old table.

Gunner climbs to his feet and wipes the blood leaking from his lip with his thumb. The whole cafeteria has gone silent, watching the interaction. Even the cafeteria monitors seem to be in shock. People aren't used to seeing Logan fight. Not on campus.

Gunner looks over at me and winks.

Bile climbs my throat and I cover my mouth, willing it to stay down while ignoring the burn.

Cooper—yes, Cooper—snaps, lunging forward and hitting Gunner so hard the crack of his jaw echoes in the cafeteria. There's a collective gasp, breaking the silence in the room. He steps forward, standing over a groaning Gunner, and says, "Don't even fucking think of looking at Danika again."

"Mr. Harris!" Principal White shouts. "In my office. Now!" He huffs, adding, "Mr. Wells, go to the nurse. You're bleeding all over my floor."

Logan kicks the trashcan hard enough to leave a dent and storms out of the cafeteria. I groan and fold my arms on the table, then lay my head down.

Today has been emotionally draining and it's only half done. I should have stuck to my gut and ditched.

Fucking Cooper.

I had everything under control. I'm not Piper. I don't need him to fight my battles. It's not like he ever has before.

I clench my fist and slam it in the locker nearest me. The sound echoes in the empty hallway. I hit it again and again until the rage in my chest dissipates. I open and close my hand and look at my bruised knuckles. *At least they're not bleeding.*

The bell rings and I realize I ran out on Danika. I turn back toward the double doors, fighting the crowd that's trying to leave the cafeteria. Everyone is rushing out to their next class.

I need to get in.

When I make it inside, Danika is gone. Everyone is gone. I run down the hall to her next class and peer through the window, but she's not in there either. I skim my hand through my hair, anxiety pricking at my neck.

I promised to keep Danika safe. I let my own issues cloud my judgment, and I failed her. Again. I slam my fist into the side of the locker nearest me. *Fuck!*

I press my fingers into my shoulder muscles and crack my neck. I'll find her. I'm sure she's fine.

I do what I should have done the moment I realized Danika was gone and take my phone out.

Me: Where'd you go?

I wait a few seconds and stare at the screen. There's nothing. No tiny thought dots. No read acknowledgment. Nothing.

Me: I'm sorry. I didn't mean to run out on you.

Where is she?

Me: Blink twice if you're alive.

Me: Just kidding. But seriously. Where are you? I'm getting worried.

It feels like I've been waiting a lifetime for Danika to respond, and still I have nothing. I run my fingers through my hair again, scrambling. *Someone* has to know where she went. It's not like she can leave. I have her keys.

Me: Have you seen Danika?

Sarah: Not since lunch. Why?

Me: She didn't wait for me to walk her to her next class and she's not here.

...

Sarah: I sent her a text but she didn't respond.

Me: She's probably pissed.

> Sarah: Why? I wasn't the one who drugged
> her.
>
> Me: She knows about the bet.
>
> Sarah: Well, shit.

The final bell rings. It seems impossible that only two minutes have passed. I hesitate in the hallway, hoping Danika will run from the bathrooms or somewhere in the nick of time to make her next class.

I'm not surprised when she doesn't.

I head to the parking lot, my last-ditch effort of where she might go, but she's not by her car. She's not anywhere. My phone dings in my pocket. I pull it out, dropping the damn thing with my butterfingers.

> Piper: Where are you going?

My heart sinks to my feet. I was hoping the message would be from Danika. I check her messages. There's no change. My texts still sit in her phone, unseen.

> Me: Nowhere until I find Danika.
>
> Piper: Stand on the trunk and look to your left.
>
> Me: I am not standing on her car. It's
> brand new.
>
> Piper: Your loss.

If the hatch dents, Danika's going to kill me, but at this point, I'm desperate. I'll fix whatever I break. I hop on the trunk first, then shimmy myself into a standing position. I look to my left, as directed, and there—under Piper's favorite hideout—are two blobs of black.

"Thank fuck." I jump down and run all the way to them.

Piper smiles up at me as I slow my stride. The oak tree's large branches fan out, shadowing the ground, offering a cool reprieve to the hot Florida sun. "Took you long enough."

I roll my eyes and plop down beside Danika. The relief of having found her is unreal. I thread my fingers with hers, finally feeling peace. "Bite me."

Piper scrunches her nose. "You're not my type."

"Are you okay?" I ask Danika. She looks fine, but there's no telling what's going on in that pretty little head of hers.

"Are you?" She flips my hand over and examines my knuckles. Outside of being a little swollen, they're fine. They've seen worse days.

She lifts my hand and kisses each red mark. A shiver runs through me. I've never had anyone kiss my wounds better. Mom used to rub her thumb over my cuts and say *you're fine.*

I nod. "I'm sorry I ran out on you."

"What did Gunner say?"

"Does it even matter?" Piper asks, saving me from telling Danika he said she was a shitty lay. I know they haven't slept together, but it still pissed me off. Gunner shouldn't be smearing Danika's name like that.

"I guess not." Danika's gaze rises to meet mine. "Can we go? I don't think I can take any more today."

I nod again and kiss the side of her head. "Yeah. Of course."

Then, I look at Piper, who has a small, sad smile, and ask, "Do you want a ride home?"

"No thanks," she says as she rips a blade of grass in half. "I'll catch a ride with Mrs. H when she comes for Cooper."

I stand first and take Danika's hands in mine to help her up. She brushes dirt off her pants and then looks down at my pseudo-sister. "Thanks, Piper. I'm not sure I could have made it out of there without you."

"You're a practically Harris now," Piper says with the first real smile I've seen in weeks. "No matter what happens, we've got your back."

Chapter 34

I t's been a long, hard week, but every day Danika gets a little better. I don't know what she's going through. And don't know how to help her because she's not talking much. So, I take a page out of Cooper's handbook and just be there for her.

I've been by Danika's side as much as possible which means I've skipped football practice all week. I drive her to and from school, sometimes in her car, sometimes in mine. And I even convinced Principal White to temporarily change my schedule to match hers. And you know what?

It's working.

Every day I see that flicker of light in Danika's eyes get a little brighter. She smiles a little more and laughs a little harder.

I'm doing it. I'm the glue that's putting her back together, and that feeling is better than any high I've ever felt.

I lift my arm and wrap it around Danika as she crawls in bed beside me. She rests her head on my shoulder and sets a bowl of popcorn on my lap. We're halfway through season one of Netflix's *Love is Blind* and Danika finally understands what all the Jessica-memes are about.

"Do you think any of it is real?" she asks.

I watch her watch the TV, trying to understand where the question comes from. There's a longing in her eyes and I think I get it. She wants to know if the love is real. If people can fall head over heels with each other in such a short amount of time. I move the bowl of popcorn off my lap and to the bedside table.

"Hey, I was eating that," she whines, but she's not angry. If she were, her brows would pinch together, creating a tiny wrinkle on her forehead.

"Have you ever been in love?" I ask.

She shrugs and looks down at her stomach. "I don't know. Maybe." Her gaze raises to meet mine and she looks so vulnerable. So beautiful. "Have you?"

"Once." I slip my arm underneath Danika and I shift her so she's sitting on top of me. I rest my hands on her thighs, which are spread open, and try to ignore the growing sensation in my pants. I clear my throat and look her in the eyes. If I look anywhere else, all bets are off. "I fell in love once. It was fast and hard, but I have no regrets."

Danika shifts her weight, unintentionally rubbing against me. I chew the inside of my bottom lip and do my best to focus on her next question. "How did it happen?"

I smirk because not too long ago I was asking myself this. "Unexpectedly. This girl, she irked the hell out of me. Consumed my thoughts and took over my dreams. At first, I thought I might have hated her, but then she started dating someone else, and I realized that fire in my chest was jealousy. From there, the floodgates opened, and I was utterly helpless."

"What happened to her?"

I shrug. "Nothing. She had some shit go down, and I never got around to making her mine."

Danika sucks on her bottom lip and zones out for a minute.

My heart races, nervous but also hoping she'll figure out I'm talking about her. I slide my hands up her thighs and give her hips a squeeze. "Hey? You okay?"

Danika snaps out of her trance and leans down. Her lips press against mine for a timid kiss. She pulls back a touch and then presses against me again. I wrap my hands around her waist, pulling her tighter against me, and her hips begin to rock. I don't think she realizes she's doing it because she lets out a small gasp and then a tiny moan and those sounds alone are the death of me.

Danika

I'm not struggling with what happened to me at the party. I get it. My drink was drugged. My friends saved me. Happy ending.

It's what didn't happen that haunts me. Every time I close my eyes, I am plagued with a different nightmare. My mind creates new horrors, new *what-ifs* every night. It's like my dreams have turned into twisted BDSM pornos I can't shut off, no matter how much they disgust me.

I should be dreaming about how epic my first kiss with Logan was, but that glorious memory was stolen.

I've thought about what it would be like to kiss Logan again a lot this week. Mostly when we're at home, lying on the couch or in his bed. I don't know why we're always at his house when mine is empty ninety percent of the time, but that's where we end up.

With my body pressed against Logan like this, I can feel how much he wants me. I want him to. Maybe not all the way, yet, but I want him to chase away my nightmares. I want him to light those grenades inside me and blow up my demons.

Especially now that I know he might be in love with me.

Call me conceited, but there's no way he could have been talking about anybody else.

I brush my tongue across Logan's bottom lip and that's all the invitation he needs. Electricity pulls down my arms, bolts of hot energy scorching me to my fingertips. I thread my fingers through his hair, finally touching those loose, disheveled curls of his.

Logan groans against my mouth and rolls me onto my back. I wrap my legs around him, our lips never breaking. My whole body shudders, but I'm not cold.

I've never been kissed like this, like the whole world begins and ends with this moment. The intensity is addicting. He draws my tongue deeper into his mouth, and I lose myself altogether. I can't get enough.

My hands are everywhere, touching everything he'll let me. I slide my fingers beneath the hem of Logan's white undershirt, needing to feel every inch of him without the barrier of our clothes. As soon as I brush against the soft skin of a scar along Logan's side, he jerks back.

I dig my elbows into the mattress and prop myself up. "What's wrong?"

Logan rolls off and sits beside me. I shiver again, this time I *am* cold. I miss the warmth of his body against mine.

"Sorry." He clears his throat. "I just...I'm not used to people touching me. Under my shirt."

"I know about the scars, Logan. You don't have to hide yourself from me."

Logan bends his legs and rests his arms on his knees. "I know. I guess I just forget sometimes how much of my past you know."

Chapter 35

I kick my legs off the side of my bed and stretch my arms up, feeling better than I have all week. I look at the clock. 6:15. Logan should be starting his morning run, which should give me thirty-ish minutes to get ready before he barges into my room. The man has been wonderful, but a little bit much. Just as I push my blanket to the side, there's a knock at my door, and half of a pause later, it's opening.

"Good morning, beautiful," Logan says, his tone far too chipper for this time of day.

"Who let you in the house?" There's a hint of unintentional malice in my voice because I thought I had more time to myself. Not that it matters. Logan saw me at my absolute worst last week and didn't bat an eye. Still, I've hit a point where I want to look good for him. I don't care what anyone else thinks and morning breath, messy hair and his oversized t-shirt is not my idea of *looking good*.

Logan saunters across the room and lays himself on my bed, hands tucked under his head, ankles crossed. "Your dad.

He's worried about you; said you went through a form of depression last year. He thinks you're slipping back into it."

Logan talks about my inner demons like they are no big deal but to me, they're everything. Dad had no business talking to Logan about my struggles. I'm frustrated but also curious as to why he's so nonchalant about it all. "I'm fine."

Logan rolls onto his side, facing me. He smells clean, freshly showered, but his hair is dry. *Did he use Piper's dryer?* "And that's exactly what I told him. Actually, I said you're better than fine."

"You are way too hyper. What's going on?" I crawl on top of his lap, my skin tingling with need. Sooner or later, I have to let Logan touch me. If not, I might just explode, but I don't want sex to ruin what we've got going.

"I've skipped my run every morning to be here when you wake up. I think all the energy is compiling into a supernova of an explosion."

I roll my eyes, shaking my head. He's such a dork. "You should go. By the time you get back I'll be dressed and ready."

Logan grips my hips and leans up. His lips are close, brushing against mine. Teasing, but not kissing. "I can think of a better way to use this energy."

He flips me onto my back and I squeal. Logan's lips find the sweet spot between my neck on my shoulder and I gasp, grasping the back of his shirt. He sinks his teeth into my skin, biting and sucking and sending a shiver of lust through me.

I arch my back, my hips rocking underneath him. I don't know if Logan realizes it, but I'm not wearing shorts. There's nothing but the thin fabric of my cotton panties and his school pants separating us.

Logan grunts against my neck as his hand slides under my shirt. *His* shirt that I fell asleep in. He stops at the center of my rib cage, fingertips grazing the swell of my bare breast.

Logan lifts his lips, dark eyes staring into mine. We're nose to nose, and I'm hyper-aware of my morning breath. Though, he doesn't seem to mind.

"Go out with me, Danika," he whispers. "Being exclusive *whatevers* isn't enough. I want the title. I want everyone to know that you're not only mine, but I'm yours too."

"That's a big commitment, Logan. One I don't take lightly."

He tilts his head, kissing my nose. "Me either. You'd be my first."

"I thought Melody was your first." I press my hand against Logan's chest. He sits back on his heels, pinning me to my bed.

"She doesn't count," Logan grunts as his hands slide to my waist. All of a sudden, his fingers start moving over my shirt, tickling me. I scream with laughter, but he doesn't stop until I'm out of breath and happy tears stream down my cheeks.

Logan's thumb finds the bare skin of my hip as my shirt bunches up by my waist and exposes my belly and the elastic of my panties. He traces circles, waiting for me to answer.

"I need time. Go slow with me, and we can see where this goes."

"So...can I officially call you my girlfriend now?"

I run my fingers down his chest, feeling every divot between those hard muscles, not stopping until they're tucked beneath the band of his shorts. "No, but I can be a girl who promises not to see anyone else and enjoys kissing you."

He sighs but smiles. "Not exactly what I was hoping for, but I'll take what I can get."

Logan

I pound my fist against the front door, then shove my hands in my pockets. It's early and Sunday. Both of which work to my advantage. No one's here yet. Not even his parents.

Jake opens the door and glares. We haven't talked since *that* party. I wasn't avoiding him or anything. I've just been preoccupied. "You owe me three hundred dollars, cocksucker."

I step through the door before Jake can close it on me, not that he would. He's my brother from another mother—so to speak—bonded through abandonment.

I've been to this house more times than I can count. Mostly because of parties, but also to check on Jake. His parents are gone more often than they're home, leaving him to fend for himself with nothing but an empty house and a credit card.

Nowadays, it's a fucking dream come true, but the first time they left Jake, he was a scared twelve-year-old with a nanny who only visited at dinner time. Sure, back then things could have been worse, but they also could have been a hell of a lot better.

"Whatever. I'll get you your money if you're that hard up about it."

Jake closes the door and shrugs. "Not really."

"Didn't think so." I walk past the kitchen toward his dad's office. It's off-limits and always locked, but I know Jake has the key. "I need the footage from the party two weekends ago."

Jake's jaw tenses. He crosses his arms and squares his shoulders, naturally on the defense. I'm not supposed to know about the cameras. "I don't know what you're talking about."

"Cut the shit, Jake. It's me. I know every room in this house is under surveillance." I turn, searching the walls until I find what I'm looking for. I point at the dark spot that looks like a hole from a mishap while hanging a picture. But I know. "Those are in every room. I don't care about the whole house; I just need the room I broke into."

Jake looks at me curiously, probably wondering what else I've figured out over the years. I know enough. Dirty money. Coverups. Crooked cops. And those are just the pieces I've put together. Whatever it is his parents actually do for a living— and I highly doubt it's porn—they're doing Jake a favor by keeping him out of it. "Why? What happened?"

"You don't watch the footage?"

He drops his arms to his sides and shakes his head, "Nah, my parents set the cameras up for security reasons. Honestly, I forget it's there half the time."

I want to smile because I know once Jake sees what went down, he'll give me the video. But I can't find it in myself to feel the least bit happy. I'm going to have to watch Danika's suffering multiple times for my plan to work. Not because I'm a twisted bastard, because I need other people to see it for everything to fall in place and I'm not letting that tape out of my sight.

I sigh, a deep frown falling. "Just watch. Then you'll understand why I need it."

~

Danika's already at the lunch table with Cooper and Piper by the time I arrive at school. It's been a long, busy forty-eight hours, but finally everything has been set in motion. Danika looks up at me as I approach. I bend down and kiss her quickly before taking my seat at the table.

"I missed you this morning," she says, her big brown eyes full of adoration. I love the way she looks at me, like I'm the only person in the world. "It was weird getting ready without you hovering nearby."

"Are you calling me a helicopter boyfriend?" I tease.

Piper's brows arch as she exchanges a silent look with Cooper. They know I usually run from relationships. Too bad when I'm finally ready, it's the girl running, but whatever. I'll wait. She'll come around eventually. Besides, it's just a label. That girl is mine in every way that matters.

"I would if you were my boyfriend." There's a playfulness in her tone I hope means she's coming around to the idea.

I nudge Danika's side with my elbow as she splits a peanut butter and banana sandwich in half. My insides flip and flutter. I'm already anxious to see how today plays out, but she brought me a sandwich. To anyone else, this is no big deal, but to me, it's huge.

"I have a surprise for you."

Excitement dances across her face. She's probably thinking it's jewelry or a trip somewhere, but what I've done is better. "What?"

"It's gonna cost you."

Danika's smile falls and she sighs. "I already told you, Logan. I need time."

"What? No." I'm kind of offended that Danika thinks I'd pressure her into anything. Let alone something she's already told me she's not ready for. I push back my frustration and intertwine our fingers, bringing her palm up for a kiss. "I need you to throw Sarah a bone. She's massively losing her shit since you've started avoiding her."

Danika looks over her shoulder at our old table. I know what she sees. Melody and Rachel gossiping about the news I'm about to break. Jake acting surprised as Tad gives his opinions on the matter. And then there's Sarah, who's probably staring at us like a lost puppy. That girl has texted me every day, sometimes twice a day, asking about Danika.

Danika sighs and pulls out her phone, shooting a quick text message. Her phone dings almost immediately. "Done. We're going to the mall after school today."

I rest my hand on Danika's lower back and lean in, kissing her cheek. It's hard as hell not touching her when we're this close, but she wants to take things slow, and I'll respect that. I need to let her call the shots and dictate when it's okay to do what. She's nothing like the girls I usually screw around with. The last thing I want to do is mess up what we've got going.

"Good." I reach across the table and steal one of Piper's french fries. Not like she's going to eat them. Her appetite is smaller than a bird lately. "So, what's the latest gossip floating around?"

Cooper and Piper look at me like I've got three heads. I know they hear everything, but I'm sure they're assuming I'm talking about Piper's rumors or possibly Danika's. Yes, there are rumors about Danika, but most of them are speculating as to what *we* are. "You mean, you guys haven't heard?"

All three of my tablemates shake their heads. I'm full on grinning now. I can't help it. I'm like a kid on Christmas who got the latest PlayStation and every game known to mankind. Fucking elated. "Gunner has been expelled."

"What?" Danika whispers as all color draines from her face. I thought she'd be excited. I thought she'd feel some sense of relief knowing that prick can't hurt her again.

Instead, she looks terrified.

I lean against the trunk of my car, smiling down at my phone. Logan sent me a gif that says: you're pretty, dazzling, wonderful, stunning, and a whole bunch of words. There are too many compliments, flicking from one word to the next after less than a second. Every time I look at it, I find another colorful word I didn't notice before.

> Me: Feeling guilty?

> Logan: More like grateful.

> Logan: Is Sarah there yet?

I lift my gaze and look around the parking lot. We agreed to meet by the movie theater entrance at four. I'm parked in the front row and it's four-oh-five. As soon as she crosses into the mall-space I'll see her.

> Me: Not yet.

"Hey!" Sarah yells, waving her arm in the air. She jogs over to my car as I send Logan one more text, letting him know she got here. "Sorry, I'm late. Melody wouldn't stop crying in the bathroom. I felt like a total bitch leaving Rachel to deal with her, but I didn't want to be any later than I already am."

Me: She just got here.

"What happened?" I ask, tucking my phone into my back pocket. I don't actually care about Melody, but my mamma raised me better than most.

Sarah shrugs and shakes her head. "Gunner. Apparently, he ended things and is moving out of state."

I bite my tongue, literally, until it bleeds. I don't want to hear about Gunner, especially if it's in relation to him and Melody. But I asked and true to her nature, Sarah rambles on, throwing more tidbits of gossip into the conversation as she goes. She talks the whole time we're shopping, throughout our food court dinner, and even in the bathroom. I'd forgotten just how much Sarah loves the sound of her voice.

A few hours later, I'm standing by my car, keys in hand, exhausted. I didn't actually buy anything, but I'm tired, none-theless. There are a few moments of awkward silence where I don't know if Sarah is going to hug me or shake my hand and say goodbye. She doesn't do either. Instead, she sets her bags on the ground and leans against the side of my car.

"So, you and Logan."

"Yup," I say, popping the P. I'm ready to slip into my paja-mas, curl up in Logan's bed, and fall asleep for the night. Dad's given up trying to make me come home most nights. I'll be eighteen next week, so there's not much he can do either way. Out of respect, I tell him where I am and he always responds with, "I'm too young to be a grandpa. Wrap it up, kiddo."

"No one talks about the Harris twins," Sarah starts, staring at her feet. "But they're not as perfect as they seem."

"Every family has their problems," I tell her, thinking about what mine was like before the cancer took over.

We were happy, but Dad worked too much and Mom complained a lot. She wanted to take family vacations and have movie nights and things like that. With Dad working so much, we'd just go on without him. Our family wasn't perfect. We had our own issues.

"True, but theirs is extra wonky. For starters, there's Piper. She's lived with them on and off for the past ten years. Not to mention she just got out of rehab for—"

"Don't talk about Piper," I snap. "I can guarantee you don't know what's going on with her. We can't be friends if you're going to talk shit."

Sarah's gaze flicks over to me and then back to her feet. "Sorry. I didn't mean to. I was just...it won't happen again."

"Thanks."

Sarah's quiet for a beat, then continues like nothing happened. "Anyway, so there's that and the Harris divorce, but there's more. You know my dad is one of the few Judges in this county, so he sees a variety of cases. Well, when I mentioned Logan's name freshman year at dinner one night he flipped out and warned me to stay away from him."

I step in front of Sarah, kind of forcing her to look at me. I don't like her talking about Logan. "Why are you telling me this?"

"I don't want you blindsided again," she huffs. I'm glad she thinks she's doing me some big favor, but without verifiable details, this is nothing more than gossip. "Look, I don't know for sure what happened with Logan, but I think there had to have been some kind of legal issues for it to make its way to my dad. I tried asking about it once, but he refused to tell me anything else."

"Probably because it's none of your business." It's none of mine, either. I can only assume this has to do with the secret

Logan thought I knew. Whatever it is, Sarah needs to stop snooping before she uncovers something no one is meant to know. "It's probably not what you think."

Sarah bends down and grabs her bags. "You're probably right, but you should be careful. Cooper's a total hothead who's in love with Piper and always getting into fights, and Logan is straight trouble."

I amble onto Logan's back porch and stare at his kidney-shaped pool. It's been years since I've been swimming. The houses in my old neighborhood were lucky if they had garages or fences. An in-ground pool was unheard of, and above-ground pools were far and few between. There was a community center, but it was run by the local gang, and I didn't want to get shot.

Besides, it's not like I had a lot of spare time to go swimming or hang out with friends. With the exception of the Friday night football games—which Mom insisted I go—and school dances, every moment was spent with her. Not that I'm complaining.

Logan presses his lips to my shoulder and runs his fingers down the back of my arms. A shiver of lust runs through me. I bite my lip, closing my eyes.

"You okay?" He asks, his voice a deep whisper. "You've barely said anything since coming over."

"How'd you do it?"

"Do what?"

"Gunner. How'd you get him expelled?" I stroll over to the patio set and sit. Logan follows, a cheeky grin on his lips.

"He actually withdrew, but I like the rumor that he was kicked out better." He waits for me to respond and when I don't, he continues. "There was a video."

"What?" Panic squeezes my throat. I swallow the lump, but it sticks going down. "Someone recorded what happened to me?"

I run my hand through my hair, scratching the back of my head. I bet it was Melody. But if she had a video this whole time, why hold onto it? Why not put it out there for the world to see?

Logan sets his hand on my thigh and squeezes. Tiny tingles spread from his fingers, momentarily distracting me from my silent freakout. "Relax, baby. It's not what you think. Jake's whole house is wired. I had him give me the surveillance video and took it to my dad. He may be the last person on Earth I want to talk to, but I reached out and he agreed to help."

I swallow hard, my insecurities peaking. "So, your dad's seen it?"

I haven't seen Mr. Harris since we moved away. Drugged and passed out in a stranger's bed is not how I want anyone to see me.

"Yeah," he says curtly. "Sheriff Tomlinson, too, I needed my threat to be as real as possible. Dad approached the matter as if *you* were pressing charges. We gave the Wells family an ultimatum. Withdraw Gunner and keep him as far away from you as possible and this all goes away... or else."

I look out at the water. The clear blue glass ripples, pushing the floats across the surface. "And if they refused?"

"We threatened his parents with a good time in court. After showing them a tiny clip of the video and Dad stressing that Gunner could be charged with a minimum of thirty years in jail for attempted rape, they agreed to our terms." Logan smiles triumphantly.

I chew on the corner of my lip. Even though it sucks people have seen what happened to me, Logan's plan was brilliant. I don't have to look at that monster anymore. I don't have to beat myself up for not seeing Gunner for what he really was.

Logan's hand falls from my thigh as I scoot the chair back and stand. He eyes me curiously as I walk to the edge of the pool. Wordlessly, I peel my shirt over my head and step out of my shorts. I level with myself—being in my mismatched bra and panties is the same as being in my bathing suit. Still, my skin pricks from self-consciousness because I'm sure Logan is taking in every inch of my backside.

I cannonball into the pool and the water shocking my body. It's not cold, but I wouldn't call it warm, either. I swim to the surface and take a breath. Wiping my eyes, I hear a splash and feel water moving beneath me. Logan pops up to my left, fully clothed, shaking his head like a dog to clear the water from his eyes.

I swim over to him and wrap my legs around his waist and my arms around his neck. He treads water, but if he's struggling, I'd never know.

"Hey, beautiful," he purrs in that deep, husky voice.

I press my lips to his and his body stops swaying. I think he's at a point where he can touch because his arms wrap around me. I pull back, press my forehead against his, and whisper, "Thank you."

Logan replies with another kiss. I slide his hand under my bra as a thank you, and my heart pounds in my chest, ready, waiting for a reaction.

Logan pinches my nipple between two fingers and I moan against his lips. We stay like this for a while, kissing and touching, until I feel his other hand slide under my ass. His finger inches painfully slow over the cotton of my panties and brushes against my center. I gasp against Logan's lips, shocked not at the touch but at the heat rippling through me. *Effing grenades.*

Logan pulls back, lust-drunk eyes smiling at me. "Should I stop?"

I swallow hard but shake my head. He moves his hand off my chest and holds onto the back of my neck. A single finger slips under my panties, brushing against my folds. He peppers my neck in kisses as he presses the tip of his finger inside me.

It's been months since I've let anyone touch me like this. My last boyfriend and I fooled around, a lot, but he never made me feel the way Logan does. I claw at Logan's back, arching my spine, instinctively trying to get away because the feeling is too intense. My whole body tingles and the pressure at my center is only growing.

Logan holds me tighter against him as he sticks another finger in, moving the two in unison. The pressure building inside me reaches its breaking point and I come undone. I drop my chin to Logan's shoulder, panting as my body hums from the aftershock.

Logan moves his hand from my panties and grips my thigh, physically steadying me. "You okay?"

I nod. Still trying to catch my breath. "Yeah. What was that?"

Logan looks at me curiously, one thick brow arching upward. "Have you never had an orgasm before?"

"Apparently not," I laugh, because if that's what Logan's hands make me feel like, I can't wait to discover what else he can do.

Chapter 39

"Hey, baby girl," Dad says hesitantly as I walk into the kitchen.

The shirt I stole from Logan falls to my mid-thigh, just short enough to see the pink donut print of my pajama shorts. The first time I strolled downstairs in Logan's clothes, Dad's eyebrows shot so far up his forehead I thought they were going to kiss the roof. Now, he's used to it.

I slump in the kitchen chair, not ready to be awake, but someone had to text me at the butt crack of dawn. Oh well. A ridiculously early text is a million times better than an unexpected-expected visitor. "Morning, Dad."

"I got called into work tonight for a seven-to-seven shift." He grimaces. "I'm sorry."

I shrug and reach for his cup of coffee. So, the thing with Dad's coffee, outside of a sip or two, he doesn't drink it. Every morning he would get up and make himself a cup of coffee—a full cup. Mom would come into the kitchen, make me breakfast, pack me lunch, and then complain about how Dad would waste a good cup of Joe. She'd then take the mug and drink it herself, also complaining that he didn't know how to make a decent cup of coffee.

Mom would pretend to be irritated.

Dad would stare adoringly.

It had been that way for as long as I can remember.

When she died, Dad still made his cup of coffee. Every morning, he'd have his sip, and then it would sit untouched for the rest of the day. One morning, I woke up earlier than usual (not on purpose) and found him crying, talking to the cup as if it were Mom. It broke my heart.

I started sharing the coffee with him the next day. It was the only way I knew how to help. And it did. Little by little, Dad pulled himself back together. So now, most mornings, we share a cup of coffee. Making sure to always leave a little left for Mom.

I take a sip and shrug.

For everyone else in the world, today is just another day. The fact that this is the day I turn eighteen doesn't make a difference to anyone but me. It sucks that my first birthday without Mom Dad has to work, but there's no sense in making him feel bad about it. He's shouldered all of the burden since Mom got sick. The least I can do is understand we can't have dinner tonight. "No big deal. You bought me a car. I'd say we're good."

He pushes back from the table and stands. He kisses the top of my head and then reaches for his briefcase on the counter. "I've got to get going."

I fight the crushing hurt twisting in my chest. Not doing my birthday dinner is one thing, but leaving me alone all day creates a new pain I haven't felt. I thought we'd at least spend the day together. He's my dad. My birthday might not matter to anyone else, but it's supposed to be important to him. I swallow the lump in my throat, pretending to be curious, yet indifferent. "Your shift doesn't start for, like, twelve hours."

"I know, but I have a meeting with Sheriff Tomlinson this morning."

I DON'T KNOW how long Dad's been gone. I've laid in bed, staring up at the ceiling for what feels like an eternity. I cried myself to sleep once, but now I'm awake, and drained, and too deep in my pool of self-pity to call anybody and beg them to hang out with me.

I don't expect Sarah or Logan to remember my birthday. It's been years and I don't have social media to remind them it's today. I also realize while counting the popcorn bits on my ceiling—so far, I'm at four-hundred and twelve—that I've been back for almost three months and only have two friends.

Two. If you don't count Cooper and Piper. Sometimes, I feel like they're only nice to me because I'm with Logan.

How pathetic am I?

I'm so lost in my thoughts and the popcorn pieces on the ceiling that I don't hear my bedroom door open and don't notice Logan until he's lying next to me. "What are you doing?"

"Counting the little popcorn specks." I can't look at him. If I do, I'll cry. Then he'll ask what's wrong and I'll have to make up some stupid excuse because I don't want Logan to feel bad for not knowing it's my birthday.

"How many are you up to?" he asks, the edge of his lips quirking into a grin.

'Four hundred and seventy-five."

We lay in silence. Me counting and him staring up at my ceiling, too. After a few minutes, Logan says, "This is worse than watching paint dry." He stands and then grabs my hands, pulling me into an upright position. "You look like you've been run over by a car. What's wrong?"

I yank my hands free and shove them under my armpits,

hugging myself. I probably look like a five-year-old having a fit, but at this point I don't care. "Nothing. Go home if you're bored. This is what I'm doing today."

Logan grunts and lays back in bed beside me. He tucks his arms under his head and closes his eyes. "I'm just saying there are way better ways to spend your birthday, but it's your day. If this is what you want to do, then so be it."

I jerk upright, my insides tingling with excitement. "What did you say?"

Logan chuckles, the sound rippling through me in the best possible way, and pushes onto his elbows. "I mean, I thought we'd go to the beach and then the haunted house tonight, but if *this* is what you'd rather do..."

He remembered! I don't know how, but Logan remembered. I cup his jaw with my hands and bend down, placing a very big, very thankful kiss on his lips.

Danika has a death grip on my hand while hugging close to my arm. We're barely out of the school's parking lot, and she's freaking out.

Every year our school turns into a massive haunted house either the weekend before or the weekend of Halloween. It just kind of depends what day the thirty-first falls on. It's a huge event that's open to the community.

Our school is three stories tall and sectioned off for themed scare zones. The first floor is meant for the lines in and out, while the second floor is zombie-themed, with two scare rooms, and the third floor is basically a living tribute to Steven King. The committee picked five movies, all of which are a secret until tonight.

Our classrooms are grouped together in pods of two, connected by a bathroom. So, if the flow is the same as last year, the guide will lead everyone on a predetermined path through each room and then back down to the first floor.

The cafeteria has morphed into a ghoulish dance party hosted by the cheerleading squad, and outside, leading back toward the parking lot, the football team has set up a series of carnival games. Basically, the whole place has one way in and one way out.

People flock by the busload to us because we are the closest haunted house that's actually scary in a fifty-mile radius. Plus all of the proceeds are sent to one of the children's hospitals in South Florida.

Danika squeezes her eyes shut and holds me so tight she nearly cuts off circulation to my hand. "Baby, relax." I shake free of her death grip and drape my arm across her shoulders. "This is supposed to be fun."

Danika shakes her head and covers her face with her hands. "I hate scary movies. They give me nightmares and I'm about to walk into one."

"Actually, you're about to walk into, like, six," Sarah declares beside us. I shoot her a shut-the-fuck-up glare, but she's too stoned to comprehend.

"Baby," I pull Danika's shaking hands off her face and stare down into her eyes. "We don't have to do this. We can do a movie or mini golf or pretty much *anything* besides the haunted house."

"No. I want to." She insists. "It's for a good cause."

I pay our entry fee and wait for our guide to start the tour and I recognize the girl dressed as not a vampire, but its victim. Tricia, is her name, and she was one of the few girls I actually hooked up with more than once last year. Four times, actually. Luckily, Danika's buried her face in my shirt and doesn't see Tricia wink at me.

Sarah catches it. Points at Tricia. Then pretends to slit her throat with her finger.

I laugh because I never pegged Sarah as the crazy type.

"Welcome. Welcome, everyone," Tricia says, her voice dripping with faux-British aristocracy. She grins and circles the group. Touches a shoulder here. Twirls a lock of hair there. "Master will be pleased with tonight's offering."

"I thought it was zombie and horror movie themed." Sarah crosses her arms over her chest. "You look like you've been mauled by The Ripper from *The Vampire Diaries.*"

Tricia smirks and dramatically steps towards Sarah. "And your name is what, little one?"

Sarah rolls her hooded eyes, unimpressed. They were both on the cheerleading squad freshman year. She knows her name. "Miss Mary-Mack."

Tricia takes Sarah's chin between her thumb and forefinger. Everyone's watching, probably wondering if this is ad-libbed or a part of the show. Even Danika's peeking through her fingers.

Tricia sticks out her tongue and licks the side of Sarah's face. "You'd taste better if you were dressed in black."

Tricia pushes Sarah's chin away and struts back to the front of the group. "Master won't be pleased if we're late."

Sarah wipes her cheek with her palm, her expression stoic, then rubs the saliva on her jeans. "That was gross."

Jake chuckles and snakes his arm around Sarah's waist. I don't know when they became an item, but I'm not about to intervene. Jake may be the closest thing I've got to a guy friend, but he's a dog. My reputation may be bad, but I look like a saint compared to him.

"Rules," Tricia exclaims, stopping at the threshold of the second floor. Her fake accent is gone and there's a seriousness to her voice. "Nothing in there can *physically* harm you. The knives are fake, the chainsaws chainless, but I warn you. Don't touch anyone. The moment you do, all bets are off. I cannot save you." Her gaze bounces from each person in line, then stops on Danika. "Will not save you."

Danika squeezes my waist, wrinkling my shirt. I kiss the side of her head and whisper, "Relax, baby. No one's going to get you. I'm right here."

Tricia opens the door and lets the group in. Danika and I hang toward the back of the crowd, letting everyone else go first. I figure we can watch where the scarers are and avoid as much of the jumping and creepiness as possible.

"Logan," Tricia says, grabbing my arm. Danika shifts under me, adjusting to hear her better. "Don't go upstairs. The stairwell at the end of the hallway isn't locked at the bottom, you can get out that way."

And then she leaves. Doubles back the way she came and disappears into the darkness. *That's different from last year.*

Danika peeks up at me. "That was weird."

I hold her closer and run my hand up and down her arm. "Nah, it's just Halloween fun. Come on."

Danika squeaks and buries her face back into my chest. I kiss her forehead and proceed to the first haunted classroom. The hallway itself is decorated to look like an abandoned town. Drop cloths with painted storefronts and tumbleweeds add to the effect. The best part about the hallway, there are no zombies. It's a scare-free zone to give everyone a mini break.

We walk into the first haunted room, a torture chamber of sorts. Zombies try to attack us from every angle, but they're *chained* to the wall and miss us by inches. As a whole, I think it's kind of stupid. The corn syrup blood is too light and whoever was in charge of makeup and costumes this year went the *Party City* route. With the budget we have every year, this could have been more realistic.

"Lift your foot." I tap Danika's leg with my hand. She peeks down at the ground, probably to see why, then buries her face in my chest again. "We've got to step over a body."

Danika blindly agrees. The *dead* body near the end of the haunted room comes to life and grabs Danika's ankle. Not a big deal until he yanks and tries to pull her onto the ground. Danika lets out a blood-curdling scream and grips my waist tighter.

I can't recognize the kid, he's got too much cheap stage makeup on, but he's determined to bring Danika to the ground, and it pisses me off.

"Dude! What the fuck? Let go."

Zombie man hisses and tries to climb his way up Danika's leg. She's hysterical and clings to me, nearly crying she's so scared. This isn't supposed to happen. I've worked in haunted halls for the past three years. There are strict rules. Even if someone touches you, *you* don't touch them. Ever.

Something's not right.

I raise my foot and kick the zombie-kid in the side until he falls off Danika. She's shaking and crying, but no longer screaming. I slip my arm under her legs and carry her out of that classroom, then kick the door shut behind me.

"I don't want to do this anymore," Danika cries softly into my ear. Her body trembles in my arms. I kiss her head and then look around the hallway. I'm supposed to follow the path of bloody footprints to the next room, but that's not happening.

"We're not staying."

I've never been more grateful hallways are the safe zones. I don't think Danika could handle another zombie attack. I don't listen to Tricia's advice about which stairwell to take. While her warning about tonight was sweet, people often forget about the North stairs—Cooper's favorite meetup spot with Piper. On the off chance that tonight is a set up by Gunner and his crew, I refuse to do what's expected of me and fall into a trap.

Am I overreacting? Probably. But considering I just fucked up Gunner's senior year, I'm not taking any chances.

I carry Dankia through the cafeteria and set her on a bench outside near one of the food trucks. She tucks her hands under her thighs, gaze bouncing from one person to the next. This was a disaster. I should have pushed for us to go out to eat somewhere or something.

I order a Coke and basket of fries from the counter, only

taking my eyes off her to collect the food, and then I am at her side again. "Here. Eat. It'll calm your nerves."

"Cooking helps. Not eating." She takes a fry and places it between her lips. "You know these probably aren't Vegan. Right?"

I shake my head and laugh. She's serious but nonaccusatory. "It's the closest we've got. Are you feeling any better?"

She takes a sip of the Coke and gives a small nod. "Yeah. What happened? Is it always like that?"

"No. Something was off tonight." We sit in silence and finish the basket of fries. I'm not ready to go home, I want to try and redeem tonight. A girl only turns eighteen once. "What do you want to do now?"

Danika shifts on the bench seat to face me. "I don't know, but I think I should thank my hero." She winks.

I turn and pull her closer by the hips. She only slides a few inches, but those inches feel like miles. I reach up and tuck long strands behind her ear. I still need to give her the gift I bought—sapphire stud earrings that match the necklace she never takes off. "And how are you going to do that?"

Danika fists my shirt and pulls my lips to hers. I cup the back of her neck with one hand and scoot her onto my lap. I don't care what the people around us think. I kiss her the way she deserves to be kissed—like the world begins and ends with her because mine does.

For as long as I can remember, there was always this feeling of emptiness I could never fill. I never could place exactly what was lacking. I just knew something was. That deep, impenetrable void doesn't exist when Danika's near. If she ever leaves me I'll be ruined, and that has somehow turned into my biggest fear.

Danika reaches behind her and lays down until her back is lying flat, and I'm on top of her. It's awkward, trying not to crush her, but I must be doing a good job because she moans against my lips.

"Jeez, no one wants to see that!" Melody complains from somewhere that isn't Danika's lips.

I break our kiss to look up at Melody. Danika giggles into my shoulder and I don't bother fighting my smile. I'm drunk on her lips and high on life. There's nothing that Melody could say or do to ruin this moment.

"Well then, don't look," I tell her, right before finding Danika's mouth again.

Danika and I have unofficially been together for four weeks now and things couldn't be better. All those stupid television moments where the couples stare at each other, smiling like the sun was made to shine on them... I always thought it was bullshit. I was wrong.

So. So. Wrong.

The sun was made to shine on Danika because the world gets a little brighter whenever she's around.

I laugh at myself. That was so cheesy I could slice it up and put it on a cracker, but that's what Danika does. Turns me into a mushy, warm, cheese ball.

I like it.

I walk into my house, Danika's hand in mine, like we've done every day after school for weeks, and stop dead in my tracks. Chill bumps break out across my skin at the sound of the voice somewhere within my walls. I swallow the knot in my throat and pray that my mind is fucking with me again.

"Are you okay?" Danika asks, eyeing me curiously. She rubs

her hand on my arm and then stares at her fingers, probably feeling the sweat seeping through my shirt.

I shake our hands free and follow the sound of that voice. My vision tunnels, only seeing the path leading me to hell. My feet are heavy with each step and they anchor themselves to the ground when I find the man I'm searching for sitting at my table.

He doesn't look much different than he did ten years ago, outside of the grays peppered through his sandy blonde hair. Then again, he never does when I see him.

I swallow hard and tell myself I'm imagining him again. Alan Shaffer isn't here. He can't be here.

I killed him.

But this man has the same angled jaw. Same pointed nose. Same dark brown eyes that never matched his complexion. *It can't be him.*

Mom waltzes over and pulls me into a hug. This woman hasn't hugged me since I was six years old, and that was an awkward side hug for a photo. I stiffen, not sure how to handle the show of affection. "Look who stopped by to say hi, sweetheart."

The man stands and extends his hand. "Good to see you, son."

My stomach quivers, and for once, I'm thankful I didn't eat lunch today. Even though I was starving moments ago, my appetite is gone. *Same fucking cologne.*

"Logan," Mom says with a light warning tone. "Don't be rude."

"H..." I swallow a boulder in my throat and force myself to speak, taking the man's hand to shake it. His skin is cold. Clammy. For a split second, I wonder if vampires could be real but push the thought away. This person is probably just *someone* and my mind is drawing parallels, seeing what it wants. "Hello, Dr. Shaffer."

I expect the man to correct me and tell me his name is Mr. Joe-schmo. He doesn't. "You've gotten big, son."

"S-stop calling me son," I growl. My emotions are all over the place. Freaked out. Pissed off. Ready to cry. They're spinning like a top and no matter what they settle on, I'm fucked. "I'm not your kid."

Mom sets her cup down and walks over to me, placing the back of her hand against my forehead. Such a doting woman when we have company. I still under her touch, the deprived child in me desperate for her attention. "Are you feeling okay, honey? You haven't stuttered in ages."

Dr. Shaffer smirks at the comment. He knows he's getting under my skin. Making me unhinged. I step back, out from under mom's touch. She doesn't care about me, not like this. Not like she does Cooper.

"I'm so sorry about Logan's behavior today. I don't know what got into him," Mom fusses. She turns her attention to me, glaring with that disappointed look I've seen all my life. "Don't you think you should apologize?"

I grit my teeth, feeling the muscles of my jaw flex with the tension. Fuck no, I'm not going to apologize. Seeing this man alive and walking around... I should've beat him harder with my baseball bat. I should have done more than destroy his office. Apparently, I didn't do a good enough job fucking him up. I mean obviously. The man's alive!

Holy shit.

He's alive.

Does Dad know? Is Dr. Shaffer here to press charges against me? I was worried about Danika remembering my truths and the trouble she could cause. But this...

This is so much worse.

Feeling the color drain from my face, and the bile churning in my stomach, I leave the kitchen without excusing myself. I hide in the bathroom, twisting the lock and lean against the door. *If* that really is Dr. Alan Shaffer, I'm fucked. Jail time fucked. Dad. Sheriff Thomlinson. Dr. Winters.

They are all fucked.

There's a soft knock at the door. I twist the lock, knowing there's only one person in this house who cares enough to seek me out. I step to the side and sit beside the toilet. I've barely given enough room for the door to open, but Danika squeezes in.

She sits on the floor beside me and takes my hand. "Are you okay?"

I shake my head and lean into her lap. Tears fill my eyes and no matter how much I want to fight them, want to set them on fire, they explode out of me. I hate that Danika's seeing me like this.

Weak.

I'm a man. Men don't cry. They bottle everything up, and eventually, all of their feelings explode out of them in some heated fight. When I was four, I fell off my tricycle. I ran up to Dad, tears in my eyes, and pointed at my knee. You know what he did? Slapped me across the face and told me not to be such a baby.

"Boys don't cry," he said, "they deal with it."

I hug my knees to my chest, desperate to curl into a ball and hide. Hide from Dr. Shaffer. From Danika. From myself.

Danika threads her fingers through my hair, lulling me until I'm calm. Mom used to do this for Piper when she'd wake up crying. A pang of jealousy ripples through me. I've never asked for much. Hell, I never asked for anything. I rarely spoke! But I should have gotten the same basic level of affection Cooper and Piper got.

Her unwavering love.

"Logan Anson Harris!" my mother demands, pounding on the bathroom door. "Open up this instant!

I hug my knees tighter and bury my face in Danika's leg.

Her tears fall onto my cheeks, and I feel lower than low. I need to be strong. I need to comfort my girl and let her know everything's fine, but I can't. I physically can't.

Mom beats against the door again. "God damnit, Logan! Open up."

Danika shifts out from underneath me. I hear her sniffle and then see the hallway light reflect against the porcelain tub.

"What the fuck is wrong with you?" Mom shouts. My back is to her, but I'm sure she's looking past Danika and at me.

"No." Danika growls. "What the fuck is wrong with you?"

"Excuse me?" My mother rears back. I can practically see her eyebrows arch and that hand settling on her hip.

"How can you call yourself a mother?" Danika scolds. "Are you too blind to see that *something* happened and your son is having a moment?"

"A moment?" Mom guffaws. "He's always been emotional. This is nothing new."

Danika tsks. "Then maybe you should reevaluate your parenting skills because you fucked up somewhere."

"Get out of my house!" My mom demands, her voice reaching a new octave.

"Gladly." Danika kneels beside me and rubs my back. "Babe?"

"Don't even think about leaving, Logan." Mom spits. "You're grounded."

Danika ignores her and helps pull me to my feet. I feel pathetic. Beyond pathetic as she wipes my cheeks. But there's no judgment in her eyes. Only love and understanding. "Let's go for a drive."

Chapter 42

We end up at the beach.

I guess it's fitting. Technically we—as a not-couple—began here. Once Danika knows about me, we'll end here, too, coming full circle.

The sand is warm, having baked all day in the sun. That's the great thing about Florida, it's the middle of November and still hot outside ninety percent of the time. I wouldn't go swimming, the water is probably colder than I like, but to sit outside in a pair of shorts this time of year is a luxury the rest of the country doesn't have. Probably why I'll never leave this state. I hate the cold.

Danika sits beside me, her long legs stretched out and crossed at the ankles. She closes her eyes, letting the sun's rays beam down on her. She's gorgeous. So much more than I deserve. Without her, I'd probably still be on the bathroom floor with Mom still screaming at me through the door. Eventually, she would have given up and left, but Mom's got good lungs. She can yell for hours. I should know.

"Want to talk?" Danika asks, squinting in the sun.

We've been sitting here for a while now, long enough that I'm half tempted to walk over to the Red Onion and grab us some drinks. Danika won't say anything in front of Cooper, but there's a good chance Mom has already called to rant about how I've embarrassed her. Cooper doesn't know the details, but he figured out that something went down with me and Dr. Shaffer when Dad refused to let me go back to therapy.

"Not really," I tell her honestly. "But for you, I will."

Danika smiles, waiting patiently. When I don't immediately start talking, she scoots closer. I lay back in the sand, tucking one arm under my head and the other around her, pulling her down with me and onto my chest. This may be the last time I have her in my arms. Might as well enjoy it.

I take a deep breath and let it out. My story is a long, one I've never shared before. I'm not even sure where to start. I run through the details in my mind, trying to figure out when this particular problem began.

"I was in the third grade the first time Piper came to live with us. I was so excited I could barely stand still. This girl—my new sister—was an outcast, unwanted and unloved by the only family she had, her mother. I've never fit in with my family, still don't, and I thought Piper and I would bond over our differences."

Danika squeezes my arm, her way of silently saying, "I'm sorry you feel that way."

I kiss the side of her head, breathing in her rosewater shampoo and close my eyes. "We never bonded, not until this year. She, like everyone else, fell under Cooper's spell and tossed me aside. She wasn't intentionally mean to me, but like my mother and Cooper, I think she forgot I existed.

Dad, on the other hand, never forgot about me. In fact, he remembered me a little too much. Especially after a few drinks.

I like to think Mom didn't know what was happening, but the truth is there's no way she didn't. Dad was smart though, he only hit where the bruises wouldn't show."

Danika runs her hand over my side. I shiver because she already knew about Dad. I broke down once in the seventh grade and told her. Showed her the black and blue welts across my back and the scars from where his belt broke skin near my ribs.

"I don't remember exactly when it happened, but at some point, Mom became worried about how Piper was adjusting and brought Dr. Shaffer, a child psychologist, to the house. He spent some time getting to know Piper, then talked to both Cooper and me individually.

There wasn't anything out of the ordinary about Dr Shaffer. He was older, maybe mid-forties, with thick blond hair. I remember he had a huge mouth and big teeth. He looked a little goofy, but it fit his face, especially when he smiled. It was easy to open up and talk to him because he was nice.

Piper was fine, but Dr. Shaffer was worried about me. Apparently, I was depressed, which, looking back, isn't surprising, but Mom acted shocked. She cried to Dr. Shaffer, complaining how she didn't know what to do because I *never* spoke up about what's bothering me."

"Maybe if she would have paid attention, she would have noticed," Danika mumbles, that same fire dancing in her tone as before.

I lace her tiny fingers with mine and kiss the palm of her hand. My heart beats wildly against my chest. I haven't gotten to the hard parts, not yet, and I'm terrified she'll pull away and leave me once I do.

"I started therapy once a week the next day. At first, everything was great. Dr. Shaffer and I played games and watched TV together. Sometimes, he'd sit on the couch beside me and read me stories. It was the first positive experience I'd had with a man because my dad and I had a terrible relationship.

Maybe that's why I didn't say anything when Dr. Shaffer's hand rested on my thigh the first time. Sure, it felt weird, him touching my leg, but I liked him. I wanted him to be proud of me so we could keep our sessions. I was eight. I didn't know that *this* was not how therapy went."

"Oh, Logan," Danika whispers.

I swallow the lump in my throat and keep going. If I stop now, I'll never finish. "We stayed like that for almost a year, playing games and watching movies together. Dr. Shaffer's hand, from time to time, would linger too long on my shoulder or rest a little too close on my leg, but overall, it wasn't a big deal. I trusted him.

I was ten the first time Dr. Shaffer touched me. He told me we were moving to the next step in our therapy, that at first, I might feel uncomfortable, but that my discomfort was normal. All the hairs on my body have only stood on edge a handful of times, and that was the first. Every time since, whether for good reasons or bad, the pin-prick-hair-rising feeling always brings me back to that moment. To the way I jumped back in fear when he touched me."

I shudder, blinking back tears at the memory because I didn't know any better. I stare up at the clouds, not wanting to see the disgust on Danika's face.

"I looked up to Dr. Shaffer. I thought he had my best interest at heart, that he wanted to help me break through my depression and become comfortable talking to people. Do you remember in the sixth grade when our school forced us to learn about sex trafficking and what to do if someone tries to hurt you? I sat in that lesson, shrinking deeper inside myself, realizing that I was a victim. There were at least a dozen things mentioned that hadn't happened to me, but a good handful did.

My stomach twisted into a million knots that afternoon as Mom drove me to my weekly session. I sat on the same brown plush loveseat, wondering if there were other boys Dr. Shaffer was doing this to, or if it was just me."

"Logan," Danika whispers, interrupting my story. "You don't have to tell me anymore. I get it. Whatever you did to that man, he deserved it."

I shake my head and sit up, bringing my knees to my chest and wrapping my arms around my legs. "You don't because he wanted *me* to touch *him*. He said we were nearing the end of our sessions. I just had to prove to him I was ready. I would have done it too had the school not shown us that program."

Danika places her hand on my back, rubbing small circles. "What happened to you wasn't your fault, Logan."

I jerk my shoulder and stand, then walk to the shoreline. The water kisses my feet as the waves crash onto the sand. It's cold, like I expected, but I don't shiver.

I watch Danika's shadow approach. She stops just outside of the water's reach. I cross my arms, hugging myself, and stare at a speck on the horizon.

"Mom took Dr. Shaffer's side when he said *I* was inappropriate with him. She never even asked for my side of the story. She wouldn't look at me the whole drive home, but I knew she was going to tell my dad and that he would wake me up in the middle of the night and drag me into his office."

Danika steps into the water and wraps her arms around my waist. "Stop," she whispers. I look over my shoulder; silent tears trail down her cheeks. "I don't need to hear anymore."

These are the demons I live with every day. The ones who take every good feeling and twist them into a living reminder of my nightmare. Just when I thought they'd been chased away forever, they're back.

"You don't even know half of it yet. What if you leave me

when you find out the rest?" I'd understand if Danika ran, if she pulled away and stopped fighting to be whatever it is that we are. We both know we aren't just friends. We've crossed too many lines.

She shakes her head. "It doesn't matter. I'm not going anywhere, and whatever you did to that man, he deserved it."

Chapter 43

Logan and I spend the rest of the afternoon in my living room watching reality TV on Netflix. He doesn't want to go back to his house, and I don't blame him.

When we pulled into my driveway a few hours ago, that same white car was still next door. Not to mention, his mom was horrible today. It blows my mind that she's never noticed what Logan went through. I'm glad Mrs. Harris welcomed Piper into her home, but she shouldn't have taken on another child when she had one that desperately needed her attention.

Sitting on the couch, we don't talk about what Dr. Shaffer did to Logan or what happened after. I don't need to know, although I'm sure at some point he will tell me. It makes sense now, why he was so worried about his secret.

He thought he'd already told me.

He was worried I'd blab.

I shake my head and chuckle under my breath. *Stupid man.*

The alarm on my phone goes off. I grab my phone off the side table and silence it with a frown. "Dad's coming home soon."

Logan pushes the button on the remote to pause the show. He stands, grabs his own phone and the cup he drank out of, and wordlessly walks to the kitchen. He rinses it in the sink and says, "I should go."

I don't want Logan to leave. He's been withdrawn ever since we got back from the beach. I get it. I do. Talking about your trauma reopens the wounds. I thought he'd cry or maybe even yell during his story. Instead, he was stoic. Even now every word, every movement is controlled and cold.

He opens the door, letting me out first, then freezes. I follow his gaze to the white BMW leaving his driveway.

"Logan?" I ask, hoping to bring him out of the darkness and back to me.

He swallows hard and closes his eyes. I reach for his hand, but Logan shakes his head, so I step back. After a few moments of silence, his thick lashes lift and he looks at his driveway again. "I need a drink."

Logan turns his head, but I touch his cheek, forcing him to look at me. I'm scared. Scared he's going to spiral backward into the jerk he used to be. Scared he's going to seek comfort in the bottom of a bottle instead of my arms. He might not be used to people having his back, but I do. I'm here and I'm not going anywhere. "Don't do that."

"Do what?" Logan reaches into his pocket and pulls out his phone, thumbs tapping away at his screen.

I feel the distance growing between us with each passing second. What's it going to be like when he walks away? Will I be able to get him back?

I touch Logan's arm, silently pleading for him to look at me. I'm trying to be strong for him, but my own armor is cracking. "Don't put up that wall again. Let me in, Logan."

He exhales loudly and shakes his head. We turn our heads

to the sound of tires on the pavement. My dad closes his car door and smiles up at us. He waves to Logan, unaware of the storm brewing beneath the surface.

"Talk to your dad." Logan's phone dings, his lips lifting at the corner. "I've gotta go."

Logan marches to his house, closing the door behind him, and my heart sinks. It's always two steps forward and then five steps back with him. Every time I think we've made a breakthrough, something happens. It's frustrating as hell.

Dad stops on the porch, greeting me with a side hug. "Hey, kiddo. I didn't know you were home."

I stare at the Harris house, mentally willing Logan to come outside again. An invisible noose wraps around my neck. Squeezing tighter with each passing second. "Yeah, plans changed."

Dad sets his briefcase down and touches my shoulder. "Honey, are you okay?"

Am I okay? No, I'm far from it.

My boyfriend was molested for years as a kid and I'm just finding out about it. His mom is an idiot who ignored the signs and his dad was an abusive prick. How Logan has coped without turning to drugs or alcohol is beyond me. Then again, he might have. I was gone for three years. There's a huge window of his life I know nothing about.

"Danika?" Dad asks, again.

I turn, my brows pushing together, and stare at my dad. He's a good guy, with thick ties in the community. Whatever Logan did all those years ago, there's a chance my dad will know about it. "Who is Alan Shaffer?"

The color drains from Dad's face. He retracts his arm from my shoulder and shoves his hands in his pockets. A screen door slams behind me. We both look over to the Harris house., watch Logan get into his car without so much as a glance in our direction, and then peel out of his driveway.

"Dad?" I pry. "Who is he?"

Dad clears his throat. "He's no one, sweetie. Why do you ask?"

I chew on my lip, wondering how much I should say. Logan's secrets are his to tell, but the way my dad blanched, he knows something. Plus, Logan told me to talk to Dad, which means he's involved somehow and keeping secrets from me. "I met him today."

"Who?" Dad asks hesitantly.

"Dr. Shaffer. He was at Logan's house today." I watch Dad carefully, waiting for him to react. He swallows hard but doesn't say anything. I think he knows what happened to Logan. I think he's kept that secret for years, and I need to know why.

So, I add, "He was super creepy. I don't like him."

Chapter 44

I take another sip from the beer in my hand, then toss the empty bottle into the grass. Forty-five minutes. It takes forty-five minutes to walk from Dumbnut's house to here. Dumbnut is not Jake, by the way.

The one day I want him to throw a party, he doesn't. No, dumbnut is some sophomore trying to make a name for himself. I am the only senior there, adding a cool factor of a billion to the kid's pathetic excuse of a party. There were maybe twenty people, but there is beer and that's all I want.

My foot slides off the edge of the sidewalk and I stumble. I left my car at Dumbnut's house, having enough sense not to drive tonight. Clearly, that's as far as my logic goes because this is a terrible idea, but I have to see it. To know if it's changed.

I stand in front of Dr. Shaffer's old office, hands in my pockets and stare at the building that ruined me. It's not a psychiatric office anymore. A few months after he died—or didn't die— it turned into a cell phone store. Another commercially operated chain store with nothing special about it.

Too bad the owners didn't know Dr. Alan Shaffer had molested dozens of kids in that hollowed-out space.

I bet they would have never bought it.

"I wondered how long it would take you to come back," a voice drawls from the shadows.

My head spins and I rub my eyes, willing the beer and whiskey to stop dancing in my stomach. They're fucking with me. Bad.

"They didn't tell you, did they?" he muses, stepping into the light. "They let you live all these years, thinking you killed me."

This can't be real. My mind is doing it to me again. Alan Shaffer is dead. This is nothing but a fucked up hallucination. He wasn't in my house today and he isn't here now.

He.

Is.

Dead.

Alan points to the edge of the building, to a small security camera I didn't have enough sense to notice. "I've waited for years. Watching. Buying my time until you came back to me, but you never did. You never once showed remorse for what you did to me."

Something in my brain flips and the anxiety and turmoil within me ignites. "What I did to you?" I step closer. Not quite on the property but not on the street anymore. "What about what you did to me? What you did to all those other boys?"

Alan smirks and looks at his old building. He's still in the shadows, barely visible in the glow of the neon *closed* sign. "I was helping those boys, just like I was helping you."

"You abused them!" I shout, taking another step. "Me. You abused me! You knew I was vulnerable. You took advantage of my trust and made me feel like what we were doing was normal."

"It was, Logan." Alan sidesteps closer to the building. "When two people love each other—"

"I don't fucking love you," I cut him off. The fire in my blood burning hotter. "The only person I've ever loved is Danika."

I suck in a breath at the realization. I love her. I love her with every fiber of my being. I hate that I realized it here, with him.

Alan smirks. "See, my methods worked. Without our affections you would not relate those feelings you have for her to love."

I see the flashing red and blue lights reflecting on the storefront windows before anything else. There are no sirens. Just lights.

"Logan!" Sheriff Tomlinson barks. His car door closes. Heavy footsteps jog over to me, and then there's a hand on my shoulder. "He's baiting you."

Alan steps out of the shadows and it's then I notice the crowbar in his hand. The fire in his eyes. The sinister smile on his lips. He was going to do it. He was going to get his revenge and beat me to death like I did him. My stomach lurches and empties itself in the grass.

"Jesus, Logan," the Sheriff mumbles.

Sheriff Tomlinson—Uncle Ryan although I rarely called him that—rubs his chin. He's my mom's half-brother, but we never see him anymore. They had a falling out around the time of my parents' divorce when he took my dad's side. Not like he had any choice. Dad had him by the balls with this secret.

"He is on my family's property, Ryan. Threatening me." Alan points to the camera again. "I have the proof this time."

"Fuck you," Uncle Ryan replies. "Did you forget the deal? I could arrest you, right now, if I wanted to."

Alan holds out his wrists and flashes a sinister grin. I don't know what's happening. What deal? I thought Alan Shaffer was four feet under in a shallow grave somewhere. "By all means, Ryan. Do it. We both know you can't."

Danika's little red Mazda skids to a stop behind the cop car.

She rushes out and runs to kneel beside me. I push her away and she comes back. *She'll always come back to me.* "Logan! Are you alright?"

"Take him home," Uncle Ryan demands. "To your home, Danika."

Danika stiffens beside me. She looks around, a question hanging on her lips, but she nods. I climb to my feet with her help, just as pathetic as I was this afternoon, and pass out in her car.

Don't ask me how I got Logan out of the car and to my dining room table, because I honestly have no idea. He's half asleep, not fully coherent, and a mess. I've never seen him like this and with his dad's history of alcohol abuse, it's a little worrisome.

The first person through my door, after me, is Sheriff Tomlinson. He drops his keys on the table and slumps into a chair like I assume he does in his own home after a long night. He's not an old man, maybe in his late twenties or early thirties. Sometimes, I forget he and Logan are related, but every so often, I see the resemblance. A brooding look. An eyebrow arch. A crooked grin. If this is what I get to look forward to ten years from now, I'll be one happy wife.

Not that I'm thinking that far ahead. I'm just saying...

"Here." I set a carton of cream and a container of sugar on the table, along with a few cups. I have the feeling Sheriff

Tomlinson won't be my only guest tonight. I pour coffee into each mug and then set the pot back on the counter.

"I'm sorry about your mom," he says, stirring some cream and sugar into his cup. "I gave Walter my condolences a few weeks ago, but never got around to seeing you."

I shrug and put some bread slices in the toaster. "Not like you've had a reason to see me, Sheriff."

"Ryan," Dad says, coming through the door. He kneels beside Logan, who's passed out and drooling on the table, and checks his pulse. "Is the boy alright?"

"He's drunk, Dad, not dead." I cross my arms over my chest and glare at him. He's too calm. They both are. I get the sneaking suspicion they were both involved with the Alan Shaffer issue long before tonight. "What's going on?"

"She doesn't need to know," a voice booms from the doorway.

Logan stirs as his dad, Jeff Harris, enters my house. He wears the same brooding expression Logan had during my first few weeks of school. I hate looking at the man. Every time I see him, I remember the lashings and scars all over Logan's body. I bite the side of my tongue to keep from saying something rude.

Jeff Harris closes the door, locking it behind him, then turns his attention to Logan. He shakes his head, tsking in disappointment. "You're a fucking mess."

"Good to see you too, Dad," Logan groans. He folds his arms on the table and sets his head down.

I pop two slices of bread in the toaster for thirty seconds, add butter when they're ready, and pour Logan a glass of water. I set them in front of him, ruffling his hair to get his attention. Jeff noticeably rolls his eyes and directs his attention to me. "Leave."

Logan lifts his head, takes a buttered piece, then sticks it in his mouth. "She stays."

"She," Jeff says, pointing directly at me, "is a liability."

"I know what happened." I feel like a sassy eight-year-old standing up to the school bully. That's all lawyers are: grown-up bullies. And Jeff Harris is the biggest bully in town.

"You don't know shit, little girl," Jeff growls.

"Jeff," my dad warns, standing at full height. "Don't disrespect my daughter. This affects her just as much as it does the rest of us."

"He's alive?" Logan mumbles, running his fingers through his hair.

I kneel beside him and take his hand in mine. Logan scoots his chair back and pulls me onto his lap, holding me tight.

"Of course he's alive," Jeff spits. "He was at the house a few hours ago. Or were you too fucked up to recognize him?"

I leap off Logan's lap and slap Jeff Harris across the face. I know his secrets. Know the abuse Logan endured for years because of him. Back in middle school, I had a hard time connecting the monster Logan described to the supportive family man I saw in the football stands. I see it now, everything Logan warned me about. I guess it's true what they say, people's true colors eventually show and Jeffery Harris' are black.

"I could have you arrested for assault, little girl."

"Do it," I growl. I'm not afraid. Jeff Harris is a bully, and I love bringing bullies down. "When the cops ask why I hit you, I'll tell them I couldn't stand to see my boyfriend be abused by his dad."

I don't miss the snapping up of Logan's head from the corner of my eye. I've never called him my boyfriend out loud. I didn't mean to let the title slip, but if there ever was a time to stand up for Logan and claim him as mine, it's now.

"Danika," Dad puts his hand on my shoulder and backs me toward Logan. "What do you know about this situation?"

Logan sits upright and holds his arms open. I find my place in his lap, sheltered from the mess unfolding in the kitchen. "I know Dr. Shaffer sexually abused Logan for years and I know this asshole never did anything about it."

Jeff Harris smirks and opens his briefcase. He drops a handful of pictures on the table. Judging by the top photo, I'd say they're evidence of the crime Logan committed. The one Sarah's dad inadvertently warned her about. "Did Logan tell you about any of this?"

I pick up one of the photos and stare in horror. It's not Alan Shaffer's mangled body surrounded by a blanket of crimson or the bruising on his skin that bothers me. It's how much blood is splattered across the walls and how destroyed the room is that gets to me. The chairs are smashed, the desk is flipped over, papers ripped to pieces and scattered across the mess. This was a crime of passion.

A reaction of rage.

Sheriff Tomlinson picks up another photo and stares at it, likely reliving parts of that night. He drops the picture back on the table and sighs. "Jeff called your dad first. Logan was panicking. Said he'd beaten Alan to death with a baseball bat."

Dad pulls another chair over to the table and sits. "Alan wasn't dead, but he wasn't doing well. We had a short window to decide what our plan of action would be. So, I called Ryan. No matter which way I spun it, Logan was in serious trouble. We needed a plan and some insight on how to make this situation disappear. It wasn't until we saw Alan's laptop that we put the pieces together."

Logan hides his face in my shoulder. His body shakes, trembling with silent tears again. I can't begin to imagine how hard today has been for him. I rub small circles with my fingertips on his back. "So, why did Logan think he was dead?"

"Because I told Logan he killed him," Jeff says nonchalantly.

I stare at him, jaw slack. *He what?* I turn my gaze to Dad, who shrugs and nods. Jeff grabs a cup of coffee that's probably lukewarm now. He sags into a chair, looking slightly defeated.

"The plan was to blackmail Alan. It worked because he signed a waiver, releasing Logan and us from all liability if we stayed quiet about his indiscretions."

"But those other boys?" I look at each of them, waiting to hear how they vindicated the other victims. All three men look down at their cups and I grit my teeth, disgusted.

"I had to think about my boy," Mr. Harris booms. "Besides, I didn't think Alan would survive, but your dad is damn good at what he does."

Dad chuckles. "I'll take that as a compliment."

"I thought I was going crazy," Logan mumbles. He looks up at his dad with sad puppy dog eyes, red-rimmed and wet. "I've seen him. For years."

"Fucking prick," Sheriff Tomlinson grumbles, shoving the table. The only untouched cup of coffee splashes and spills onto the wooden surface. "We've got to do something, Jeff."

Jeff Harris runs his hands through his short black hair. Logan got his coloring from his dad. Dark hair. Olive skin. Ember eyes. Cooper, he took after Mrs. H. "We can't do anything, Ryan, not without legally jeopardizing Logan."

"Do you have the agreement you all signed?" I ask.

Jeff looks at me like I'm stupid. Maybe I am in his eyes, but it's been years since they read over the document. Maybe there's something they overlooked. "Why? Think you can find something I missed? I wrote the damn thing, little girl. It's airtight."

"Fresh eyes, Jeff," my dad defends.

With a grunt, Mr. Harris shuffles through his briefcase. He drops the contract in front of me and leans against the counter, arms crossed. It's smaller than I anticipated, only two pages, so it doesn't take long to read. Even with the fancy verbiage, it's pretty straightforward.

"Here," I touch one of the sentences. "Conditions of abuse. The whole document you're talking about Logan. Nowhere does it state any other child. This makes the sentence sound like Logan's abuse."

"Don't be so sure." Jeff snatches the agreement from my hands. He reads over the contract again and mumbles, "Well, I'll be damned."

Sheriff Tomlinson holds out his hand and takes the paper. He skims over it and asks, "Will this hold up if we prosecute the other cases?"

Mr. Harris rubs his chin and paces the kitchen. After a few minutes of silence, he says, "I'll have to approach the other families. They have to be the ones to press charges, but yeah. It should."

"I love you," Logan whispers. It's the first time he's said those words and while it wasn't some big romantic gesture like when Gunner homecoming-proposed, Logan's announcement was better. It came from a place of true vulnerability.

I kiss his cheek. I'll tell him later. I love Logan, I do, but I want him to feel my words. Not assume I'm saying them just to say.

"Things could get messy the next few days. Logan, I think you should leave town. I can't risk you causing a scene again and fucking things up," Jeff says, scrolling through his phone. "I booked you a room in Miami for the week."

Sheriff Tomlinson nods. "I think that's a good idea."

"I want to go, too. Logan shouldn't be alone." I say and even though Dad has a look that says sending us across the state together, alone, is a terrible idea, he doesn't disagree.

"Oh, my god. Logan! This is beautiful!" Danika says, walking into our room.

She looks around, sets her backpack on the couch, and pulls back the grey curtains. Our room has a full living room, kitchen, dining room, and California-king in the bedroom. Dad must have assumed Danika was coming with me when he booked the room because this can't be the standard suite.

"You've got to see this view," she gasps.

I drop my duffle bag by the door and wrap my arms around Danika's waist, resting my chin on her shoulder. Our room looks out at the ocean, but I'm more interested in what's in front of me. I've spent the last two and a half hours keeping my hands mostly to myself, distracting my mind from everything related to Dr. Shaffer by thinking about all the things she and I might do this week.

I dip my head and kiss the exposed skin of Danika's shoulder. She squeals and spins in my arms. Hands on my chest, she looks up at me with those big Bambi eyes. "I love you, Logan."

My heart pounds against my ribs, each beat echoing the weight of last night's confession. When I told Danika I loved her in her kitchen, I meant it. I never expected her to say it back. That's not how she works. Hell, it took her weeks just to call me her boyfriend. So, I thought I'd be waiting just as long for this.

"You do?"

She doesn't answer with words. Instead, she presses her lips to mine, a reassurance stronger than anything she could say. It's exactly what I need. I slide my hands beneath her thighs and lift her into me; she wraps her legs around my waist, locking us together. Our mouths stay fused as I carry her across the room, until we tumble onto the bed, her squeal breaking through the moment. Her hands find the hem of my shirts and both layers over my head.

I swallow hard. My scars are on full display now. I never take my undershirt off unless I'm alone—not even then, if I can help it. Most of the marks are on my back, out of sight but never out of mind but I hate that they're there.

Danika trails her fingers across the marks marring my back. Her lips follow, pressing gentle kisses to my collarbone, my shoulder, my neck. Her nails graze each mark like she's memorizing them. I never realized how sensitive that skin is. The sensation ripples through me—not painful, not unwelcome. Just... different.

"You okay?" she murmurs.

I find that sweet spot on her neck and kiss it, dragging another squeal from her lips. "You stole my line."

Danika pulls her shirt off and then unbuckles my belt, looking me directly in the eye. "I'm perfect," she says as her hands dip into my pants and her fingers wrap around me.

I unclasp her bra, shove it out of the way, and suck her nipple between my lips. Danika moans, and that sound alone has me on the edge of coming undone. I pepper her chest with kisses up to her neck, her back arching, those hips grinding against me. I love it. I love her. But it's too much.

"Baby, you've got to stop, or I'm going to cum."

Danika pushes me onto my back and smirks. "Are you, now?"

Danika pulls me out of my pants and sucks me into her mouth. I grip the bedsheets beside me because the girl's got a mouth like no other. I don't know if I want her to stop so I can drag this moment out or savor it and take my release.

"Fuck, baby." I moan, too far gone to stop on my own. "I'm about to..."

She sucks harder. Deeper. And takes every bit of my seed, swallowing. I lie there, my body humming for the high. That was the best blowjob I've ever had and the fact that it came from Danika makes it even better.

"Holy fuck," I whisper, lifting my head to see where my queen went.

After that performance, she's been promoted to queen, and I am but her humble servant.

Danika sits cross legged beside me with a grin a mile wide. She wipes her mouth with the back of her hand and chuckles. "Tangy."

"Is it just me, or is this pool way better than yours?" Danika relaxes in a blue and white lounge chair nestled on the deck of the rooftop infinity pool.

I chuckle into the rim of my beer bottle and take the last sip. The best thing about my uncle being Sheriff in a small town is he can do whatever he wants. Such as giving his nephew and his girlfriend fake IDs that match perfectly to their driver's licenses, except for birthdays. Yeah. He's that good.

I set my empty beer bottle on the little table beside me and then fold my arms behind my head. "Mine is better."

Danika rolls onto her side. "Oh, yeah. Why's that?"

I was going to say because we can go skinny dipping, but the poolside waitress checks on us. Again. The girl is very attentive. Annoyingly so. She picks up my beer and Danika's empty glass. "Want another?"

"Yes, please," Danika replies with an innocence that almost gives us away.

I lift my Oakley's and smile. Our waitress is pretty in that wears-too-much make-up-and-tries-too-hard kind of way. I glance at her nametag, which sits over her tiny chest, and purr her name. "Mariella. That's a pretty name."

Danika rolls her eyes and turns onto her back, adjusting herself in the sun. Any other girl would be pissed. Accuse me of flirting—which I kind of am— and probably throw a fit. Not my girl. She knows I'm one hundred percent hers, and there's nothing to worry about.

Mariella bats her thick lashes, and her red lips lift at the corners as she gives me a once-over. Here, in a town where no one but Danika knows me, I don't bother wearing my undershirt at the pool. Danika has already seen my scars, both real and emotional. She's not ashamed of them. I shouldn't be either.

Mariella takes Danika's empty glass and my bottle and I follow her as she walks back toward the poolside bar. "Hey," I say, quickening my pace to be beside her. "I have a question."

"No," she replies, her lips lifting at the corners. "You can't have my number."

This just got awkward. I rub the back of my neck and smirk. "Not what I was looking for."

Mariella blushes and looks down at her hands. "Oh, sorry." She clears her throat and meets my gaze again. "It's my first day here. A lot of people have asked me for it. What's up?"

"You look to be about our age. I want to take my girl out tonight. Any suggestions on where to go?"

Mariella arches a brown and gives me another once-over, really studying my features this time. "How old are you? Really?"

"Twenty-one," I say, flashing her my signature crooked grin.

"Sure you are," Mariella says on an exhale. She shakes her head, then grabs a bar square and scribbles an address onto it. "Here. Tell the bouncer, Jack, Ria sent you and you'll have no problems getting in. If you do, hand him this napkin."

"Thanks." I turn back to the pool when she whistles, grabbing my attention.

"Don't you want your drinks?"

The driver stops in front of a dimly lit building on a dark street. Aside from a big man guarding a door, there's no one outside. No signs of life. This street—Wicker Street—looks like the kind of place where people get stabbed and left to die. The tiny hairs on my body bristle. I don't like it here.

"Are you sure this is right?" I ask the driver, a middle aged Hispanic woman.

"*Si.* Yes. 1800 Wicker Street," she says.

Logan takes my hand and brings the palm to his lips, wrapping a thin blanket of comfort around me. "Relax, baby. Tonight is supposed to be fun."

He steps out of the car first, holding the door open for me. I slip close to his side. He's got all of the money and our IDs—so there's no purse for someone to snatch—but that doesn't make me feel any safer.

The bouncer at the door looks down his nose at us. He's

huge. I'm not just talking large, even if his arms are the size of my head, but tall. The man fills the whole doorway and then some. He grunts and shakes his head. "I don't think so, kid."

"Ria sent us," Logan says with a confidence I can only dream of having in a place like this.

Apparently, Ria was our poolside waitress, whose shift conveniently ended right after her chat with Logan. Not gonna lie, I was grateful. I know Logan isn't a cheater. He had plenty of opportunities to stray or break up with me in the six weeks we were kind of dating, but he stayed faithful. Even without the title of a boyfriend, he showed me that I'm the only one he wants. Unfortunately, knowing this doesn't stop me from feeling jealous when pretty girls hit on him.

"Nice try," the bouncer chuckles. "Go around the front and wait in line like everyone else."

This is a back entrance? I look around again at the unmarked doors and dumpsters. Makes a little more sense now. Except, I can't understand why we're back here and not at the front.

Logan fishes in his pocket for the napkin Ria gave him. He holds it out for the bouncer, who takes and inspects it. "You're a lucky son-of-a-bitch. You know that?"

"Does this mean we're allowed in?" I ask.

The dude chuckles, shaking his large belly and steps to the side. "Yes, ma'am, it does."

When I think of a nightclub, I picture what you see in the movies: flashing lights, pounding music, and a sea of people. After walking through a dim hallway that leads to a second-story V.I.P. suite, this place is no different—except, here, the noise fades in the room we've stepped into.

A woman, wearing nothing but feathers and a bikini, brings

a bottle of champagne to our table. She pops the cork as Logan says, "We didn't order this."

The woman ignores Logan and fills two skinny flutes with the bubbly liquid. "Compliments of the club." She sets the remainder of the bottle in a bucket of ice, then disappears.

Logan hands me a flute and then takes the other for himself. "Cheers."

We clink glasses. The champagne is sweet, but not too sweet—refreshing, even. I take a sip, savoring the taste, while Logan drains his in one go. He grabs the bottle, refilling his glass without a second thought. "How much do you think something like this costs?"

I shrug. I've never been to a club, and my guess is based on what I've seen in TV shows. "In a place like this? Hard to say. A few hundred bucks, maybe."

Logan takes a slower sip this time, his eyes drifting to the mass of bodies below, writhing and drinking in the chaos of the dance floor. "Want to go down there?"

Not really. A nightclub is an overhyped party, and I'm not big on those. I would've preferred staying in our quiet room. I don't even know what's come over me lately. Maybe it's because I finally called Logan my boyfriend, or because I've said those three words to him, but all I can think about is touching him. Everywhere. All the time. And I want him to touch me, too.

I set my drink down and reach for Logan's hand. He turns to me, a playful grin tugging at the corners of his mouth, and sits back on the couch. I swing my leg over, settling on his lap. His hands immediately find my waist as mine tangle in his hair.

"Places like this have cameras, baby," Logan warns.

I'm not going to screw him, although I'm sure said-cameras probably have recorded that kind of stuff before. I just want a kiss. One kiss and then we'll drink, and we'll dance, and we'll forget everyone else in the world exists.

Chapter 48

We stumble into our room, hours later. Danika heads straight for the window again, pulling back the curtains and staring out at the vast darkness of the ocean. I find the couch and kick my shoes off. My feet hurt. We ended up going down into the crowd to dance and once Danika started, she didn't want to stop.

I sink back into the cushions, my head lolling against them as I fight to keep my eyes open. If I close them, the room will spin, and the night will slip away too soon. I drank too much. Hell, we both did—because why wouldn't we? Everything was free, and for once, life felt weightless. When I see Ria again this week, I'm giving her a ridiculous tip. Tonight was unforgettable.

Danika crawls onto my lap, her body warm and unsteady, the scent of smoke and alcohol clinging to her—yet beneath it all, she still smells like rosewater, soft and familiar. My hands find her waist, fingers curling into the fabric of her dress as I pull her closer. She tilts her face to mine, and I don't hesitate.

I crash my mouth against hers, and she parts her lips without a second thought, letting me in. If my head wasn't already spinning from the liquor, it would be from this—the way she kisses me, hungry and reckless, like she's been waiting for this all night. Maybe longer.

And maybe, just maybe, so have I.

My hands roam her body, skirting up her stomach, across her braless chest, and eventually tugging her dress over her head. Don't ask me when or how, but my shirt ends up haphazardly across the room, too.

I lift her nipple to my lips, swirling my tongue around the taught nub while sucking. She moans again. Arching. Digging her nails into my arms. Too much more of her grinding on me and I'm going to explode like a pre-teen with his first hard-on.

"I need a minute," I say, trying to control myself.

"Stop talking," Danika's mouth brushes against my ear. Her warm, wet lips send a jolt straight to my dick. "Stop thinking. I want this. I want you, Logan. All of you."

I want her, too.

I lift Danika, easing her back onto the couch as our lips stay fused, slow and unrelenting. She hooks her legs around my waist, her touch searing through me as her hands work my pants and boxers down to my ankles in one effortless motion.

I pull back, meeting her gaze—steady, searching. The past twenty-four hours have been a whirlwind. *Boyfriend. I love you.* Two monumental steps. And while every fiber of me aches for her, we don't have to add *this* to the list just yet.

I brush my thumb over her cheek, my voice low. "We don't have to do this, you know."

Danika cups my face, her touch soft but insistent. Her gaze locks onto mine, dark with need. "I know," she murmurs, her thumbs stroking my jaw. "But I need you—I need *this*—to satisfy the ache rippling through me. Please."

I nod, kissing her quickly. Danika sits up on her elbows and watches me walk across the room to my duffle bag. I open the new box of condoms I bought—just in case—and rip one free of its wrapper. "Do you want to move to the bed?"

She shakes her head and pushes her panties down to her ankles. "No. I like it here."

I roll the rubber over my cock and lean over her again. The only time I've ever been nervous to have sex was my first time. I was fifteen, drunk and did nothing but lay there while the girl rode me. I thought about everything—football plays, cars, World of Warcraft—whatever I could to keep myself from coming in two-point-five seconds.

The nerves I felt that night are nothing compared to what I'm feeling now.

I spread Danika's legs, feeling her shudder. "You okay?"

She nods, and I stare at her, waiting for her to change her mind. We've never talked about how far she's gone with guys before. I've never wanted to know because she's always seemed so pure to me. *Until the last few days.* "If you ever want to stop, just tell me. Okay?"

She nods again, swallowing hard.

I lift her legs onto my shoulders and slide Danika closer by the hips until my tongue kisses her warm, wet folds. She gasps, back arching at the first lick. I feel her instinctively pulling away, but I hold her in place, licking every bit of the honey seeping out of her. Her legs shake and I can tell she's getting closer. I pull my face back, wiping my mouth with the back of my hand, then slide a finger in. Her tight muscles clench around me, and when I can't take it any longer, I line the head of my dick up with her opening.

I hesitate and stare down at this wonderful, beautiful woman I have the honor of calling mine.

Danika's panting, her body glistening with sweat. She bites her lip and those wide brown Bambi eyes almost send me over the edge. "What are you waiting for?"

Nothing. She's told me more than once that she wants this. The moment she says otherwise, I'll stop.

I ease the tip in and pause, letting her stretch around me. She's so tight my dick feels like it's being squeezed to death, but in a good way. I press deeper, barely halfway, when Danika gasps and winces. "Are you alright?"

"Yeah," she whispers. "Keep going."

Danika closes her eyes and bites her lip. I'm hurting her. The last thing I want to do is hurt her. I know I'm big, but I'm not horsedick big. This shouldn't be painful. I should have loosened her up more. "Honey, we can stop."

"Keep going, Logan. Please." Danika wipes a tear away with her palm but keeps her eyes shut. I swallow the lump in my throat and push myself in using Band-Aid logic—get the hard part over with.

I pause once I'm all the way in and wait for her to look at me. She doesn't. Her eyes stay shut, quiet tears still leaking from the sides. I kiss each one and then rock my hips. Panic and worry override all pleasure I should be feeling. I'm worried about her, and even though I think we should stop, I keep going.

After a few slow, steady thrusts, Danika exhales a moan. It's the first sign that she's enjoying this and my balls tighten. Danika opens her eyes and smiles. And then her back arches and her legs curl around my hips, like a flip switched inside her. I do my best to stay strong, thinking about anything but how warm and tight she feels. The last thing I want to do is gyp her the moment things start to feel good, but I'm not going to last much longer.

I move a little harder, faster, and feel her tighten around me. Danika's eyes close again, but this time, it's because I've made her feel good. She bites her lip, trying to keep the wave of pleasure to herself until it's too much. She moans and then gasps, "Oh, Logan."

And I can't fight it anymore. I let loose, filling the condom, my orgasm so intense it's almost painful. I collapse on top of Danika, a sweaty mess but proud of myself, until I look at the clock.

I lasted five minutes. A new personal worst. *Oh well.*

I ease out of Danika and sit back on my heels. "You okay?"

Danika nods and scoots into a sitting position. "Yeah, just a little sore."

I look down at the condom to roll it off and notice a pink hue. "Babe." I run my fingers across her opening and swallow hard. "Are you a virgin?"

She smiles shyly, cheeks as red as the cream in my fingers. "I was."

Morning light seeps through the curtains. I pull the blanket over my head, unsure of when I made it to the bed. I bend my legs closer to my chest and wince at the dull ache between them. I lost my virginity last night. I was drunk and pushy, but I wanted it.

I wanted him.

Logan slips beneath the covers behind me, his warmth instantly melting into mine. His arm drapes over my waist, pulling me closer as he presses a soft kiss to my cheek. The faint taste of mint lingers on his breath, sending a warm shiver down my spine. I may be sore, but the ache only reminds me of last night—of him. And God, I want him again.

"Good morning, beautiful," he murmurs, his voice thick with sleep.

"Morning," I whisper, a slow smile curling my lips.

His fingers trace lazy patterns along my side, his thumb pressing gentle circles into my back. "How are you feeling?"

"I'm good." I shift in his arms, turning to face him as I hitch my leg over his hip, pressing closer.

He chuckles, kissing my forehead. "Someone is feisty." He grabs my ass, pulling me against him and I moan, that ache pulsing through me again. "What do you want to do today?"

"You."

Logan

We spend the rest of the week in bed, tangled under the sheets, only coming out for room service and the occasional swim at the pool. I don't see Ria again, and when I ask about her no one knows who she is.

I don't dwell on it long because Danika steals my attention every chance she gets. We taste, and we touch, and we explore each other's bodies. Relishing in what I'm calling the best week of my life. It's lazy, and carefree, and absolutely perfect. If I could stop time and stay here forever, I would.

I always thought people were full of shit when they said having sex with someone you love is a million times better than simply screwing someone who is there. I thought sex was sex. I liked it, but I could go without it.

Now that I've tasted Danika and felt her from the inside, nothing compares. She's by far the best experience I've ever had.

And I can't get enough.

I THOUGHT it would be fun to squeeze in one more quickie before checkout. Can you blame me? It's like I was made to fit inside Danika. Besides, once we go back home, we have to face reality. Not only will we be forced back to school, but there's the whole Dr. Shaffer mess. I'm not stupid. I know that a lawsuit could take months, years even, to settle.

Everything is perfect, just like the other times. But when I pull out of her, the condom flopped like a sticky, wet balloon. I sit back on my heels and stare at my dick, willing my eyes to see something different.

I must have mumbled something because Danika flips onto her back and asks, "What do you mean it broke?"

There's only one thing I could be talking about, even if I didn't know I was talking. I point down and raise my eyebrows. My heart pounds in my chest, each beat pumping a shot of nervousness into my veins. We can't have a kid. Not until we're married and I know that Dr. Shaffer is safe behind bars. "I mean *it* broke."

"When?" Danika sits up on her elbows. Her eyes bounce from the broken rubber to my face too many times. "How?"

"I don't know, Danika. It's not like I attached a camera to my dick and can tell you." She glares, apparently not finding my comment funny. Truthfully, it sounded better in my head than it did out loud. "Couldn't you feel it?"

"No, Logan," she spits, climbing out of bed. She grabs a towel from the bathroom and tosses it at me. "I couldn't feel it."

Danika stands beside the bed and begins jumping up and down, holding her massive tits in place with her hands. I try not to laugh but can't help the grin that takes over my face. "What are you doing?"

"I'm helping gravity pull all the little yous out of me!"

I grab Danika's wrist and gently pull her into my arms. "I don't think that's how it works, baby." I press my face against her chest, breathing her in as she wraps her arms around me. Her heart is racing, a frantic rhythm against my cheek. I can only imagine the storm of thoughts spinning through her head.

"I'm sorry for freaking out," I murmur.

"Yeah. Me too." She exhales a shaky sigh.

I tilt my head up, meeting her worried gaze. "Hey. It's okay. We'll grab the morning-after pill on the way home. Things like this happen all the time."

I stroke my thumb over her wrist, grounding her. "We'll be fine."

The past few weeks since coming home from our week-long vacation have flown by. We had two days of school and then Logan and I were off for Thanksgiving break. Unfortunately, under the direction of her ex-husband, Mrs. H took Logan, Cooper, and Piper out of state for the week.

Thank God for texting and Facetime. Although, while I had all the privacy I needed, Logan was almost always surrounded by someone. So, there was no hot sexting or dirty video chatting, but we made up for lost time when he got home.

When school resumed again, we had ten days of mundane work. Mrs. H made Logan take a shift at the Red Onion three nights a week. Apparently, she thought he needed to expand his extracurriculars outside of the bedroom since the football season had come to an abrupt end. That sucked too, but it gave us somewhere else to hang out beside our houses.

"Are you okay?" Logan asks, running his fingers through my hair. It's Wednesday, Cooper and Piper's day to work, which means I get Logan all to myself tonight. It feels like an eternity has passed since we've been able to curl up on the couch like this. I really *really* miss Miami.

"Yeah. Why?" I roll onto my back and look up into his ebon eyes. Logan has his glasses on today, something he's started doing more since coming home. To the rest of the world, Logan is a sexy jock with a temper but here he's my soft, cuddly nerd. I love it.

He shrugs, twisting my locks into a failed attempt at a braid. "Tomorrow is your first Christmas without your mom."

"I'm trying not to think about it." I turn back to the TV, blinking the tears that have begun to form back, and tuck my arm under my head. I've done well to force tomorrow from my thoughts, but now that Logan has brought it up, I can't hide from them. "I don't know what we're going to do for breakfast this year."

"What do you mean?"

"Mom used to get up before us, before Dad even, and bake French Toast. She did that every year up until she got sick. I'd wake to the smell of vanilla and a warm cup of hot cocoa. In the hospital, she would beg, bribe, and plead with the staff to help keep our tradition alive. Even if French Toast wasn't on the breakfast menu, someone would always bring it in for her."

I smile, remembering last year. Dad brought a twin-size blow-up mattress for me while he slept in the awful reclining chair, Christmas Eve. It didn't matter we lived minutes down the road. We knew our time was running out and that every minute counted.

I woke at the last check-in before shift change when the nurse came to take Mom's vitals. Mom smiled sadly at me, her hollow cheeks even more skeletal in the dim lights. Even in her weak state, covered in wires, and wearing a faded hospital gown, Mom was beautiful. She didn't wear a wig, instead opting to rock the straggly hair that had begun to grow back. At first, we thought the hair growth was a sign the treatment was working. We were wrong.

"I'm sorry," she whispered.

I shushed Mom, letting her comfort me when, in our twisted reality, I was actually comforting her. I crawled into bed with her, careful not to pull on her wires and laid there until the sun came up. Dad had just begun to stir when there was a knock on her door.

I climbed out of Mom's lap, figuring it was that morning's nurse, when the door opened. I'll never forget her—Tammy, the tattooed, twenty-six-year-old who carried in two massive bags from IHop.

Tammy set them on the foot of Mom's bed. "I'm freaking starving this morning. I hope you don't mind, I brought breakfast."

It wasn't vegan, but it didn't matter. That was the last Christmas we'd have together. There were presents, but nothing that mattered. Everything store-bought was mundane compared to the memory that the nurse gave us.

I wipe my eyes with the back of my hand and try to stop the tears fro flowing. Not only is tomorrow my first Christmas without Mom, but it's the first one I'll wake up to alone because Dad has the graveyard shift tonight.

I WAKE on the couch to the warm, nostalgic scent of vanilla drifting through the house and, for a blissful moment, I let myself believe it's real. I open my eyes and see it's only six-forty-five. Dad is still at the hospital for another fifteen minutes, which means I'm alone. I realize the smell is nothing more than a memory-tinged dream, and I'm in some semi-lucid form of consciousness.

I force my feet to move, knowing that everything about this

moment is fake, but I'll bask in it and allow myself to see Mom again because I haven't dreamed of her since she died, and I miss her.

I miss her more than words can convey.

I push myself up, feet moving instinctively toward the kitchen, where I expect nothing but silence—only to stop short, caught between a laugh and a sob.

Logan stands at the stove, a ridiculous Mrs. Claus apron tied around his neck. Cooking. French. Toast. He senses me before he sees me, turning with a grin that's all mischief and warmth.

"Good morning, beautiful."

"Hey," I say, breathlessly.

"Sit." He motions to the table with his spatula. I take a seat in front of a bowl of fruit and a pre-poured glass of orange juice. "I really, *really* hope you like them. I was up all night testing out different recipes. I think I finally found one that works using coconut milk."

My gaze snaps to his, wide-eyed. "Wait. These are—"

"Vegan." He sets a plate in front of me and kisses my forehead. "I'm a dick and didn't buy you anything for Christmas. So, I thought I'd make you breakfast."

"This is better than anything from a store, Logan. Thank you." I take a bite and moan. The Frent Toast is heavenly. Fluffy and full of flavor. Not quite Mom's, but still delicious. "Oh my God, Logan," I mumble with my mouth full.

The front door swings open before I can brag how amazing my French Toast is. Dad has a take-out bag in one hand and carnations in the other. He looks exhausted, but he remembered breakfast, too. I guess I know what we're having for lunch today.

Dad pauses in the doorway, his gaze flicking between us. "Merry Christmas," he says slowly, suspicion laced in his tone. "Tell me he didn't stay the night again."

"No, sir." Logan, completely unfazed, holds out a plate, waiting for Dad's hands to be free. "Just broke in at the crack of dawn."

Dad sighs, shaking his head. "Remind me to fix that window in your bedroom, kiddo." He sets his bag and the bouquet of flowers on the counter before taking the plate from Logan.

Sliding into the seat across from me, he lifts a forkful of French toast to his mouth. The moment he takes a bite, his eyes widen.

I grin, warmth swelling in my chest as I glance at Logan—so proud, so unbelievably in love with him in this moment.

"Yeah, Dad," I say softly. "They're just like Mom's."

cDonald's meatless egg McMuffin sandwich.

Trying to eat that sandwich was the moment I knew I had a problem. I stare down at the yellow paper and my stomach twists in protest.

"Are you okay?" Logan eyes me suspiciously. He takes a bite of his McGriddle and just watching him eat makes my insides feel like they're on a roller coaster.

"Yeah," I nod, pushing my food away. "I think I'm coming down with something."

"Shit," he mumbles against his straw. "Do you still want to go to the beach or skip it?"

I take a sip of my Frappuccino. The cool sweetness tangles with whatever war is raging in my stomach, but it stays put—for now. "I think I'll be okay. It's probably all the grease they use messing me up."

Logan points to the tray, silently asking if I'm done. I nod and he tosses the trash in the bin.

For December, it's ungodly hot, but this is normal. Unlike the rest of the country, which is buried knee-deep in snow right now, winter-only vacations in Florida. It hangs out, just long enough to get everyone sick, then it gets stupid hot again.

The ice cream store that afternoon is where everything goes south.

Logan buys me my favorite—a chocolate chip cookie dough nice-cream cone—and I only make it three licks before I feel disaster stirring. I shove my cone at Logan, who thankfully takes it without question, as I cover my mouth. I run to the bathroom, barely making it to the stall before expelling everything in my stomach into the public toilet. At least the bathroom is clean. Small blessings.

I sit back on my heels and grab a few squares of toilet paper to wipe my mouth. *What the hell?*

At the sink, I wash my hands and then splash some water on my face. I hate getting sick. I've been lucky and haven't caught the funk floating through the hallways, until now. So many kids were out those last two weeks of school with one thing or another. I guess it was only a matter of time until it was my turn.

When I sit back at our table, Logan holds my ice cream out for me. I shake my head and he takes a lick of it. "Are you okay?"

"Yeah," I say pushing my hair back from my face. I'm hot. Sweat pools at my hairline and my shirt sticks to my back. I think if I take a shower and lie down, I'll be okay. "I don't feel good. Can you take me home?"

"Sure." He tosses what's left of his shake and my melting cone in the trash. "Want some company?"

I shake my head. I don't want him catching whatever it is I've got. "I think I'm going to take a nap. I'll text you when I get up though. Okay?"

Logan links his fingers with mine and kisses my palm. "Of course, baby."

I GLANCE over at Logan's house and make sure no one is looking, then lock the door. My pulse pounds under my skin, making me tremble. I've dodged Logan the past two days, claiming to have a contagious stomach bug. Every time I thought I was getting better; I'd throw up again. Morning. Noon. Night. It's all the time. I didn't think anything of it until Sarah cracked a joke about me being pregnant.

I don't track my periods. They've always been regular, but I figured when it didn't come last month, the morning-after pill threw it off track. It didn't occur to me that I hadn't had a period this month either until Sarah said something.

"Did you bring it?"

Sarah holds up a Pharmacy bag. My contents are hidden inside. "Of course. Do you really think you're—"

"Don't say it!" I point my finger at her, cutting her off. "I don't want to even put the possibility into the universe."

Sarah smirks and shakes her head. "Sorry, chicka, but you did that the moment you called me. Why not just drive down to the pharmacy and grab a test yourself?"

"Because I told Logan I'm too sick to see him. He'll call my bluff and try to come over." I grab the bag and head upstairs. I don't need Dad coming home in the middle of us waiting for the results. "I don't want him worrying or trying to come see me. *If* I am pr..."

I can't say it.

The thought of being a teen mom sickens me. I had a plan. I was going to go to UF. I was going to study medicine and become a Physician's Assistant. I was going to get married— hopefully to Logan— and wait until my late twenties, when I was financially stable, to have a child. This...

I exhale a shaking breath.

This would ruin everything.

Sarah pulls me into a hug, her arms tightening around me as if she can feel the storm raging inside. And maybe she can—because I'm barely holding it together. My thoughts spiral, tangled in fear and uncertainty.

What if Logan doesn't want the baby? What if I have to do this alone?

The weight of possibility presses down on me, suffocating. Could I go through with adoption? Could I... end it? The thought alone sends a shiver down my spine. I never imagined myself standing at this crossroads, never thought I'd even let these choices flicker through my mind.

And yet, here I am.

Lost.

Terrified.

And completely unsure of what comes next.

"Hey, hey. Don't cry."

I didn't realize I was. I pull back, sniffling, and wipe my cheeks. "I guess I should get this over with. No sense in freaking out yet."

"No sense in freaking out at all," Sarah assures me. "Everything will be fine."

In the privacy of my bathroom, I read the directions on the box. Three times, just to make sure I don't screw it up. They're pretty straightforward. Pee on the stick. Wait three to five minutes and either jump for joy or break down in tears.

My bladder, of course, chooses this moment to be shy. Figures, when I need to pee, it doesn't want to. Eventually, after enough pushing to move a tiny poop, I *finally* pee. I cap the stick. Set it on the counter. Pull my shorts up, then reach for my phone. I want to set a timer, but the stick decides my fate before I can open the app on my phone.

I look down at the test, all color draining from my face, and I must make a noise because Sarah barges into the bathroom. "What? What's wrong?"

I hold the stick out and she takes it. My legs give out and I fall to the ground. Sarah's by my side in an instant, rubbing soft circles on my back. Whispering what I think are comforting words but I can't hear them.

All I hear is my mind reading the results aloud.

Pregnant.

Chapter 52

Logan slinks up behind me, his arms wrapping around my waist, pulling me flush against his chest. I go rigid, but he doesn't notice—too caught up in the excitement of our surprise reunion. I

It's only been a week. Just seven days away, under the excuse that my Nona needed an emergency helper after her hip surgery (which she really did). But the way he holds me, you'd think it had been a lifetime.

His head dips, lips brushing against the crook of my neck. The scent of whiskey clings to his breath—an odd detail that sets my nerves on edge. I've seen Logan drink, but I know the truth. The party-boy persona is a carefully crafted illusion. He indulges, but rarely more than a few sips. Only once before has he smelled like this. And that night... that night was bad.

Teeth graze my shoulder, sinking in just enough to send a shiver through me. Fear threads beneath my skin as his grip tightens. I step forward, prying myself from his hold, and turn to face him.

I reach up, fingertips brushing against his cheek, and he

leans into my touch like it's an anchor. His deep brown eyes are liquid warmth, pools of adoration, and my resolve wavers.

I'm running out of time. But I can't do this. Not tonight.

"I should go."

"Baby." Logan grasps my arm. He studies me, a crease forming between his brows. "What's wrong?"

"I..." I bite my lip, swallowing hard against the tears threatening to surface. I can't break down. I've spent too many nights crying, curled up in my room, drowning in my own thoughts. "I don't feel well."

"Are you getting sick again?" Logan doesn't wait for my reply. His fingers slide down my arm until they tangle with mine. "Let's go. This time, I'm taking care of you."

A chill runs down my spine. I hate this—lying to him, hiding from him—but I need time. Time to figure out what the hell I'm going to do. I should've waited until tomorrow to have this conversation, but it took every ounce of courage I had just to get this far. And now that the moment is here, I'm not ready.

I shake my head. "No, stay with your friends."

He lifts my hand to his lips and kisses my palm. "The only reason I came out tonight is because I thought you were still visiting your Nona. I missed you."

I nod and swallow the lump in my throat. I missed him, too. More than words can convey. I guess we can hang out tonight. One more day won't make a difference, won't change my mind.

And God, I missed being in his arms.

"Are you good to drive?" I ask, my voice barely above a whisper. "Or should I?"

Logan

The drive back is silent. The only sounds are my heartbeat thundering in my ears and our shallow breaths in the car. Occasionally, Dani sniffles, wiping her nose with the back of her hand. Maybe her stomach flu turned into a head cold. Or maybe she picked up something on the flight back from Georgia. I stretch my arm across the center console, palm up. She slips her fingers into mine, but everything feels off. Her touch—usually warm, grounding—is cold and lifeless. I squeeze her hand, searching for the comfort that's always been there, but find nothing.

"So," I say, gripping the steering wheel so tightly I'm sure I'll leave marks. I know Dani was worried about me drinking and driving, but I'm not drunk. Not even close. If she'd walked in five minutes earlier, I wouldn't have needed that shot of whiskey. It just...helps. Helps me get through the days without her. Helps me drown out the noise in my head.

The local paper released an article today about three families pressing charges against Dr. Shaffer. Mom lost her mind when she read it. The way she reacted... I'm starting to think they had an affair, which makes what he did to me even more fucked. Cooper eyed me like he was putting the pieces together, but I bolted before he could say anything. Of all the days for Danika to come home, I needed it to be today.

"Is everything okay?"

Dani turns her head, gaze fixed on the passing streetlights. "Not here."

Three more blocks and we'll be home. Three more blocks and I can finally hold her in my arms. I don't sleep well when she's not by my side. I toss and turn and wake up just as tired as when I laid down. Sick or not, I'm sleeping by her side tonight. "You know I love you. Right?"

She exhales a small, pained laugh. "I know."

That's not good. She always says I love you back. I have this feeling in my bones that tonight's conversation isn't going to end well. I rub my thumb over her palm, hoping that somehow, she can feel how much I need her in my life. After one week, I'm falling apart. What will happen to me if she leaves?

"You are my forever, Danika. No matter what happens with us, I will never love someone the way I love you."

She finally turns to me, her green eyes shimmering under the glow of the streetlights. "Those are big words, Logan. You can't possibly know what the future holds."

I pull into my driveway and hold her hand a little tighter. Shifting the car into park, I turn in my seat and look her dead in the eye. "There is no life without you, only a veil of darkness. My world revolves around you, craving your light. My words aren't thoughtless sentences. They are promises, Danika. A promise to always be yours even if you don't want to be mine."

She shakes her head and looks up at the ceiling, blinking fast, but a single tear slips free, tracing down her cheek. "Don't do this, Logan. Don't make promises you can't keep."

"I never do." I reach up and brush the tear away with my knuckle. She leans into my touch, and for the first time since getting into the car, warmth radiates from her skin. We're going to be okay.

"What's wrong, baby? Talk to me."

Danika drops her gaze to her lap. More tears spill over, silent and steady. Then, barely above a whisper, she says, "I'm pregnant."

I don't move. I don't breathe.

I couldn't have heard her right. That whiskey must've hit harder than I thought, because there's no way—

"What do you mean you're pregnant?" My voice comes out raw, unsteady.

"It's not a hard concept, Logan," Danika huffs. She reaches for the handle and gets out of the car. She's pissed which I don't understand because she can't be pregnant. We were always safe. Careful.

I take a breath and exhale loudly. There has to be some mistake. I take a deep breath and step out of the car, watching as she leans against the trunk, arms crossed, eyes locked on the sky. The moonlight catches on her skin, making her look ethereal and... fragile.

"How far along are you?"

She shrugs, refusing to look at me. "I don't know. Six, maybe seven weeks."

Six or seven weeks. That puts us at the end of November. My stomach drops.

She's known since *November* and didn't tell me?

A slow burn ignites in my veins. This isn't just news. This is a *secret*. A huge one. One she had no right to keep. And now, we have fewer choices.

"What the hell, Danika? How long have you been keeping this from me?"

She shrugs and wipes her cheek. I get it, this is hard for her. But what about me? I can cope with the fact that she's pregnant. Fine. We'll deal with it however she wants. What I don't understand is how she could keep such a big secret from me. Any secret for that matter. "Were you even visiting your grandmother this past week?"

Danika shakes her head.

The betrayal slices through me, deeper than I expected. My fingers rake through my hair as I take a step back, trying to process. With everything going on—the court case, the weight of my past suffocating me—this feels like too much. "What the fuck, Danika? What else are you hiding?"

"Nothing. I swear." She reaches for my arm, but I step out of reach.

Tears stream down her face, but they only fuel my anger. How can she cry like that—so easy, and on cue? If I weren't so pissed, would she even be crying?

I turn on my heel and march toward the porch, my mind spinning. The baby is *whatever*. Not ideal, but manageable. The lies, though? The secrets? That's something else entirely.

How do I know this wasn't planned? *She* provided the

condom that broke. *She* insisted on taking the morning-after pill alone. What if she never took it? What if she's been waiting for the right moment to drop this bomb on me?

"Logan! Please talk to me," Danika sobs.

I slam the door behind me, shutting her out.

Piper looks up from the couch, brows furrowed in confusion. I ignore her and head straight to my room, collapsing onto my bed. I bury my face in the pillow, my chest heaving.

I don't know if I want to scream or cry.

I've never felt so fucking betrayed in my life.

I LIE in bed the next morning, the sharp ding of my phone cutting through the silence before my alarms. I glance at the screen and chuck it across the room. Eight missed calls. Thirty-two texts.

Funny how, when Danika was supposedly with her Nona, she could barely manage two messages a day—now she won't stop. My mind churns with questions, each one twisting into something worse. *What was she really doing last week?*

Going to baby appointments without you.

I grab the pillow beside me and press it over my face, exhaling a silent scream into the fabric. It doesn't help. If anything, it makes the pressure in my chest worse. I stay like that, buried in my own self-inflicted darkness, until a knock at the door drags me back to reality.

"Go away," I yell, my voice hoarse.

The door creaks open anyway. Which means it's one of two people. I grit my teeth and peek under the pillowcase, bracing for the worst. But it's not my lying, possibly cheating girlfriend.

It's Piper.

Relief seeps into my limbs, though I'd never admit it. She perches on the edge of my bed, wearing Cooper's basketball shorts and an old concert T-shirt, her face scrubbed clean of makeup. It's the best she's looked in months.

"Danika's been texting me all night," she says, stretching her legs out in front of her.

I frown. "Didn't know she had your number."

Piper shrugs. "Not like a ton of people want it." She smirks, then sobers. "She asked for it a while back, so I gave it to her."

I roll onto my side and pull my blanket over my body like a cocoon. I don't want to talk about Danika. She was the one person I thought I could trust. And now...I don't know anything anymore.

"Go away, Piper."

The bed shifts as she stands, but she doesn't try to talk me down or force me to vent. She just closes the door behind her, leaving me alone with my thoughts.

Too. Many. Thoughts.

Hours later, my phone dings again. I pry myself out of bed, staring at the screen. *Danika.* Same message as all the others.

I hover my thumb over the keyboard, but I don't know what to say.

I don't know *if* I want to say anything at all.

> Danika: Logan we have to talk.

> Danika: I'm sorry I lied about where I was, but I needed time to figure everything out.

> Danika: Please. Please. Tell me you're okay?

> Danika: I'm trying to be understanding, Logan but you've got to give me something.

> Danika: Don't push me away, Logan. I need you.

I shut my phone off again, not wanting to see anymore.

SCHOOL STARTS AGAIN ON MONDAY. I'm dreading it. I'm not ready to face Danika. Piper calls me a coward, and maybe I am—but I'm a coward who's hurting. Every day, new articles surface about kids coming forward against Dr. Shaffer. There are more families than we'd originally thought and Dad has agreed to help every one of them pro-bono—turns out he does have a heart—and the one person I'm dying to talk to is the person I'm pissed off with.

Not only do I not trust my girlfriend, but I also can't talk to my best friend—because they're the same person.

I sit on the floor, guitar in hand, mindlessly picking at the strings when my door flies open. Piper storms into my room, barely pausing to find me with her gaze before she starts chucking books from my desk at me. Her aim is garbage, but eventually, one lands a solid hit to my head.

I set my guitar on the ground and raise my arms defensively. "What the hell, Piper?"

She stops throwing and stalks toward me, hands on her hips, fury radiating off her like a heatwave. "No. You what the hell, Logan. How could you?"

I stand, forcing Piper to look up at me. Like Cooper, I'm a head taller than she is, and I'll use every inch of my height to regain dominance in this conversation. "You've got to be more specific there, Piper. I've done a lot of shit in my life."

"Danika!" Piper yells, eyes flashing. "She's scared and pregnant, and you're avoiding her." And then she slaps me.

The sting spreads across my cheek as I inhale sharply, biting down on my frustration. I step around her, shutting the door. This isn't a conversation I want anyone—especially my mother—overhearing. She'd throw a fit and probably kick me out. If Cooper hypothetically knocked up Piper, though? She'd throw a damn party. She hates my dad, and I remind her of him. I get it. But it's not fucking fair.

"Have you told anyone?" I ask, my voice low.

Piper rears back, brows furrowed. "Of course not."

"Good. Keep it that way. It's probably not even mine."

She slaps me again, harder this time, and I grunt. I'm about tired of her hitting me.

"You're a dick," she spits. "That girl is so in love with you, she'd cut off her left tit before cheating."

"Then why hide it from me?" The words explode out of me before I can stop them, my anger slipping through the cracks. I haven't talked to anyone about this. It feels good to finally let some of it out. "She's, what—eight weeks pregnant?"

Piper stares at me like I've grown another head. "You're a fucking idiot."

I scowl. "Excuse me?"

"She's at most three weeks pregnant, dumbass."

I blink. "What the hell are you talking about?"

She sighs, pulling her phone from where she apparently stashed it in her bra and starts typing furiously. "Doctors track pregnancy from the first day of her last period. Sounds like that was around Thanksgiving, which means she missed hers at the end of December and took a test."

I rub the back of my neck. "That's confusing."

"Tell me about it. I spent an hour Googling that shit just so I could explain it to your dumb ass since you won't call her back." She shoves her phone in my face, the screen open to some medical website.

I skim over it, my stomach twisting. I feel like a jerk for assuming Danika cheated. But I'm still pissed. "Whatever. She still lied. She kept it from me."

Piper groans, throwing her hands in the air. "Really, Logan? You're mad because she took a week to process the fact that she's pregnant before telling you? She's eighteen. Her whole life is ahead of her. That's a huge decision! I'd need more than a week to figure out what the hell I'd do in her shoes."

"It's not just her decision to make." I hand Piper her phone back, pissed off for a whole new reason. Danika has already decided what she's doing with her child. *Our* child. She should have told me as soon as she found out she was pregnant and let me shoulder some of that burden.

Piper's expression darkens. "Have you even given her an option?" Her voice is softer now, more controlled. "The abortion window is small. I'm not saying that's what she's considering, but if that's what she needed to talk to you about, you guys are running out of time."

My stomach drops. I rake a hand through my hair, the weight of everything pressing down on me. I need a drink—but I refuse to turn into my father. And yet, by the way I've been acting, maybe I'm already halfway there. Maybe Mom has a reason to hate me after all.

"Shit," I mutter. "I've been a dick, haven't I?"

Piper nods, a triumphant smirk on her face. This girl hardly ever smiles, especially since her incident. Even if the smirk is to rub my nose in her win, I'm glad to see it.

"A massive dick." She bends down and grabs my phone from its new home on the floor beside my dresser. "Call your girlfriend. She shouldn't have to do this alone."

~

Me: Can we talk?

Danika: No need. The decision has been made. Everything will be taken care of on Tuesday.

Me: Want me to go with you?

Danika: No.

Me: What time are you leaving?

Danika: Early.

Me: Can I see you?

Danika: I don't think that's a good idea. I won't
be able to go through with it if I do.

Me: Ok. I'm sorry for being a jerk. I love you
Dani.

THERE'S a long pause between my text message and the three little dots on my screen. Each time they appear and disappear, they gut me. I guess this is karma.

Finally, finally she writes:

Danika: I love you too. You'll always be it for
me, Logan.

T he weekend passes mind-numbingly slow. I thought last week was bad, the hours creeping by, feeding my insecurities, but I was wrong. Waiting for Tuesday is worse.

I look at the clock again. It's only 2:42.

Only Saturday.

I have three more days until I can hold Danika and tell her how sorry I am for how I reacted. Tell her how brave she is and that everything will be okay.

On Monday, I don't go to school, fearful we'll bump into each other because I want to give her the strength she needs. I spend the day searching the internet for what to expect after an abortion. Outside of smothering Danika with love, Tylenol, and possibly chocolate, there's nothing I can do.

I spend the rest of the day and most of the night wondering if it's a boy or a girl—not that it matters at this point.

Or should I have proposed? Is that still the right thing to do?

I mean I could easily see myself spending the rest of my life with Danika, but is that what she wants? Would she even say yes?

I know I've been a dick in the past, but I royally screwed this situation up. Is it even possible to fix the damage I've done?

I don't sleep. Too many questions. Too many thoughts.

By the time the sun rises, I have a plan. I will be better. I have to be. Danika is the most important person in my life. I need to show her as much.

I watch the clock. Each minute is a lifetime in and of itself. I know Danika doesn't want to see me and I know I should respect her wishes, but she needs to know I'm all in. No matter what she wants. I'm. In.

Finally, when it reaches seven o'clock, I decide it's late enough to go over.

I barely make it out the door before my heart sinks to my feet. Mr. Winters' car is gone. Their house is empty and dark. I've missed them. Missed my opportunity to let Danika know that whatever comes our way, I'll be her rock.

I step onto the bottom step of my entryway and drop my face into my palms. I always fuck things up. Somehow, some-way, I make a mess of things.

Hours pass, the day fading into night before Mr. Winters green sedan pulls into the driveway. I rush over to the passenger side, prepared to help Danika out of the car. Every-thing I've read says she will be hurting, the pain ranging from mild discomfort to unbearable.

"Logan," Mr. Winters exhales. He sounds tired. I get it. This has been a long day for him, but for me, it's been a long week. Hell, it's been over two weeks since I've taken an easy breath. "She's not here."

I look in the window, not processing what he said. The passenger seat is empty. The back seat is empty. Danika's not anywhere in this car and I'm officially freaking out. "What do you mean she's not here? Did something happen?"

Mr. Winters shakes his head and runs his hand over his face. "Ah, shit. I thought she told you."

"Told me what?" I run both my hands through my hair. *Did she sign a DNR? Did something go wrong, and she bled out on the table? Where the fuck is my girlfriend?*

My chest squeezes. I can't catch a breath. Each inhale feels like it's being sucked through a straw and spots cloud my vision. "I don't understand what's happening right now."

Mr. Winters walks around the sedan and squeezes my shoulder. "Logan, Danika's decided to move in with her Nona in Georgia."

"What?" I look up at him, utterly confused. The weight on my lungs builds with each passing second and my head spins. This has to be a dream. Some fucked up dream I'm going to wake from any minute now.

"Nona is her mom's mother, and she's getting old. We've talked about putting Nona in a home, but Danika wouldn't hear of it." Mr. Winters guides me closer to my house and my feet move without my permission, going wherever he takes us.

Nothing he's saying makes any sense. Where is Danika? What has happened to our baby? "What?"

"The details don't matter, son. What I'm trying to say is Danika's gone, Logan and she doesn't want to come back."

Three months later

I stare up at the popcorn ceiling in Danika's bedroom. I shouldn't be here for a multitude of reasons, the top being that Mr. Winters could charge me with breaking and entering, but I can't stay away. The room still smells like Danika, although the scent is fading. I've sniffed every shampoo, soap, and perfume bottle I could find in every store I've gone into and have yet to find the particular blend that is Danika. Soon, this room won't have her smell anymore, and that terrifies me.

I bring the rim of my Sprite bottle to my lips. I carry one everywhere I go these days, the mixture gradually becoming more vodka and less Sprite, but it helps. The ache that ripples through me from the moment I wake up becomes more bearable with each sip, but it doesn't go away.

I never wanted to be this person, a man who depends on a crutch to get through life, but sometimes our paths are chosen for us. No matter what, though, I will not turn into my father.

When he drank, he was both verbally and physically abusive. Drinking amplified his problems.

It dulls mine.

Tonight, I need a drink more than ever. It's prom. The dance Danika promised we'd go to together. I had it all planned out, too. I found a horse-drawn carriage company down in West Palm that was willing to transport their items up here. Our house is only fifteen minutes by car to the Horizon Hotel, roughly thirty by horse. We'd take the carriage to the hotel and ride the private glass elevator to the penthouse suite, where I planned to hire a private chef to cook for us. Once the dinner was over, we'd go down to the dance and enjoy the night. I take another sip and close my eyes.

Tonight would have been perfect.

My phone vibrates beside me, pulling me from the depths of sleep. I blink, disoriented, unsure of when I drifted off or how long I've been out. A soft, amber glow filters through the curtains—it's early. My body feels heavy, sluggish, like I'm still caught between dreams and reality. I reach for the Sprite bottle that's rolled off the bed, its cool plastic a small comfort against my palm.

My phone buzzes again. Over and over. No stopping, which means it's a phone call. I give up my attempt at getting my drink and swipe at my phone screen. "What?"

"Where are you?" Mom asks. Her voice shakes like she's been crying. I force myself to pay attention and not fall back asleep. I'm tired a lot lately.

"Not far. Why?" It's not a lie, but I'm not going to openly admit that I passed out in Danika's bed again.

"Piper's been shot!" Mom cries. "Cooper is with her at the hospital."

"I'll be home in five minutes." I hang up before Mom can protest or threaten to leave without me. I straighten Danika's comforter so her dad will never know I was here and grab my bottle off the floor.

WE SIT in the ICU waiting room—Me, Cooper, Rex, and Mom —anxiously waiting for someone to give us an update on how Piper is doing. My hands shake. The everyday darkness that I fight is heavier today.

Hurts more today.

I need a drink to lift the veil and find the light, but I don't want to leave and miss anything.

After hours of waiting, a tiny woman covered in blood pushes through the double doors. "Lovelace family?"

We all stand, but mom is the first to speak. "It's Harris, but that's us."

Cooper takes Mom's hand. She's a mess both physically and emotionally. Between her unkempt appearance, Cooper in shorts and a scrub top, and Rex's rust-stained attire, we must be a sight to see.

"I'm Dr. Roe," the woman says. "The bullet lodged itself into Piper's shoulder blade, but we were able to remove it and fix the artery it nicked."

I exhale a breath of relief for Piper, but my head is spinning. My legs feel unsteady as I make my way back to the chair I've claimed as my own, sinking into it heavily. My stomach twists, a sharp reminder that I haven't eaten since lunch yesterday—not that I could keep anything down right now. I'm barely holding myself together when I hear it.

Coma.

Piper is in a coma.

Holy. Fuck.

I stumble into the bathroom, shoving open the nearest stall just in time to hunch over the toilet. A violent heave rips through me, purging a toxic mix of stomach acid and vodka. When there's nothing left, I sag against the stall door, wiping my mouth with the back of my hand. My phone slips from my pocket, landing face-up on the grimy tile.

I stare at it, my fingers twitching. Another text. Another unanswered message.

Fuck it.

What's one more?

> Me: The sky was clear last night. The moon was large, too. It was beautiful.

What am I doing? Danika doesn't care about the moon. Hell, she probably doesn't realize that last night was prom or how similar the sky was to Homecoming night.

> Me: You know that guy Rex Piper started dating? He took her to prom last night.

I need to stop doing this. Texting Danika like we're still friends. She never responds, but she also hasn't blocked my number, which gives me hope that she reads them. That she misses me. And that she might come back.

> Me: Anyway, I don't know how it happened, but someone shot her last night.

> Danika: Is she okay?

The air sticks in my lungs. I bring the screen closer to my face, making sure I'm not imagining this. Three months. Three long months of being ignored and finally, *finally,* I get a response.

> Me: I don't know. The doctor said she's in a coma or some shit.

Danika's reply is instant and I take the easiest breath I've taken in months. She may be miles away, but the same relief of having her in my arms washes over me.

> Danika: OMG. Logan. Are you okay?
>
> Me: Not really.
>
> Me: I miss you.

Three tiny dots appear under the chat feed and disappear a dozen times. I shouldn't have said that. I drop the phone in my lap and pull at my roots. She's probably going to ghost me again.

> Danika: 24 hours. I'm giving you 24 hours, but you can't talk about us.
>
> Danika: I'm serious. The second you do, I'm done.
>
> Me: I'll take what I can get.
>
> Me: Can we Facetime?
>
> Danika: No. This is hard enough, Logan. If I see you, I'll cave and come home. I can't do that.

The corner of my lips tugs upward—an unfamiliar, genuine sensation. I can't remember the last time I smiled without forcing it. Danika still has feelings for me. And if she has feelings, then I have a chance.

It doesn't matter how long it takes or what I have to do.

I'm going to win her back

> Me: Okay.

A SNEAK PEEK AT PART 2

Chapter 1

Danika

Present day

The world spins in a not-so-good, probably going to throw up later, kind of way.

I carry my heels in one hand and what's left of my hard cider in the other while I amble across the closed pool deck to the sandy beach and stumble in the dark into a lounge chair.

Tonight was the rehearsal dinner for a wedding I'd rather not be attending. A wedding I tried my hardest to get out of, but when your plane ticket is non-refundable and the bridesmaid's dress comes in the mail with the invitation, it's hard to say no.

Especially when the person getting married is your father.

Too bad he's marrying the Wicked Witch of the West, Tessa

Harris. Aka Mrs. H. Aka Mamma T. Aka Logan Harris' pathetic excuse of a mother.

So, not only is my dad marrying the worst woman in the world, he's turning the man who crushed my heart into my step-brother.

Peachy. Right?

Even though I was the one who ended our relationship, leaving Logan broke me. If I'm being honest, I'm still not one hundred percent over him. Every so often, bits of memories flicker in my mind, reopening old wounds and making it impossible to move on.

I rub the sore spot on my shin and continue my journey to the beach. The soft sand under my toes is just what I need to settle the churning in my stomach. It's unhappy from both the environment I've been forced into and the six hard ciders I've drank while hiding from my family.

Needless to say, they found me.

Well, my best friend Sarah Archer found me peeking through the doorway. Thankfully, it was at the tail end of the rehearsal dinner, meaning I didn't have to mingle and pretend to be happy to be back at the Horizon Hotel.

Don't get me wrong, I am excited to see Piper Lovelace and Cooper Harris and spend time with Sarah. There are just too many other people in that ballroom I'm less than excited to be around.

So, after the quickest hello in the history of time, I ran away. The people in that room might be my family at the end of this weekend, but *we* are not *a* family. Of course, the one person I want to get away from most has his elbows resting on the driftwood banister, preventing my toes from feeling the wind-chilled sand.

I could turn back and head up to my room.

It's what I should do.

After all, I've never been able to trust myself around Logan.

He has the ability to get under my skin and eat away at my resolve without trying because, like a moth to a flame, I'm drawn to him.

The wind blows, carrying the scent of his cologne with it. It's different, not the same smell I spent hours in department stores searching for.

If not for my Nona, I would have caved and come running back home after day one. I owe her everything. She ran her fingers through my hair, lulling me each night I cried myself to sleep. She didn't judge me when I refused to wear anything but pajama shorts and Logan's shirt for a month. She accepted every emotional outburst and tear-filled breakdown with grace. She reminded me daily that I made the right decision, that Logan wasn't ready to be a father, and that until he found a way to manage his demons, he wouldn't be.

I don't have her tonight. I have this mirrored sky, where the stars and the moon are just as bright as they were on homecoming. I have Logan's scent swirling through my head, replacing my semi-happy drunk with longing. And I have a mostly empty bottle of hard cider.

Had a mostly empty bottle of hard cider.

"The fuck?" Logan grumbles, rubbing the back of his head. He turns, face pinched in pain and anger, but softens his expression the moment our gazes lock. He bends down and picks up the bottle with a chuckle. "This yours?"

"Yup. I missed my mouth." I take a step forward and hold my hand out. "I'll take it back," I say, adding *please* for good measure. I may be drunk and slowly burning up from the inside out, but I will not let Logan think he unnerves me. Even if he does.

Even if my world is spinning and I'm not sure if the cause is him or the alcohol.

The corner of Logan's lip lifts into a smug smile. He leans his elbows on the banister behind him. "Come and get it."

I shake my head, losing my balance and stumbling a step to my right. I raise my hand and point my finger at his chest. That chest... god, how does his shirt even fit over those muscles? Like seriously! I can practically see the broad lines of his pecs through the thin white material. *Walk away, Danika.*

"You, sir, are drunk."

I open my fist and block Logan's face with my hand, ignoring the deep rumble of his chuckle and the warm air between us as I descend the stairs. I need to put some space between us and get the fluttering in my stomach under control. Too bad I don't make it. My ankle gives out as I try to go down the first of only five steps.

I should be tumbling to my sandy demise, but strong hands grip my hips and fire ignites my skin through my dress. I feel sweaty, and clammy, and like I need to take the flowing black fabric off or jump in the water to cool myself. Both of which I know would be terrible ideas because this is the nicest dress I own and there are scars across on my body that Logan doesn't need to see.

"Easy there, killer." Logan doesn't pull me against him and I can't decide if I'm disappointed or grateful. "If you sprain your ankle, you won't be able to walk down the aisle with me tomorrow, which would be a shame, considering it's the only time I'll have that privilege."

Guilt stabs at my insides. Was that an intentional dig at what our relationship could have been? Or am I just drunk and overthinking things?

I push Logan's hands off my body, then grip the handrail, taking each step painfully slow. When my toes finally meet the moon-kissed sand, a chill slithers through me, bringing my body temperature a little closer to normal.

I walk through the soft grains. My ankles roll, and I topple to the side a time or two, but eventually, I make it to the solid stuff—the sand and the water teases, making it hard just so she can run away.

I drop my shoes just out of the tide's reach and walk knee-deep into the waves. I don't care anymore that the hem of my dress is wet or that I'm ruining my perfectly painted toes from the first pedicure I've had in months. All I care about is slowing my heart and making my body feel a bit more normal. A hard feat, considering that I am most definitely drunk.

I close my eyes and drop my head back, allowing myself to become one with the waves. But then there's a jingling of keys hitting sand and a grunt of frustration from behind me. I exhale, pulled from the tiny moment of peace I found.

I strain my ears, listening to the sound of a buckle being undone and the soft thump of pants falling to the sand. I'd be worried anywhere else in the world, but no matter how much time passes I know Logan would never let anyone hurt me.

Water sloshes and my skin is hot again. Heat bounces between us, the tiny hairs over my body standing on edge, waiting for Logan's voice or touch, anything.

Finally, he speaks, his voice almost to a whisper. "How do you do it?"

"Do what?"

There's something about this moment that feels so beautifully wrong. Like a painted sky before a missile sails through it and destroys everything in its path.

"Suck the air from my lungs while breathing life into me at the same time."

Also By Bailey

Looking for some love in your life? Bailey's contemporary romances range from sweet to spicy, with everything in between.

Enemies to Lovers, High School Bully, Athlete Antihero, First Love, Girl Next Door, Completed Duet

Book 1 in the Broken Love Series

Piper

Most people don't think about the day they'll die. They coast through life, blissfully unaware of how their time is ticking away. I wasn't like most people. I welcomed death, wanted her to take me away from the prison I called life, but she refused. I tried twice only to survive. And then, when I thought I had nothing left it came.A reason to live.Rex was a small, unexpected ray of light my world of darkness that blossomed into a beam of sunshine. I thought, maybe this was why Death didn't take me. Maybe she knew that if I held on a little longer things would turn around. But the third time Death came to my door wasn't by choice. Someone else brought her, and I fear this time she might take me.

Rex

Being the son of a country star sucks. My parents are never around, I move every year or so, and I have no real friends. Everyone around me has an agenda. Everyone except Piper Lovelace. I can't get that girl to notice me. Trust me I've tried.Thankfully, fate stepped in and gave me the break I needed. I've got her attention, now I need her to give me a chance.

Enemies to Lovers, High School Bully, Athlete Antihero, First Love, Girl Next Door, Completed Duet

Book 2 in the Broken Love Series

She's beautiful. Fierce. Nothing at all like the girl I used to know, which is absolutely terrifying because Danika Winters is the only person outside of that room who knows the truth. She could ruin me, and I'm not talking about my reputation. I couldn't give two shits about what the kids at St. A's think. I'm talking major, life-altering, jail time ruined. I'll do whatever it takes to keep her quiet. Even if it means destroying the only person I've ever cared about.

Fall In love with a
Bailey Black Book Here

Frienemies to lovers, Fake dating, High school romance, Love triangle

Asher Anderson is a dick.

We aren't friends, so when he seeks me out in the cafeteria on the worst day of my life, I'm suspicious. When he tells Liam Heiter that we're dating, which couldn't be farther from the truth, I want to kill him...Until I see Liam's reaction.

Liam—my best friend, the guy who crushed every hope of us *officially* being together—is jealous. He has never looked at me this way and I love it.

So, I play along. Maybe watching me with someone else will make Liam suffer like I have the past four years. And maybe, just maybe, he'll come to his senses and realize we belong together. It's not like I actually *like* Asher. At best, I tolerate him. What's the worst that can happen?

**Fall In love with a
Bailey Black Book Here**

Small town, Opposites attract, Cowboy, New girl in town,
Unexpected parenthood (+denial)

Josh

Josh Andrews hadn't expected to meet the girl of his dreams in a church parking lot—especially not while his best friend was hooking up in his truck. But there she was, parked two spaces away, pretending not to notice his predicament. Layla was gorgeous, sharp-witted, and completely immune to his charm. He should have walked away. Instead, he couldn't stop thinking about her. Layla wasn't like the girls who usually fell for his easy smile and smooth lines. She challenged him, saw right through him—and he liked it. For the first time, he wanted more than just a fleeting connection. He wanted her. Winning her over won't be easy, but Josh has never backed down from a challenge. And Layla? She might just be the one risk worth taking.

**Fall In love with a
Bailey Black Book Here**

Second chance, The dare/bet, Insta chemistry, Learning to love, Shared Pasts

I've sworn off men forever! Okay, not forever, but for a few months. After my last hook-up, my vag needs a reset because the last man to touch me broke it in the worst of ways. Not a problem until my new dance partner comes into the picture. He's turning into my forbidden fruit, tempting me in ways I didn't know possible.

I have three months of celibacy ahead of me and eight weeks to whip my new dance partner into shape.

Someone save me.

Scan to Read a
Sample

Fake dating, Second chance, Friends to lovers, Everybody can see it, Short and Spicy novella

A wedding. A lie. And regret.

I'm in over my head with not one but two ex-boyfriends at the same wedding. Both of which I haven't seen in over a year. When the one who ripped my heart into pieces backs me into a corner, I grab the other and kiss him.

Yup. This is how I ended up fake dating Noah Ruckers, and let me tell you, it's an emotional roller coaster. I thought I'd put my feelings for him behind me. We spent years as friends after our break up, nothing more. But no matter how hard I try I can't forget what his lips feel like. Or the way his arms wrap around me.

In two days, I'm walking away. There is no future for us. But that doesn't mean I can't pretend.

**Fall In love with a
Bailey Black Book Here**

Fake dating, Second chance, Friends to lovers, Everybody can see it, Short and Spicy novella

Holly Flynn is a leprechaun who grants wishes—but with a dangerous twist. Each wish comes at a price: once it's fulfilled, the "victim" forgets everything before their wish—and her.

When a gorgeous stranger asks for one unforgettable night, things take an unexpected twist. The chemistry between them is electric, and soon, Holly's struck by a terrifying thought: She doesn't want him to forget her.

Then, a week later, he knocks on her door. And he remembers everything.

Why does he remember, when no one else does? Is it fate—or is her magic betraying her?

**Fall In love with a
Bailey Black Book Here**

How About a Fantasy Adventure?

Dive into the completed Neverland Novels. Characters have been aged up for this darker, grittier version. If you like your fairytale retellings with hot, ruthless, morally gray love interests, you'll enjoy this series. The Lost Darling is the first book in the main storyline. Please read this series in order.

Twisted Fairy Tale, Peter Pan Retelling, Multiple Love Interests, Morally Gray Males, She's Mine, Scorching hot lost boys, Spice, and more!

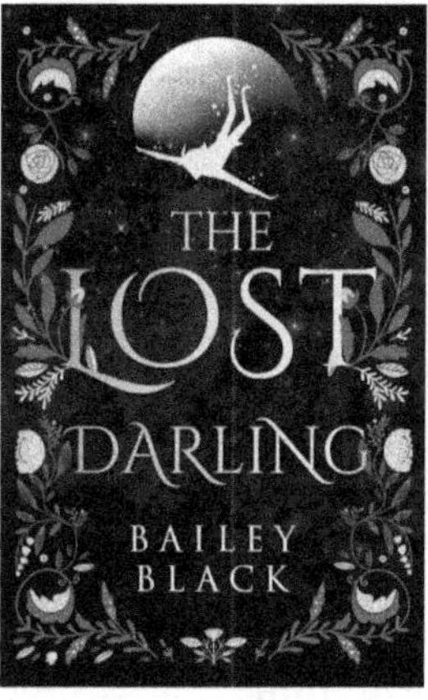

Second star to the left and continue until morning.

I got that line tattooed on my wrist the day I turned twenty-one. So much symbolism in such a simple sentence. At the time, it was a nod to the future and the infinite possibilities to come, while reminding me to remember the past and to look for magic in the world.

Growing up, nothing was ever what it seemed. The shift of leaves on a tree was a faery skipping by. Shooting stars were a chance to make wishes. Shadows were souls stuck between this world and the next, mirroring a life they once had.

My imagination was limitless, the world a wonderful adventure waiting to unfold.

It's easy to lose that sense of wonder with the weight of life on your shoulders and I wanted a reminder to get me through the hard days.

Most importantly, it was an ode to the boy who earned the title of my first crush, even if he was animated. Peter Pan wasn't a *save the damsel* kind of prince. He was daring, and selfless, and took care of the ones he loved. He was a friend to all but never afraid to fight the Pirates when their moral compass broke. Wendy was an idiot for leaving him. She rushed home to a heartless world full of men willing to lie through their teeth to get down her pants.

But that's the beauty of a book, the characters are perfectly flawed. Damaged just enough that we still love them. Whereas reality is nothing but empty promises and baggage the size of mountains.

The day I got my tattoo, I would have given anything to be whisked away into a fairytale. My world was crumbling, and all I wanted was to go back to when life was simpler. I didn't realize I had sealed my fate in ink.

Branded myself as one of the Lost.

Neverland was everything the stories made it out to be. Beautiful. Full of magic. Filled with handsome men and debonair pirates. But the author of my favorite tale left out one crucial detail.

In order to get there, you have to die.

**Fall In love with a
Bailey Black Book Here**

A witch in a world where magic is illegal, A revenge mission, A rescue mission, Death. People die. Sorry, not sorry, 2 love interests (not a RH and not a triangle), A touch of enemies to lovers. He falls first she falls harder

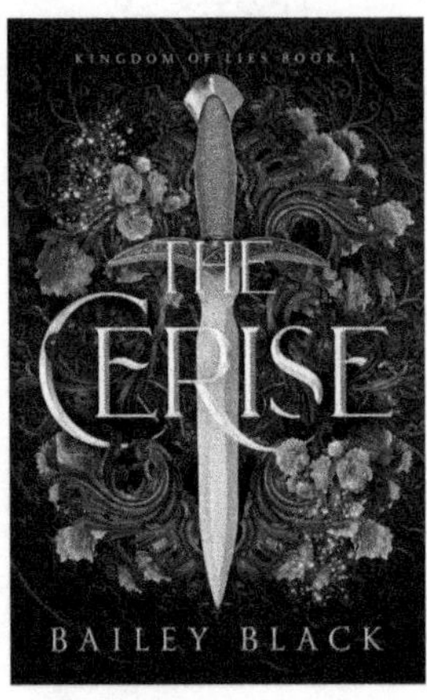

I had a plan. Find the soldier who killed my family and make him pay. It should have been an easy feat. I'd done it over a dozen times, taking out each member of that regiment one by one, but the mission went sideways. It all started with the man in the woods. The one my webs of magic couldn't sense even when he stood before me. Then my partner made a mistake, and now he's lying in one of the Crown's dungeons, fighting for his life. I couldn't leave him to die, but I couldn't just walk into the castle either.

Or maybe I could.

With the help of some unexpected allies, I entered the Culling—a one-in-a-lifetime chance to become queen. I have no interest in winning the prince's heart, or the crown. My only goal is to get into the castle, find my friend, and get out before someone realizes I'm a Cerise.

But when the welcome ball turns from a grand event into a

nightmarish dance of death, all eyes are on me. As if that's not bad enough, the soldier, the one who took my family, he's here.

If you loved "The Selection" by Kiera Cass and "From Blood and Ash" by Jennifer L. Armentrout, get ready to fall in love with this enchanting fantasy romance!

I want to start by saying thank you to my family. Writing a book takes sacrifice and sometimes my mom guilt eats at me that I'm not doing enough with my kids. So thank you to my husband for pushing me to write and to my kids for reminding me every day just how loved I am.

Thank you to my Mom for believing in me and helping me through the first stages of this book. It challenged me more than you know but I'm glad I kept it split the way it is.

A super bit thank you to Melissa for helping me polish this beauty to near perfection.

Thank you to my amazing ARC team! You guys are the best. Thank you to all of my friends at Bailey B's Besties. I have fun hanging out with you guys not quite daily but more than I do anyone else outside of the house.

Thank you to the bloggers.

Lastly, I want to say a huge thank you to you, the reader. Without you, there would be no book.

If you enjoyed IHYILY and have the time, please leave your reviews on Amazon, Goodreads, and Bookbub if possible.

Reviews are the lifeblood of a book and without you it would pretty much die.

Also, if you'd like to join my mailing list to find out what's happening next first, you can do so here.

Xoxo
  -Bailey

ABOUT THE AUTHOR

Bailey B is an up and coming New Adult author. She lives in Lehigh Acres Florida with her husband, twin girls, and two fur babies. She enjoys (but doesn't get to take part in because of her crazy daughters) the simple things like Disney+ binge watching, Netflix romcoms, reading and sleeping. She reads two to three books a week and thinks if narwhal's are real animals then unicorns might be too.

www.ingramcontent.com/pod-product-compliance
Lightning Source LLC
Chambersburg PA
CBHW070413310726
48977CB00003B/664